Grave Things Like Love

SARA BENNETT WEALER

DELACORTE PRESS

GetUnderlined.com

Educators and librarians, for a variety of teaching tools, visit us at RHTeachersLibrarians.com

Library of Congress Cataloging-in-Publication Data
Names: Bennett Wealer, Sara, author.
Title: Grave Things Like Love / Sara Bennett Wealer.
Description: First edition. | New York : Delacorte Press, 2022. | Audience: Ages 12 and up. | Summary: "Elaine—aka "Funeral Girl"—not only has to decide between two boys, her best friend from childhood and the dangerous new boy in town, but also must contend with the fact that the funeral home her family has owned for centuries may be haunted"— Provided by publisher.
Identifiers: LCCN 2021039519 (print) | LCCN 2021039520 (ebook) | ISBN 978-0-593-70355-7 (trade pbk.) | ISBN 978-1-9848-9630-8 (ebook)
Subjects: CYAC: Dating (Social customs)—Fiction. | Ghosts—Fiction. | Funeral homes—Fiction. | Family-owned business enterprises—Fiction. | LCGFT: Novels.
Classification: LCC PZ7.B447111 Fu 2022 (print) | LCC PZ7.B447111 (ebook) | DDC [Fic]—dc23

The text of this book is set in 11-point Dante MT.
Interior design by Ken Crossland

Printed in the United States of America
10 9 8 7 6 5 4 3 2 1
First Edition

Grave Things Like Love

ALSO BY SARA BENNETT WEALER

Now & When

For M, who is spreading her wings.

And for B, who is just finding hers.

Grave Things Like Love

CHAPTER ONE

There's a dead body in my house, and before the day is out there will be at least two more.

The one here now is in the basement. The second is at the hospital getting unhooked, untubed, and readied for final discharge. The third is in a van, lost somewhere between here and Shasta Falls. I know this because the bell at the delivery bay hasn't rung yet. And when I went to the main floor twenty minutes ago to bring my mom a sandwich for lunch, she was on the phone with the medical examiner's office.

"He left at eleven?" I heard her say. "He should definitely be here by now."

I snuck away to eat my own lunch up in my room on the third floor. I group-chatted Madison and Sienna about the Harvest Home concert tonight. I forgot about the bodies. And when I went back downstairs to see if the *Dragonfly* hoodie I ordered had been delivered, there'd still been no buzz from the door where our recently deceased clients arrive.

Mom's head pokes into the hallway.

"Elaine. Can you get on the phone with Dakota and figure out how to direct him to the highway? He seems to have gotten himself turned around."

I pause, thinking about my own phone upstairs in my room and my friends waiting to finalize our concert plans. Helping our clueless apprentice find his way back to the funeral home is nowhere on my list of things I want to be doing right now.

"Dakota's phone has GPS," I say.

Mom glances around, making sure no living clients are lurking in the foyer or the parlor or the visitation rooms. There aren't any, but her eyebrows stay up and her voice keeps its even, friendly tone.

"GPS is what got him lost in the first place. Phones *are* fallible, you know. I put a map on the dash in the van, and from the way it's been neglected I'm beginning to wonder if anyone even knows how to read one anymore."

"I know how to read a map." I brush past my mother into the office. "I also know anyone could have predicted that Dakota would get lost."

"Well, he's all we had. Your dad would have gone, except he's busy with Mr. Pagoni. And who knows when the hospital will release Mrs. Keener? Dakota was drafted and now here we are. I swear if this day gets any more hectic, I'll need a cocktail by two."

She scrubs a hand through her hair, dropping the placid façade that we are all expected to maintain while on the main floor of the house, where there's always a chance of running into somebody grieving the loss of a loved one. I'm lucky not to have been roped into corpse chauffeur duty; I know this. The least I can do is help out.

Dakota picks up after just one ring.

"Lainey, hey," he says. "Sorry to bug you but I am literally out

2

in the middle of nowhere. GPS wanted to take me around some construction; now I'm on this dirt road going through a big-assed cornfield."

I smile, picturing Dakota in his hipster glasses and bow tie, driving a fully loaded funeral-home van through the back roads of Clark County. He just finished mortuary school, and he's supposed to be learning the ropes of the funeral business with us. But sometimes it seems like all he's really learning is increasingly creative ways to mess up. I almost wish I could be there to witness if he runs out of gas and has to ask a farmer for help. But that would back things up even more, and Mom already looks like she's ready for wine-o-clock.

I sit at her desk and pull up a map on the computer.

"What was the last sign you saw?"

"Ummm . . ." Dakota always does this humming under his breath thing when he's trying to concentrate. "I don't know. Shelbyville? That was, like, five miles back."

"Shelbyville is the exact opposite direction of where you want to go. Can you pull over and turn around?"

I hear him sigh, then hear the crunch of gravel as he maneuvers the van to the side of the road.

"If you're near Shelbyville, then you're close to Philipsburg and Lester," I tell him. "Route Eight runs through both of those. Whichever one you hit, find Route Eight going north. That will take you back to the highway. I assume you can take it from there?"

"Yeah, I can find it. Thanks, Lainey, you're the best."

It's what everyone says—the elderly ladies when I play piano for their friends' services; Mom when I update the software on the office computers; Dad when I make coffee at 3:00 a.m. after the business phone rings, summoning him to the hospital or someone's house.

You're the best, Lainey. We always know we can count on you.

"He should be on his way," I tell Mom as I start for the door, my mind already back with Madison and Sienna.

"Not so fast!" she says. "Did your dad talk to you about the parade?"

I freeze. The Harvest Home parade kicks off the big community fall festival, and it's the reason I'm not at school today. We're off because every scout troop, marching band, sports team, politician, and local business within a thirty-mile radius takes part. People love Harvest Home because it's fun in a carny-rides-fair-food-and-has-been-country-band kind of way. School closing for a day doesn't hurt, either.

Mom reaches to the top of a shelf sagging with casket catalogs. She takes down a top hat with a veil cascading from its brim. She hands the hat to me.

"We need you to drive the buggy."

"Seriously? No!"

"The buggy" is what we call the Victorian hearse that is parked under a canopy next to the house. It's been in our family since Victorian times, which is when my great-great-great-grandfather Leathan Gillies established the funeral home. The buggy is made of polished black wood that rises in a big rectangle with windows on all four sides. The windows are decorated with purple velvet curtains, GILLIES FAMILY FUNERAL HOME emblazoned across the glass in silver script. A gleaming mauve casket sits inside—empty, of course.

The buggy is pulled by two horses, which my parents borrow from an Amish farm outside of town. It's a rolling advertisement. It's our brand: time-honored and trustworthy—a single family serving the community for generations.

When I was little, I rode with my dad, and he would show me how to control the horses. I used to love how the wood-and-steel

4

wheels clacked down the road. Now the thought of it makes me cringe. Not so much because I'll have to steer two massive animals from eight feet off the ground by myself, but because when the buggy comes out for things like the Harvest Home parade, it entails dressing up in the hat my mom currently holds, along with a fitted black coat, high-collared shirt, and a skirt complete with bustle, under which must be worn an actual, honest-to-God corset.

Driving the buggy in the Harvest Home parade means riding through town dressed up like a character from a Dickens novel.

No thank you.

"Dakota will be back soon. Have him do it. Please?"

"After this morning's GPS confusion, we are giving Dakota a break," Mom says. "Dad needs help downstairs. Besides, it looks better if someone from the family does it."

That's my mom, always thinking about appearances. Dad handles the bodies and everything that goes with them—caskets, vaults, death certificates, stuff like that. Mom takes care of stuff like finances and public relations. She goes to every festival, fair, and fundraiser, schmoozing and networking and making sure we are the first one people think about when Grandma or Grandpa dies. She should be wearing the corset and top hat.

"I'm riding in the vice mayor's car," she tells me before I can even suggest it. "We're being recognized for underwriting the new auditorium at city hall."

"What about Astrid?" My sister is a long shot, but I'm desperate. My anxiety has been barely noticeable these past couple of days; now I feel a warning zap as the worry starts flickering to life.

"She's marching with the pom squad," says Mom. "I know it's outside your comfort zone, but your father and I both think you're responsible enough. Do you have something better to do?"

Actually yes. I do. I was planning to meet my friends at the cook-out after the parade for the festival's kickoff concert. I did *not* plan on doing that dressed like an old-timey Morticia Addams.

Mom pulls a garment bag out of the closet and hands it to me.

"You'll be great, I'm sure." She lowers herself into her desk chair, flashing a smile before starting to clack away on the computer. "They want everyone at the fire station by three for lineup. Thanks, Elaine. You're the best."

The veil from the hat drags on the floor as I trudge back into the hall. Anger sprouts inside me, making me want to drop the hat and stomp on it. I strangle the anger at its roots. One lesson I learned a long time ago is that one does not throw a tantrum in the foyer of a funeral home.

My little sister bounces down the main stairs, a sequin-overflowing weekend bag at her hip. She is not dignified or unobtrusive or any of the things we are expected to be on the first floor of the house. If a grieving client walked in, they'd be greeted by the sight of a thirteen-year-old in false eyelashes and booty shorts, checking her slicked-back ponytail in the mirror over the guest-book table. From his frame above the table, Great-Great-Great-Grandfather Leathan looks on with the same grimly disappointed expression he's worn for more than a century.

"Is something wrong with the back way?" I ask.

"Sophia's picking me up out front," Astrid says. "The back creeps her mom out."

She says this matter-of-factly, like it's no problem to have your friends think the back of your house is creepy. And yet it *is* creepy—or at least a lot of people would think so—because that's where the garages are where we park the vans and the actual hearses that we use for actual funerals. It's also where the delivery bay is, where in the next hour or so two more bodies will be dropped off.

The back is where my family is supposed to enter and exit on our way to the second- and third-floor living quarters. It's where dead people enter and exit too. That's the way things have always been, and to know that Sophia's mom is turning up her nose at it makes me mad all over again. I'm mad she said it. I'm mad Astrid didn't set her straight. I'm mad that I have to wear a Victorian undertaker's costume and drive a horse-drawn hearse while my sister marches in a cute pom uniform like a normal person.

"I could take you," I offer. There was a time, not long ago, when she would have dropped everything in a heartbeat if it meant getting to hang out with her big sister. I actually miss that, plus driving her wherever she needs to be would let me stall on getting where I need to be.

"Yeah . . . no." She side-eyes the hat and garment bag. "Did Mom tell you where they're putting you?"

Ouch. I work my face into a smile that says I'm joking but also sort of not.

"I don't think we find that out until we get to the parade route," I tell her. "But I hope it's right behind you guys so I can yell how much I love you as loud as possible for the whole . . . entire . . . way. I'll make sure I do it by name, cool?"

She shudders as a car honks from the street outside. Astrid trots out the door and down the walk to a big SUV. I can just glimpse Sophia's mom in the driver's seat, all shiny hair and designer sunglasses. She's talking to the other pom girls in the back and doesn't even glance this way. Apparently, she's too busy to be creeped out now.

How nice of her.

I watch them drive off. Then I head back up to my room in the attic, using the back stairs because it's the right thing to do.

My phone sits on my bed, the screen crawling with texts from my friends.

Jaxon is for sure going tonight so I need to get him on the Ferris wheel. That's Sienna, the hopeless romantic, obsessing over the guy she's had a crush on since fourth grade. **Ferris wheel = cuddles & kisses.**

Ferris wheel also = dangerous af, warns Madison, who is even more type A than me, a rule follower to the extreme. **Those rides are never inspected properly—they just load them off a truck and set them up and hope nobody gets killed.**

It's fine, says Sienna. **If it breaks down that's more time together— and if I'm scared then he'll have to cuddle.**

Madison posts an eye-roll emoji. **Still dangerous. Elaine will back me up on this, right, Elaine?**

> Elaine?

> Hello . . . ?!

I scramble to get back into the conversation.

> Sorry! Got stuck downstairs—and I avoid rides even when they're not assembled by carnies, so my opinion is probably not valid here.

Yes it is! says Madison.
Boo, says Sienna.

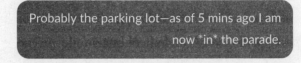

But don't do anything until I get there—I just got told I have to meet you at the end of the parade.

K—at the fountain? asks Sienna.

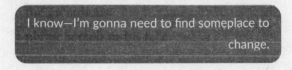

Probably the parking lot—as of 5 mins ago I am now *in* the parade.

Oh God . . . , says Madison.

I know—I'm gonna need to find someplace to change.

I send them a photo of the top hat sitting on the garment bag.
Sienna: **Uhhhhh . . .**
Madison: **This could only happen to you.**
Me: **Tell me about it.**

Sighing heavily, I pull off my leggings and sweatshirt. Then I pull on a pair of black tights and a chemise. Next, I lace up the corset and step into the bustle cage. Petticoats, skirt, high-collared shirt buttoned to my chin, and my braid fastened into a bun at the nape of my neck . . . I'm almost ready to go.

I tie the black ankle boots, grab the jacket, gloves, and hat, and then head back out, down through the living room and kitchen, down the back stairs again, past the door that opens onto the first floor, and down another level to the basement, where my dad is hard at work on dead body number one.

CHAPTER TWO

At the bottom of the stairs is a world completely different from the warm woods and fresh, fragrant flowers of the main floor. Passing through a nondescript door just beyond the back parlor, you descend into white walls, tile floors, and the faintest trace of a chemical smell.

The second of our two prep rooms sits at the end of a short, wide hallway. That's where I find Dad. He wears a white lab coat over his dress shirt and slacks. His suit jacket hangs on a hook just outside the door, ready to be put on should he be called upstairs to meet with a family.

Mr. Pagoni lies on a table that looks like an oversized dentist's tray. He's got to be older than eighty, and he's naked except for a towel covering his private parts. But it's not weird. When a body is old, it doesn't look like the body of anybody I know, except maybe my grandparents, but when I see them they have clothes on, so I'm not thinking about how they look naked.

So yeah. Old, naked, dead guy. Not weird. At least not to me.

Dad did most of the work on Mr. Pagoni when he came in two days ago, including what morticians call setting the features—inserting tiny cones behind the eyelids, placing cotton inside the mouth and sewing it shut so the person's face looks as natural as possible. With the visitation tomorrow morning, it's time to cosmetize. Dad whistles as he lays out vials of airbrush foundation on a tray by Mr. Pagoni's head.

"Aw, sweetheart," he says when he sees me all dressed up. "Thanks for taking one for the team."

I deposit the hat and coat on a chair in the corner of the room, lifting my skirt as I move in case the floor is wet.

"I guess it's no good begging you to use your veto power over Mom and make Dakota do it instead?"

"Since when have I had veto power over your mother?" he says. "Besides, Dakota doesn't fit the tux."

This, unfortunately, is true. The male version of this costume—a reproduction 1870s tuxedo with tails—was custom-made for Dad. Dad is taller than average, while Dakota is oddly petite for a guy. He would be swimming in it.

"I'm going to try and get there for the barbecue." Dad holds bottles up to Mr. Pagoni's cheek, trying to match the skin tone. "That's if I can get caught up. Today turned out busier than I'd thought."

He doesn't say what we both know—that busy isn't a bad thing, especially when we've been having a series of slow patches. It might be awful for whoever is going through the loss of a friend or a family member, but the very nature of our work is that when other people are having the worst days of their lives, we are doing well. If I let myself think too much about what my family does, it's hard not to feel guilty, because I want the things that come with having a family that does well: nice phone, nice clothes, a car to drive. But I get to have all those things because somebody else lost someone they love. Dad says we perform a necessary service, and there's no shame in taking payment for it. I don't feel ashamed necessarily, just . . . aware. And Dad says that's a good thing too.

"Looks like you're almost done with Mr. Pagoni," I say. "Maybe you can do the parade after all? Mrs. Keener's not going anywhere. Neither is the guy from the medical examiner's."

"Now see, as soon as I make a promise, the phone will ring with another death call." He tosses me a bottle. "Can you look in the drawer over there and check if we have any more of this in ivory beige? I'm pretty sure Mrs. Pagoni doesn't want Mr. Pagoni looking like he just got back from Aruba."

I find a lighter foundation, bring it around to Dad, and watch as he starts applying the makeup to Mr. Pagoni's face and neck. Once Mr. Pagoni has been dressed in the suit that hangs in a cleaner's bag nearby, Dad will put color on his hands as well. The goal is to make him look like he's sleeping or resting. But honestly, that's impossible. Dead people do not look like they are sleeping. Dead people look dead. Still, people always compliment my dad on the care he takes with everyone he touches. I like watching him work.

"What if I can't control the horses?" I ask.

"You've done it before. They're Aaron's best-trained Belgians. They practically drive themselves."

"But you were always with me. I'm going to look ridiculous."

"Stop by the drugstore and get a few bags of candy," he says. "That's always a hit with the kids."

"Throwing candy from a hearse?" I mock-cringe. "That's not a weird juxtaposition or anything."

"It's joy in the face of sadness. It's the juxtaposition of the universe. Also you look beautiful."

He winks at me over Mr. Pagoni's head, and even though he's smiling I know I'm treading close to the limits of his patience. My dad has two main modes: Whimsical Fun Dad, which is who I'm dealing with now, and Disappointed Dad. Refusing to do the parade would disappoint him, and when my father is disappointed, he gets painful to be around at best. At worst, he's straight-up intimidating. He becomes very formal. He speaks to you only when absolutely necessary. And the most excruciating thing about it is that you don't know what will un-disappoint him. You can spend days doing whatever he asks to the very best of your ability before things finally feel normal again. When I was little, Mom said I inherited my silent-treatment temper from him. I also inherited his dark brown hair and hazel eyes, which people have told me are striking. Whether I truly am beautiful, no one has ever said except for him, but it's not something a person hates to hear.

"Fine." Flattery has chipped away at my resistance. "But no candy. It'll just get squished on the road."

"That's my practical girl." He smiles. The delivery-bay buzzer goes off, sending an echo down the hallway. "Ah, Dakota's finally found his way home."

"I'll help him. I have to get going anyway."

I make my way to the door at the other end of the hall, where Dakota is trying to wrestle a gurney with a body bag on it over the lip in the floor. One of the wheels has become stuck, plus the door isn't latched open the way it should be. Dakota alternates between bumping the door with his butt and yanking at the gurney in what looks like some nerdy dance move.

I grab hold, pushing the door until it catches. Then I bend over (which is not easy in this outfit) and free the gurney wheel from the threshold. The whole thing lurches forward with Dakota still hanging on.

"You could have opened the door correctly before bringing in the body," I inform him.

"Sorry," he says. "The latch wasn't working."

"Whatever. Prep room one is ready."

My phone pings from the depths of my black crepe skirt. I fish it out, thinking it'll be Madison with more concert details. Instead, it's her twin brother, Miles, aka my fellow *Dragonfly* geek and the fourth member of our friend group.

> Did you see this? Look!!!

I open the link he sent to find the website for DraCon Central, the midwestern arm of the annual *Dragonfly* fan convention. *Dragonfly* is famous for being one of the most complex science fiction/fantasy series ever made, and fans have three annual Convergences around the country where they meet to hang out and bask in all things out-there. Miles and I have been watching *Dragonfly* since it started. We've been in fandom long enough to be semi–big names. But we've never been to a con.

Now, plastered across the top of the Central website, is a banner announcing that Magnus Tiedemann, the actor who plays Pax on the show, will be attending as a special guest.

Magnus never goes anywhere, says Miles. **Now we have to go.**

> Really?!

> Yes really!

> But you never go anywhere either.

> Maybe I didn't have any place I wanted to go until now.

DraCon Central always takes place in November. Going would mean driving four hours to Chicago, probably finding someplace to stay overnight, and being away from all the things that need us here at home. But Miles is obsessed with Magnus. With Magnus so close, he just might try to go see him.

I text back.

> You and Magnus in the same room = blinding brilliance.

> My brilliance is nothing without you to reflect it—we go to conquer. See you tonight?

Grinning, I thumb in my response.

> Yes but later, thanks to some late-breaking shenanigans.

> Uh-oh? Good shenans or bad shenans?

> Let's just say my plans to watch the parade from the sidelines have been foiled—you marching with cross-country?

> Yep, then helping get the grills started.

Come find me after.

Always.

And again, I'm grinning. I'm also feeling bad for being so hard on Dakota, so I turn around and help him get the gurney into the empty prep room. Then I shove my phone back into my pocket and take the stairs to the main floor two at a time, leaving Dakota and Dad to deal with dead body number two.

CHAPTER THREE

The one good thing about driving the buggy is that I'm up so high I don't have to talk to anyone. It's good because the longer I sit here, the more I'm having déjà vu.

This déjà vu goes all the way back to kindergarten, when people started calling me Funeral Girl. The reason for the nickname is obvious (duh, my family runs the local funeral home). But there's more to it, because the funeral home—my home—is supposed to be haunted.

The Gillies Ghost, so the story goes, is a woman who jumped from the third-floor attic window back around the time the old hearse I'm driving carried actual bodies in it. People claim you can still see her standing in the window, which means we get regular gawkers peering up at the house from the sidewalk, especially on Halloween, when they also leave candles and flowers and other offerings by the sign in our front yard. The Gillies Ghost story is horse doo-doo, even stinkier than the massive pile that just got dumped into the manure bag in front of me, and I should know because the

17

third-floor window where people say she appears is *my* window. If there was a ghost in my bedroom, I think I would have seen it.

Funeral Girl! Funeral Girl! It was the soundtrack to every lunch and recess until fifth grade, when kids started to outgrow stupid name-calling. Or maybe I shrank myself and my temper into a small and quiet-enough space that they finally got bored and forgot about me. Most of them don't notice me anymore. But still. Here I am, dressed like *an actual funeral girl,* and I'm just glad I'm perched high enough above everybody's heads to avoid making conversation.

I am not, however, high enough to escape the stench of horse poop, or the embarrassment of watching my other horse pee all over the pavement.

"Ew, nasty!" The trombone section from my school's marching band wanders into view. Stepping around the pee, they wave to a couple of guys from the drum line as I dip my head over my phone, hoping the brim of my hat hides my face. Meanwhile Aaron, the farmer Mom and Dad rent the horses from, speaks soothingly to the animals until the drummers rat-a-tat to another part of the line.

Aaron rode with me to the staging area. On the way, he gave last-minute pointers on how to keep the buggy on a steady roll and get the horses to stop, slow down, and work together, basically preventing the whole thing from turning into a parade-crushing stampede. We are now sandwiched between kids from Strickland's School of Tae Kwon Do and mini-ballerinas from Miss Bobbi's Twinkle Toes dance studio. Aaron is on the ground, while I sit up on the driver's platform, watching a kaleidoscope of colors shift and morph inside my favorite relaxation app. When you live with anxiety, little strategies help, especially in stressful situations like this.

"Elaine!"

I look down to see Mom in her red power suit, craning to catch my attention.

"Elaine, put away the phone. It ruins the effect."

"The parade hasn't started yet," I tell her. "And the only people who can see me don't give a crap if I'm on my phone."

"Language, Elaine." She pats one of the horses and turns to Aaron. "Tom is up to his ears at home. He won't be able to make the barbecue, so can you drive the buggy back?"

Aaron assures her he will. Mom shoots me a conciliatory smile.

"Oh, and I hate to ask this, Lainey, but we *just* got a call from Blanchester. Dakota doesn't know how to get there. It can wait until after the parade, but would you mind riding along for that pickup?"

"But I'm going to the concert with Sienna and Madison."

"I know and I'm sorry," she says. "But there's nobody else to ask. We're sponsoring the arts council ice cream booth, so I have to be here. Otherwise, I'd go myself."

"Am I not doing enough right now?" I run my hand along my corset-clad torso, sweeping it out to include the horses and the hearse. I've been looking forward to the concert with my friends all week; it's a Harvest Home tradition.

"I don't know, are you?" Mom snaps back. "We're having our first truly busy day in months. But if you can't be bothered, your father can leave all the work he has to do and handle the death call too."

"No, I'll do it." I let submission bloom in anger's place. This happens all the time, and I hate the helpless way it makes me feel. But I can't just leave them hanging.

"Wonderful," says Mom. "You're the best."

She turns, just in time to collide with a guy handing out postcards. He presses one into her hand. She looks at it and scowls.

"Who gave them permission to distribute these?" She passes the postcard up to me. It's from Memories, the funeral home that just opened in Philipsburg, and the reason Mom and Dad are so grateful for a busy day. Up until recently, Philipsburg was one of the drabbest of the drab little places that make up our little corner of Illinois. But the area near the highway has been reinventing itself as a modern oasis, starting with the big megachurch that went up a couple of years ago and the strip mall that's being built as we speak. Memories took over Bud Nolan's funeral parlor when he retired and turned it into this sleek, touchy-feely place that calls itself "a new concept in honoring lives well lived," whatever that means. The postcards are advertising a raffle for a MacBook Air and a free consultation on "planning for a beautiful and meaningful transition."

"This is too much." Mom grabs the postcard back. "We've been supporting this festival for decades and we've never had to deal with competitors before."

What she really means is that we've never had to deal with competitors, period. The Nolans' business was a lot smaller than ours. But Memories expanded it, and now they're bringing in the competition big-time. Part of the reason Dad's at home now and not here at the parade is because he doesn't want people calling Memories if no one's available at Gillies.

Mom goes off to complain to the vice mayor, and the guy with the postcards wanders toward the police cars at the front of the lineup. One of the cars whoops its siren. The others start swirling their lights. Miss Bobbi's baby ballerinas start toddling forward in their tutus. The marching band strikes up the school fight song. Aaron clicks his tongue, and I scramble to pull on my gloves and grab the reins. The horses walk, the buggy bounces, and I can't worry anymore about competing funeral homes or being forced to miss the concert because I am rolling toward Main Street, trying not to run anybody over and create any more dead bodies for my father to deal with today.

❧

"Candy! Where's the candy?"

Up and down the sidewalk, little kids dart in and out, grabbing bubble gum and rolls of Smarties off the pavement. When they see me, they start jumping and shouting, and part of me wishes I'd followed my dad's advice to pick up some Dum Dums on the way here. The other part is glad I didn't because controlling the horses takes all my attention, especially with a bunch of Shriner guys in tiny cars zipping in and out of the other marchers. I must be doing an okay job because I haven't heard anyone screaming about their child getting trampled, nor has the parade stopped to free one of the Shriners from underneath the buggy. Of course, it is pretty loud, so screaming might be hard to hear. And the parade marshals are so militant about keeping things moving that I'm not sure they would actually stop, even for a dude in a tiny car getting dragged under the wheels of a Victorian hearse. If I focus on what's just ahead of me, I can pretty much tune out the kids and keep the horses on track. My fingers unclench inside my gloves. I start to relax.

"Hey! Watch out!"

At the edge of my peripheral vision is a figure. This figure stands still while everything else keeps going forward, including my horses.

My focus adjusts, and all at once I make out what the figure is. It's a guy in a cross-country T-shirt. He's facing me, but his actual face is blocked by a camera. A woman from the sidelines screams at him to get out of the way; he doesn't hear her. I yank the reins, the horses rear up, and I shout—to warn the guy but also because I'm teetering on my seat, afraid I might fall into the street.

The boy lowers the camera. Our eyes meet, and this must be that thing you hear about where time slows down as you hover on the brink of a catastrophe. The moment stretches. We look at each other, and something sparks in my core, like a match against the side of a box. It's his eyes. They're big and dark and just the slightest bit sad.

Another heartbeat and the moment's over. The boy seems to realize he's about to get pulverized. He bolts away. I lose sight of him in the sea of kicking, spinning tae-kwon-do kids. And now people are shouting at me to go, go, *GO!*

Heart pounding, neck sweating, I start rolling forward again, but slower now—a lot slower.

Who *was* that boy? Our school takes kids from all of the towns within a ten-mile circle, so I can't say I know every one of my classmates, but I'm certain I've never seen him before. We looked at each other no longer than a second, but it felt like much more. And even though I should have been terrified, the adrenaline shooting through my body did not feel like terror; it actually felt good.

As I continue down the parade route, I look for the boy and don't see him again, which is probably a good thing because I'm not sure I could avoid a second crash. And wouldn't that be fun for people in this town? They'd love a new addition to the local lore: FUNERAL GIRL KILLED IN A VICTORIAN HEARSE WIPEOUT. My spirit would haunt Main Street, wandering among parade spectators every year at Harvest Home, accompanied by the hoofbeats of ghostly horses.

That's what people would say, but they'd be wrong. Because if I died, this would be the last place I'd hang around. I'd say bye to Dodson, bye to driving the buggy, and bye to worrying about competition from a slick new funeral home called Memories. If I could go anywhere I wanted, I'm not sure where I'd go exactly, but I would definitely be moving on to bigger, better things.

CHAPTER FOUR

The parade might be the official kickoff to Harvest Home, but things don't really get started until the Masons fire up their grills for the barbecue at the park. Reaching the end of the route, all the marching band people, the tae-kwon-do kids, and the baby ballerinas peel off to meet their families. I, however, am stuck until Aaron comes to get the buggy. So I climb down and stand beside the horses, texting to let Madison and Sienna know where I am.

Astrid drifts by with her pom-squad friends. I catch her eye, and for a second I think she might say hello. Surely I'm not *so* embarrassing now that we're not in front of an audience of everybody in the county anymore. But nope. She moves away without even waving.

I envy my sister a lot of things, but right now the biggest is the amount of skin she's exposing. It might be the end of September, but the weather is sweltering. And this costume is hot as hell. Sweat drips down my back. Even my legs are sweating. I take off the hat, wiping my forehead and feeling my soaked hair.

"Nice horses."

"What?" I turn to find myself face to face with *the boy*—the one who nearly caused an epic crash by taking parade photos from the middle of the street. He looks like any regular boy, with messy hair the color of sand and a sprinkling of zits on his forehead. But his eyes. Up close I can see they're a shade of brown so deep it feels like they could swallow me if I looked at them long enough. Heat flickers at the edges, and it's all I can do not to look away while I wait for him to answer.

"Nice horses," he repeats. "They were terrifying when they were about to run me over, but they seem perfectly nice now."

He reaches out to pet the mane of the one closest to me. The horse lifts its head for a scratch on the nose before going back to munching the hay I put down on the pavement.

"You shouldn't have been in the street." I cross my arms, then uncross them, suddenly aware of the pit stains that I'm sure are visible through my jacket.

"I know." He holds up the camera around his neck. "I'm taking photos for the *Daily,* and I was just trying to get this one shot. It took longer than I thought it would. But . . . success! I got it. Just in time."

"You also almost got us both killed."

"Sometimes you have to put yourself at risk to capture something amazing." He smiles a smoldering smile, and my voice catches in my throat. What do you say to a guy with startlingly gorgeous eyes who literally steps in front of you and brings your world to a screeching halt?

"What's so amazing?" I ask as I look around at the dumpy park with the dumpy carnival rides and the people hanging out, waiting for cookout food. "I can't think of a single thing here that's worth dying for."

He raises an eyebrow as he gives my outfit a once-over.

"This is just a costume," I say. "I don't wear this every day."

He looks at me like *Duh, why would you wear that every day?*

"It seems like a pretty sweet job, though," he says. He steps back to get a better look at the hearse. "Did you get hired for this?"

"No. My family owns it. The funeral home, I mean."

"Wow, serious?"

"Yes. So technically it is my job, but no I didn't get hired because I'm already in the family, so . . ."

I scan the park for my friends, desperate to be rescued from this new affliction of oral diarrhea. I'd probably be an awkward mess anyway, but cute boy plus me in full buggy getup? This is pure nightmare fuel.

First, I look for the Thespian Club tent, because that's the most likely place to find Madison and Sienna. They're theater kids, both in Pops Choir and Chamber Chorale with me, where I am *not* a theater kid. I'm the accompanist, which means I play piano for rehearsals and concerts. The bright red comedy-and-tragedy banner dances dramatically in the wind, but they are not underneath it.

Over by the coolers, I spot the rest of the cross-country team. Miles is easy to recognize, not just because he's a head taller than the rest of them, or because of his red hair, but because he is a laughing, joking tornado who pulls everyone nearby into his vortex. They're all cracking up, guzzling Gatorade, but this boy in front of me doesn't seem in a hurry to join them.

"I didn't know working for a funeral home included horse driving," the boy says. "You're good at it."

"They're Amish-trained, so they're really well behaved," I tell him. "I have other things I'm better at."

"Oh yeah?" His smile turns wicked. "Like what?"

Now I really don't know what to say and thank God I don't have to figure it out alone. In a stroke of ridiculously good timing, Madison and Sienna appear from around the other side of the buggy.

Madison studies me, her lips pursed in amusement.

"You look hot," she says. "And not in a good way."

A rivulet of sweat rolls from underneath my corset down past my underwear, along my tights and into my boots.

"Thanks." I fan my face. "Maybe I'll spontaneously combust and destroy this costume forever. That'd be a worthy sacrifice, right?"

"Well, I like your dress," Sienna says. "It's very operatic."

"Which means a lot coming from you," I tell her. Sienna is an Audra McDonald doppelgänger who looks like she should be leading Valkyries into battle or decked out in miles of lace, charming infatuated suitors while secretly dying of consumption. If anyone could find the romance in a corset and bustle, it's her.

"I'm worried Elaine will get heatstroke." Madison frowns, always the mom of the group. She looks like what Anne of Green Gables would look like if she had a pixie cut and did show choir. As much as I love her, I'm constantly amazed that someone so tightly wound could be twins with Miles.

I don't think I've ever seen Miles with any other expression on his face but near laughter or full-out laughter or a raised eyebrow that suggests he's on the verge of cracking up. Like this very second, when he sprints over and throws an arm around the shoulder of the boy in the matching cross-country shirt.

"Hey, X, there's a hot dog missing from the grill. I said I'd check with you, but I'm pretty sure nobody wants your little smokie."

The boy laughs and says, "Watch the camera, Drummond!" but still lets himself get noogied.

"And you . . ." Miles turns to me. "You survived the paradapocalypse. I'm relieved to be in the dimension where we all end up safe and sound and ready to listen to the sweet country stylings of the Doc Bakers."

Madison and Sienna shake their heads at his mash-up of *Dragonfly* and Harvest Home fair references. But it makes me laugh.

"We almost ended up in the dimension where everybody got trampled to a bloody pulp," I tell him. "Thanks to this guy."

I have a wardrobe of smiles I put on for various occasions. There's my sympathetic smile that I use when I'm working with grieving people. There's my aw-shucks-it-was-nothing smile that I use when our choir director, Mr. Ferrara, acknowledges me during concerts. And then there's my trying-not-to-look-too-eager-to-find-out-who-you-are-but-it'd-be-really-nice-if-you-told-me smile, which I use now on the boy standing next to Miles.

He looks confused by the banter. Clearly, he doesn't speak *Dragonfly* either. I give up and thrust out my hand. "I'm Elaine."

A beat goes by where everyone tries not to notice that I've reverted to funeral home formality. Apparently, the heat has short-circuited Work Elaine with Normal Person Elaine.

Play it off, I tell myself. *Don't make it weird.*

I pull in a calming breath and keep my hand out. The boy gives it a little shake. His fingers are dry and rough, like he bites his nails.

"I'm Xander," he says.

"Xander moved here this summer, right before practice started," Miles tells us. "You're in Philipsburg, right?"

"Yeah," says Xander. "My dad's a chef, and—"

"Really?" I interrupt, suddenly even more fascinated. "A chef?" I have visions of a kitchen in a big-city restaurant producing delectable dishes for celebrities. I've always wanted to go someplace like that—sit at an elegant table sampling new and interesting food while watching new and interesting people. "Where did you move from?"

"Springfield, Missouri," Xander answers. "My uncle owns the nursing home in Philipsburg and they needed someone to run the kitchen. He hired my dad, and here we are."

So, not elegant. I guess it should be obvious that there are chefs everywhere, and Missouri is as likely a place to have moved from as Boston or San Francisco. I wait for the glamour to evaporate—for Xander to go back to being just a boy again, but my stomach keeps cartwheeling every time he glances at me.

From the stage at the back of the park come the sounds of microphone feedback and a guitar playing a country lick as the band warms up for the concert at dusk.

"Sounds like . . . music?" says Xander.

"It's the Doc Bakers," says Madison. "They had that line dance everybody used to do, the 'Little House Shuffle'?"

"They're trash," says Sienna. "But the concert is a tradition, so . . ."

Her voice trails off, and I know she's looking for Jaxon. Dusk has started to fall, the carnival lights are blinking on, and even though Harvest Home is cheesy, right now there's a definite hint of romance in the air.

"You can stay, right?" Miles asks Xander.

"I can stay," Xander answers. "My dad works all the time so it's not like there's anything going on at home anyway."

Sienna raises an eyebrow at me just as Aaron materializes out of the crowd like some reverse fairy godmother reminding me it's time to leave the ball.

"Hey, Elaine, we need to go," he says. "Your dad's asking when I'll have you home."

Ugh. Right. I forgot I promised to help Dakota.

"You have to go?" Madison says it like she already knows the answer. My friends have grown used to me canceling plans for funeral-home stuff.

"Why would you have to go?" asks Xander.

The Masons start ringing their big bell, which is the Harvest Home way of saying the food's ready, and as if to inject a fresh dose of get-your-butt-home guilt, I see that the guy from Memories is now handing out postcards to people in line.

"Something came up," I say. "I have to go do this one thing that hopefully won't take too long."

"That sucks," says Sienna.

"But okay," says Madison.

They turn away, already engrossed in a new private conversation. Miles rests a hand on my arm.

"You good?" he asks.

No. It's not fair that you all get to stay and have fun while I have to go. The Doc Bakers may be trash, but I was sort of looking forward to doing the "Little House Shuffle." I want to say all that, but I don't want to complain in front of Xander, so I simply nod. It is what it is.

Miles tilts his head, the corner of his mouth rising in a way that tells me he gets it.

As Aaron helps me back up the hearse, I lose my grip on the top hat. It tumbles, and a breeze sends it skittering across the parking lot. Xander scrambles after it, plucking it out of a bush. He climbs up the side of the buggy and holds it out to me.

"When you're done with whatever you have to do, come back," he says. "Okay?"

He has a little mole on his right cheek. It stands out from the freckles sprinkled there like a speck of brown sugar. When I lift my gaze to his eyes, I feel the regret of leaving even stronger.

"I'll see you?" he says hopefully.

"If I can," I say.

"We'll wait for you by the funnel cake stand!" He hops down as Aaron starts turning the buggy around.

I resist the urge to look back as we head out of the park. The sounds of the warm-up band follow us on the early evening air. The farther away we get, the more muffled the music gets until it's nothing more than echoes off the buildings along Main Street.

Aaron turns the corner, and home looms into view with its massive wraparound porch and steps that lead down to the front walk, where a sign announces GILLIES FAMILY FUNERAL HOME—SERVING OUR COMMUNITY SINCE 1878.

Dad emerges from the back of the house to meet Dakota, who's just pulling the van into the drive, fresh from the hospital with dead body number three.

Aaron whistles. "So, you have to go back out again tonight? You really are having a busy day."

"Yeah." I lift my skirt to the side and let him give me a hand down to the curb. "Guess I'll go make some coffee."

CHAPTER FIVE

"Astrid, come on. We're going to be late."

Silence from behind my sister's bedroom door. I lift my fist to pound on it. The door opens and she slinks out, ducking under my arm in a new sweater with her hair in waves. I rush after her, the two of us bumping down the back stairs and around to the garage where we keep the family cars. I hop into the front seat. She slides into the passenger side.

"Seriously?" I say once I catch my breath. "If you can't be ready on time, you can take the bus."

"Sorry." She punctuates it with half an eye roll. I want to say more, like how the least she could do is talk to me so I don't feel like an Uber driver. But I'm not in the mood for another argument, not when we're so short on time.

Astrid and I are in the same building now, which means I've added transporting her to my list of family duties. And it means we're spending a lot more time together because it's a twenty-minute drive on a good day. Our school sits in the middle of five towns. They all have elementary schools, but none of the towns is big enough to have its own high school, so everyone comes together starting in eighth grade at a big building surrounded by soybean fields.

When school started this year, I thought driving together would help us get close again, like we were when she was a grade-schooler. I figured she'd feel better knowing I'm here, a junior and the comfort of a home base. But every morning it's the same: She texts with her friends, who are all waiting for her on the sidewalk when we pull up, and I don't hear from her again until she gets home from pom practice too tired to talk with anyone, let alone hang out.

This morning, she's on her phone before I start the ignition. Nothing.

"Ugh." I try to start the car again. Still nothing. "Great."

"Now we're really going to be late," Astrid says unhelpfully.

This car is two years older than I am, with an odometer racking up a whopping 150,000 miles. Dad got a deal on it from his friend at Jake's Discount Auto, and it ticks off all the things he and Mom think are important in a car for a teenager: Number 1, It's huge, "so if you get in an accident, more of the car will be hurt than you." Number 2, It was cheap, so it's paid for, "because cars are terrible investments, best to stay out of debt." And number 3, It doesn't make me look like a spoiled rich kid. "We don't want to send the wrong message."

But I guess *running reliably* wasn't a top item on their list. This is the second time in the past month that the car has refused to start.

We get out and start looking for a plan B. Mom's at a breakfast meeting for the Rotary Club, and Dad's meeting with a family behind closed doors.

"Where's Dakota?" Astrid says.

"Who knows? Playing Fortnite? Drinking kombucha some-where?"

Instead I find him in the prep rooms, unpacking supply boxes.

"We need a ride to school," I say. "Are you super busy with that, or can you help?"

"I can help." He unclips his bow tie and unbuttons his dress shirt to reveal a faded tee with a cartoon of Jesus riding a dinosaur on the front, and I find myself wondering for the hundredth time what in the heck he's doing training to be a funeral director.

"You want a hearse, or you want my car?" he asks as we make our way back outside.

"Your car!" Astrid and I both say. But the only improvement Dakota's orange VW Bug offers over a hearse is that it isn't a hearse. Dakota's car is filthy, inside and out. Apprentices make decent money, but I know Dakota has a ton of student loans, plus he's helping put his little brother through a special school for kids with autism. I once heard him video-chatting with friends, saying he'd probably be homeless if my parents didn't provide room and board in the house behind our main one—the house that was the original funeral home back when Great-Great-Great-Grandfather Leathan started the business. Back then, it had enough space for Triple-Great-G-Father to work and live. That's hard to believe when you see it today, just a one-bedroom apartment with a tiny kitchenette, a tiny bathroom, and a tiny sitting room. It's even harder to believe when you see the massive house that the funeral home moved into as the business grew.

"You know, when I was your age, I took the bus to school," Dakota says as we pull out of the front drive.

I make a half-interested sound from my spot in the back. Up in the passenger seat, Astrid stares out the window.

"Of course, that was in Cleveland," he continues. "We had neighborhood schools, so we didn't have far to go. The buses out here are picking people up at six a.m. to get to school by eight, and these old country roads are bumpy. I can see why you'd want to drive yourself."

Now that we're on our way, I'm actually glad someone else is driving because Miles has been texting me links to some sketchy takes on Saturday's *Dragonfly* episode. It's Nelson, a fanboy we both despise, going off with an already-disproved theory about bootstrap paradoxes. Lots of people hate *Dragonfly,* but Nelson hates it in the most annoying way. His whole personality is deliberately misreading things. But rather than direct arguments to him, Miles directs them to me. He's already up to eleven texts.

> I mean, if you don't like it or you don't get it, maybe just don't watch?

How long have you been up? I ask, interrupting his rant. It's not even seven-thirty, and he's clearly been at this awhile.

Since five, he answers. **New baby calf out at the Schmidts + litter of piglets due soon.**

Of course Miles was up. His mom's a veterinarian and he goes along on calls because he wants to be one too; he gets up early nearly every day.

Even though I know Nelson's analysis will piss me off, I open the link anyway. Three sentences in, I've already seen enough to think someone needs to hit him with a truck.

"What a load of crap!" I mutter, and then immediately regret it because Dakota is now eyeing me in the rearview mirror.

"What are you reading, Elaine?"

"Probably something about *Dragonfly*," Astrid tells him. "It's so weird."

"Um, excuse me." I kick the back of her seat. "No it's not. Maybe be quiet?"

Too late, Dakota's ears have perked up.

"You're into *Dragonfly*?" he says. "Wow! I gave that show a try and thought it was a massive mindscrew."

I resist the urge to say, *Well, of course* you *would think that, Dakota*, because—to be honest—he is far from the only person to hold that opinion. There are dozens of characters in *Dragonfly*, windingly weird plots, and imagery that even in a dull episode could be considered out-there.

But there's also something that pulls me in—on the deepest and not-so-deep levels.

When I first started watching, I felt an instant connection to Pax and Skye, soul mates who must meet lifetime after lifetime in order to advance to perfect enlightenment. It's the same with every other soul, except they are the alpha and omega, and once they reach their final level, all humanity will end. As they unlock the truth about their destinies, and as other entities work for and against them, the universe changes and evolves.

I love *Dragonfly*, but I also appreciate how absurd it can be. Three years ago, when Miles outed himself as a fellow stan by skewering the episode where the Night Queen hosts this ridiculously campy orgy of the gods, I started riffing along and it was like jazz, like a great game of tennis, like hilarious improv. Finally, someone else understood the perfection of this strange cake batter of escapism and profound existentialism. We watch every episode together now, either in person or via video chat. Then we spend the rest of the week analyzing, appreciating, and angsting with the rest of the fandom.

> And . . . Look at this.

Miles sends a screengrab of the DraCon Central registration list. Nelson is on it.

Of course he's going, I respond. **His mom needs to air out the basement.**

> Now we really have to go. We have to troll him—damn what if Magnus trolls him too? We can't miss that!

I've only been to Chicago twice: once for my cousin's wedding, and once for a school field trip. The school trip was a blur of shuttling between the museums and the aquarium to the soundtrack of chaperones screaming at everyone to stay together. And for the wedding I was seven. So, I don't feel like I've ever really *been* to Chicago. I imagine going there now with Miles, doing the convention, exploring the city, feeling like we're part of something bigger. My thoughts start to swell with excitement and possibility.

I text him back.

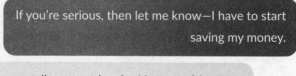

> If you're serious, then let me know—I have to start saving my money.

> We can talk more at lunch—I have to drive to school. Speaking of . . . How are you texting me right now?

I smile, imagining Mom Madison getting into the truck next to Miles, scolding about the dangers of texting and driving.

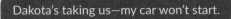

Dakota's taking us—my car won't start.

Ugh. Great start to a great day, huh?

I look around the disgusting VW, at my sister planning to meet up with her friends as soon as we get to school, and roll my head to work out the tension creeping into my neck and shoulders.

Yeah, I reply. It can only get better from here.

CHAPTER SIX

wouldn't exactly say the day's gotten better, more like it's gone into a sort of sideways skid that includes getting a D on an AP chemistry quiz. By the time lunch rolls around, I'm ready to hit the refresh button. But when I get to our table, Madison and Sienna are comparing notes on how awesome Friday night was without me.

"Did he really do that?" Sienna is saying. "Tell me he really did do that, and I didn't just dream it."

"Yeah, he did it," Madison says with a mixture of admiration and disapproval.

"Who did what?" I ask as I slide into my usual seat.

"Xander," says Madison. "After the Doc Bakers, we went to the quarry. A bunch of people were having a bonfire."

"You know that old tree that hangs out over the pit?" Sienna says. "Xander climbed that thing and tied a rope to it. Then he *freaking swung on it*. We thought he was going to fall, but then he swung back and landed on his feet right in the parking lot."

"A few other people did it too," says Madison, now looking firmly shocked. "They could have died."

"It was wiiild!" says Sienna.

"Wild," I repeat, wondering why this is the first I'm hearing about it. Neither of them mentioned a bonfire before now, and when I asked how the concert was, all I got was "pretty good" from Madison and "trash, as expected, but Jaxon and I danced to 'Be My Beth,' so now that's our song," from Sienna. Miles at least told me about the party when we watched *Dragonfly* on Saturday, but I had no idea it was so exciting—especially not that this new boy dazzled everyone with death-defying stunts.

"I heard he got kicked out of school in Springfield," Sienna says. "That's why he's really here."

"Yeah, he broke into the building at night, and they caught him," adds Madison.

"What was he doing?" asks Sienna.

"Probably something pretty bad if it got him kicked out."

I listen to the two of them, trying not to look forlorn. This has been happening a lot lately: Madison and Sienna do their own thing, have their own secrets, go their own way without me. I do bug out a lot on plans because of stuff that comes up at the funeral home; it's only fair to admit that. But they used to keep me looped in. Lately, I feel like I'm getting left behind.

"I heard the spring musical's going to be *Sweeney Todd*," Madison says.

My ears perk up—music is one topic I can actually be a part of.

"Sweet!" I say.

"Ugh," says Sienna.

"Why?" I'm confused. "*Sweeney Todd* is an amazing musical."

"Yes, but the lead cast is tiny. And the female leads are a white middle-aged lady and a young white girl." Sienna runs her hand along her cheek, as if showcasing her brown skin to a stranger.

"That shouldn't matter," I say.

"It shouldn't, but the fact that you think it wouldn't shows your privilege, Elaine. You have no idea what it's like being one of the only Black people in this school. You don't see all the ways I have to work twice as hard as everybody else."

Madison is nodding, like this should have been obvious, and now my cheeks are burning. I feel like an idiot.

"I just meant the parts can be played by anyone," I say.

"Or Ferrara could pick shows with a more diverse cast," Sienna shoots back. "There are tons of options if he wanted to put in the effort."

"But still, you would make the perfect Mrs. Lovett," Madison tells her. "It's just right for your voice, and Johanna is perfect for mine. But Jasmine apparently thinks it's perfect for hers too." She bristles at the thought of her archrival, who, as a senior, is better positioned to snatch up a lead.

I have an idea—a way to stay in their musical orbit.

"If you want, I could help you practice," I offer. "Since I play for auditions, it'll help you be prepared."

Sienna's face lights up. "Now I like how you're thinking." She reaches across the table to give me a fist bump, and I can feel my world shifting back to normal.

Madison opens her mouth to add something, only to be interrupted by Miles slipping into the seat next to her.

"You guys look like you're plotting some trouble," he says as he plops down a tray stacked with pizza slices. He grins at us while another boy sits next to me. My gaze slides first to his tray; it's loaded with chicken nuggets, which are being smothered in ranch dressing by said boy, the one I almost ran over at the Harvest Home parade.

Xander.

"Hey." He nods. "You're Elaine. Girl with the horses."

"Right." My head feels a little light at the sound of his voice, especially when that voice speaks my name. I've been wondering if I'd see him around school. Saturday afternoon I went back to Harvest Home with my dad, and the whole time I kept an eye out, thinking he might come back too. I even asked Miles if he planned to bring any friends to the fair, but he told me that he (and thus, Xander) had a cross-country meet.

Now Xander is here. Same messy sandy hair, same mole dotting his suntanned cheek, same deep brown eyes. The only thing missing is the camera around his neck.

"You never came back for the concert," he says. "We stayed by the funnel cakes until everybody else left, just in case, but you stood us up."

A flush of pleasure runs through me that he noticed. Not only that, he waited for me.

"I had to work," I say.

"At the funeral home, right? That's so cool."

"It's not that cool."

"It's pretty cool," he says. "Especially if what I heard about you is true—there's a ghost at your house?"

I swear I hear actual screeching brakes as everyone at the table stops what they're doing. The atmosphere hovers between *This could be interesting* and *Prepare to run for cover*. My friends know the ghost thing is a sore subject for me.

Miles lets out a weird giggle.

"Elaine's not a big fan of that rumor," he says. "The Gillies Ghost is like your weird uncle who keeps coming over for dinner. You have to be nice to him, but he's cringey to have around and he won't take a hint and go away."

But Xander won't let it go.

"I heard it's a woman," he says. "Maybe she jumped out a window?"

"It's wrong to glorify suicide," Madison tells him.

"Right. Sorry."

He blushes, and the sight of it melts whatever prickliness I might have been feeling.

"Supposedly somebody jumped out the third-floor window," I tell him. "Depending how out-there you want to get, she can either be seen up there still or she actually comes down and eats your brains."

"Mmmm . . . brains . . . ," says Miles with just the right timing and intonation to make everyone laugh.

But it's not really that funny, considering our business is comforting people as they deal with the very not-funny reality of death. My parents try not to make too big a deal about the Gillies Ghost because they know the last thing mourning loved ones need is to be thinking about restless spirits.

"Seriously, though. My dad says that story has been around forever," I say. "And there's no evidence to back it up."

"Plus let's face it, people can be idiots," Sienna adds. "So who knows if any of it is true?"

I shoot her a thanks-for-having-my-back smile.

Miles nods. "Mr. Gillies is cool with the ghost stuff up to a point, but I wouldn't want to push it too far. He can be scary when he's mad."

"But you live there, right?" Xander presses. "At the funeral home?"

"Yes," I say.

He blinks, and wow. Those eyes. I'm actually a little woozy.

"What's it like?" he asks.

"It's like a regular house," I tell him. "When you're upstairs you don't even know you're above a business, let alone a funeral home."

"But do you ever think about what's underneath you?" asks Madison.

I gape at her in disbelief. "What do you mean? You've been to my house a million times. Do *you* ever think about it?"

"All the time, but I didn't want you to know I was thinking it. I didn't want to be rude."

I look over at Sienna, who's nodding along.

"We only go there for a couple of hours at a time," she tells me. "You're there all the time—and at night. I've always wanted to know, is it creepy?"

Now I do feel prickly. I'm used to strangers thinking what my family does is weird. I never knew my friends thought it too.

"It's not creepy." I pick up my sandwich and bite into it, hoping they'll move on.

"Have you seen the ghost?" asks Xander.

"No," I say through a mouthful of chicken salad. "It's just a story."

"So your house isn't haunted."

"No." Take away the beautiful brown eyes, and Xander is starting to feel like every other thrill-seeking jerk who's showed up over the years thinking they were going to be the ones to finally see a local legend.

"You sound pretty sure of that," he says.

"I am sure. I've lived there my whole life, and there haven't been any unexplained footsteps or cold spots or doors opening and closing by themselves."

"Maybe you just weren't open to it."

I put down my sandwich and cross my arms.

"No offense, but why is this such a thing for you?"

"Yeah," says Miles. "Are you obsessed with haunted houses or something?"

"I wouldn't say *obsessed*," Xander replies. "But I do have what you could call an intense interest. Investigating the paranormal is sort of what I do."

I raise an eyebrow. "Like a job?"

"Not exactly a job. Yet."

"So you're one of those ghost hunters," says Madison. "Like on TV?"

"God, no." Xander makes a face. "Those guys are douchebags. Most of what they do is fake. I only do legit investigations."

Something about the way he says that makes me burst out laughing. The whole thing just sounds so ridiculous.

"Okay, I don't know what you consider to be 'legit'"—I hold up my fingers, making air quotes—"but I can tell you all of that is pretty much BS."

"So you don't believe in ghosts?" Xander asks.

"I didn't say I don't believe in them. I just don't think spirits would be all that interested in a dude lurking around going, *Say something into this tape recorder to let us know you're here.*"

"You're skeptical," he says. "I can respect that. But I'm not just an investigator, I'm a photographer too."

He pulls out his phone and opens Instagram. We all lean in to take a look.

"Whoa, you have a ton of followers," says Sienna.

"People like my stuff, I guess," Xander replies.

"I guess," says Madison.

But I'm not paying attention to his follower count. The first thing I notice is how beautiful the actual photographs are. Some are in daylight, some in darkness. There are a variety of subjects: empty rooms, landscapes, people doing random things—and they all seem to have been captured at peak honesty, by which I mean there's something in the images that makes you feel like you know whatever you're looking at on a deep and true level.

"I've been doing some freelance work for the *Daily*—like the parade." He points to a photo of a girl in a pageant sash waving from the back seat of a convertible. "But capturing paranormal phenomena is my specialty."

"What are those little lights over there?" Madison asks, pointing to a photo of what looks like an old library.

"Those are orbs," Xander says. "They're the most common spectral forms to capture in a photograph."

"By forms do you mean actual ghosts?" asks Sienna.

"Yes, the orbs indicate the presence of spirits. But what's really cool is when you get an apparition."

He scrolls until he finds an image of a mistlike form in a doorway. It ends halfway to the floor and appears to be roughly shaped like a human head and shoulders.

"Whoa," Sienna says. "That's wicked."

"That's just a partial; I have one full-body." Xander scrolls some more, then holds out the phone again. "This was taken at an old house my friend lived in."

The photo shows a living room that could be any living room in any old-ish farmhouse. In the corner is a semitransparent shape— the silhouette of what looks like a woman in a bonnet and hoopskirt. No details are visible, certainly not a face, but the form would be hard to dismiss as anything other than human.

"That could be fake," Miles says. "It wouldn't be hard to do with Photoshop."

"I had this photo professionally analyzed, and they didn't find any evidence of tampering," Xander tells him. "I'm actually semi-famous for this one. Nobody can disprove it because there's nothing to disprove. It's real."

Madison and Sienna look impressed. Miles looks annoyed. I nibble my sandwich, trying to decide how I feel. Something about Xander feels dangerous—and it's not just that he likes to swing over quarry pits. But then I always play it safe. Just because I've never dared to do something like that doesn't mean it wouldn't be fun.

Miles is the one who finally speaks up.

"Well, this has been thrilling, but the bell's going to ring and I'm starving, so . . ." He takes a bite of pizza and chews exaggeratedly to make his point. Everybody else starts wolfing their food too. The bell goes off just a couple of minutes later.

We all get up to leave, Sienna and Madison and I breaking off down the music wing for choir. Halfway there, I hear someone calling my name. I turn to see Xander running up.

"Hey," he says, holding out his phone. "So I wanted to get hold of you. Would it be okay if I got your number?"

Surprise. That's my first reaction. Then I realize with a tingling rush what's going on. He wants to *get hold of me*. Does he maybe want to ask me out?

If that's what's happening, then it's something I've never experienced before. This is a small town. Everybody pretty much knows everybody. Most of the time, dates around here look more like ending up at the same party as someone else and deciding it's worth trying to make out. For me, that kind of thing always stops pretty fast because no one has made much of an impression in the making-out department, and because I know pretty much everybody. So I'm new to the world of actual dating, if that's even what this is.

"Right," I say. "Yes, you can have my number."

Xander hands me his phone, and I thumb it in.

"I've been hearing a lot about the old homestead on Route Eight," he says. "People say weird stuff goes on out there."

"It's just another urban legend," I tell him. "Or in this case, a *rural* legend."

The homestead has been a thing around here for decades. It's an old farm where nothing is left but the foundation of the house and the skeleton of a barn. A short ways away is a small cemetery, almost completely taken over by brush and tall grass, that belonged to the family that lived there. Local legend says if you drew a pentagram over a map of the state, the homestead would be one of the intersections, which means it's a gateway to hell or some such nonsense. People go there to party and try to see ghosts. The most daring of them lie down in the cemetery at midnight, which is supposed to invite the devil to drag you into his fiery abyss.

Or whatever. Like I said, it's nonsense.

"Every legend has a basis in fact," Xander tells me, and I'm suddenly gripped by an oh-no-here-we-go-again feeling. We're talking about more than the homestead.

Before he can bring up the Gillies Ghost, I say, "If weird stuff is happening there, it's because people are smoking weed and *doing* weird stuff."

"We'll see." He lets the words hang before adding, "Want to see with me?"

I pause, thrown off. "When?"

"Friday night?"

"I'm going to the football game."

"We wouldn't go until later. Preferably after midnight. My goal is to be there for the witching hour."

Confusion mixes with a growing sense that I'm heading for a disappointment. My patience crumbles and my defenses go up.

"The witching hour? That is such bull! You're not going to find anything out there."

"What if I do?" he challenges.

"Then it'll be a figment of your imagination."

The bell rings. I don't know where Xander's next class is, but he should be getting there. Instead, he follows me as I start walking toward the choir room.

"I can't believe someone like you wouldn't be more of a believer in the paranormal," he says.

I keep my eyes straight ahead, telling myself to *breathe in, breathe out . . . stay calm.*

"What do you mean, someone like me?"

"Where you live," he says. "What your family does. If you let me investigate at your place, I'll bet you anything we could find things that would blow your mind."

I stop walking, a million thoughts and emotions blindsiding me at once. Is he only talking to me because he sees me as a ticket to a ghost hunt? And how dumb have I been to let myself get all fluttery and mushy over him? I feel shocked, embarrassed, and epically let down.

Underneath it all is a voice repeating over and over: *Funeral Girl! Funeral Girl! Someone like you . . . Funeral Girl!*

He smiles, like he's expecting me to say *No problem!* and open up my world for him to poke around in, as if it were just some curiosity and not my actual life.

"You barely know me," I tell him. "And you're asking if you can ghost hunt at my house? That's pretty . . . wow."

I can see him realizing how it looks, see him starting to back-track.

"I—I didn't mean it like that," he stammers. "And it wouldn't be a ghost hunt, it would be an *investigation*."

Enough. If this wasn't my life, I might think it was funny in a screwed-up kind of way. It's one thing always having to leave my friends because I'm needed at the funeral home, but now I can't even meet a cute boy without my family's business getting in the way.

Or maybe this cute boy could forget about my family's business and try getting to know me instead.

I wait to see if he'll go that direction and suggest something more traditional, like a movie. When he doesn't, I hoist my backpack onto my other shoulder and look straight into his coffee-colored eyes.

"You'll never know what I believe in, and you'll never *investigate* where I live," I tell him. "Because I'm not going to let my house be a sideshow for your social media followers. I hope you get to explore all the haunted places this Podunk part of the world has to offer, and I hope you find what you're looking for. Just do us both a favor and leave me out of it."

CHAPTER SEVEN

"How's school going?"

Dad smiles at Astrid and me over BLTs made with the last of this summer's tomatoes. Mom grows them on the deck that runs along the back of the house, and they're as good as the ones you can buy at the farmers market downtown. She also grows herbs, peppers, and even roses in pots around the table where we eat outside on nights when it's not too hot or cold. We may not have a real backyard, but we still garden like other people.

"School's good," I tell Dad, and his smile widens.

"Glad to hear it," he says. "What about you, Astrid?"

My sister shrugs and says, "Okay."

"Astrid," says Mom. "You left your pom gear on the kitchen floor again this afternoon."

"Sorry," she says.

"I tripped on it and almost sprained my ankle."

"Sorry." Astrid takes a drink of her milk.

"So maybe don't do that again?" Mom's getting frustrated, and Astrid's rolling her eyes doesn't help. Dad jumps in.

"How about a little more consideration?" he says.

"Fine." Astrid's smile is now exaggeratedly polite. "But if we're talking about gear, I actually need new shoes. Coach decided the white gets too dirty. She wants to switch to red."

"We just spent eighty dollars on those white shoes!" Mom sneezes, then pushes away her plate. A flu bug is going around, and it looks like she may have caught it. "Don't tell me the red ones are that expensive too."

"Don't worry," Dad says. "We'll make it work."

"If things don't pick up soon, we might have a hard time making anything work." Mom stands and moves to the other end of the kitchen to blow her nose. "Ugh. Did you see this?"

She holds up the *PennySaver* magazine from a stack of mail on the counter.

Dad squints. "No, what is it?"

She brings the *PennySaver* over and points to the ad on the back with the logo that's too familiar to all of us these days: Memories.

"They have a new website," she says. While Dad takes a closer look at the ad, she pulls out her phone, thumbs in the URL, then hands it to me. "They're also on Instagram."

Memories' website is slick, with lots of impeccably curated photos. It looks like an influencer opened an Airbnb that offers embalming plus visitations with brunch. The Gillies website is some basic thing Mom designed using a free template. Next to Memories, it's old-fashioned and amateurish. We have a Facebook page too, but nobody's posted to it in ages.

"What do we think?" says Mom. She always uses "we" when

discussing the business with Dad. "Is this something to be concerned about?"

"Let me chew on it," he says. My father doesn't like to do anything rashly, but I can tell he's concerned.

He turns to me and changes the subject.

"By the way, I was thinking Elaine and I could take some road trips over the next couple of months. Check out some schools? Cincinnati's not far away, and they have one of the best mortuary programs in the country. With your grades and experience, I would imagine you could get a scholarship."

My teeth grit behind my that-sounds-cool! smile. Because it feels like Dad just barged into my brain, right into the space where I've been thinking about college. And in that space, there are so many ways it could go—so many types of schools that could be right for me. There's artsy, there's rah-rah, there's Ivy, there's urban . . . I've been envisioning myself at basketball games with my face painted the school colors, or having deep discussions at coffee shops, studying all night in ancient libraries, or living in a city and planning my next social justice project. When I picture what I might be doing with the rest of my life, it's not embalming bodies or comforting widows. I could do music, I could do journalism or philosophy—the world opens up when I think about college, not narrows in.

But how do I tell that to my dad, who's looking at me with an expression that says I am the key to the future of the business that's been in his family for 150 years?

They've never expected Astrid to take it over, probably because she's made it clear she isn't interested. I, on the other hand, help without complaining. That's partly because I like being with Dad. I like seeing how he works with the families, and even the bodies. It's science. It's art. It's interesting. Did my helping somehow say to my parents that this was what I wanted for a career?

And if I don't do it, who will? Dad's an only child, and no one on my mom's side of the family would be caught dead in the funeral business (no pun intended). So it's just me, with no way to escape the eager, proud, vulnerable look on my father's face as he makes plans for us to visit mortuary schools.

I put on my Good-Daughter smile. I say okay.

"Great!" He claps his hands together. "I think Kevin Berland still has a funeral home in Cincy. I'll see if he knows someone at the school who can show us around."

The conversation moves on. Mom decides she doesn't have the stomach for dinner, and Astrid slinks away soon after that. Over on the couch in the den, my phone pings.

"Who's that?" Dad asks as I pick it up.

"Probably Miles," I reply. "He's pumped about the *Dragonfly* convention coming up. Probably wants to talk about costumes or something like that."

"People are really that involved with a TV show?" Dad shakes his head in wonder. "Amazing."

I always hate when he talks about it that way. My parents have never understood my obsession with *Dragonfly*. Mom says it gives her a headache, and Dad won't try watching at all. Anytime they overhear Miles and me riffing on it, they act like we're aliens that landed in front of them speaking some totally foreign language.

"As much as you love talking about the universe, I would think you'd really like *Dragonfly*," I tell my dad.

"That show is above even me," he says. "I'll leave it to smart people like you and Miles."

He starts doing the dishes while I wake up my phone.

> How are the horses?

I frown, thrown off until the pieces of my memory start to snap together: Deep brown eyes with a mole under the right one like a punctuation mark. A request for my number, and then a suggestion so totally out of line that it still enrages me. No *Hey, it's Xander* or even *Hi*. He just jumps in with a random question.

I should ignore him. Instead, I text back.

> I assume the horses are enjoying some hay at the farm. I don't know. I'm not really a horse girl.

I wince at how lame that looks on the screen. Dots flash under my words as he replies.

> You're a girl who's mad at me and I totally get why—I was a jerk. I'm sorry.

I have to admit I wasn't expecting an apology. And this one is better than most—not that I've had many guys apologize to me before. It doesn't make up for what he did, but it helps.

> Thank you—apology accepted.

> Whew—I'm relieved!

His next text comes as I'm climbing the stairs to my room.

> I was going through my roll from the other day and just wanted to send you this.

He's attached a photo: me in the Harvest Home parade. In the background you can see Gardner's Drugstore, plus the blur of the crowd on the sidewalk. I'm in the driver's seat of the buggy, but I'm not struggling to keep the horses from hitting anyone, nor am I shouting in terror at the person behind the lens. I'm laughing, my eyes wide in surprise, fixed on something out farther ahead. My hair is coming down in tendrils from under the top hat, and my cheeks are flushed from the heat or the laughter—or both.

When did Xander take this? And when did I laugh like that? I want to respond but I don't know what to say.

Xander doesn't text again.

I hover my finger over the image, enlarging it until my face fills the screen. Then I hit download and watch as it saves to my photos.

🙰

Equilibrium means forward reaction equals reverse reaction . . . Forward equals reverse . . . Forward, reverse . . . God, I should not have signed up for this class.

Whimpering, I bow my head over my AP chemistry book. I knew AP chem would be hard; I took it because I'm good at science, and I thought I was up for the challenge. But now my brain's taken one tough lesson and turned it into a loop of worst-case scenarios. *You'll never get it, you're going to fail, your GPA will be trashed, and you'll never get into any college anywhere.*

That's the thing about generalized anxiety disorder, which is the official term for what I have. It's not about what's really going on, it's more this fear of some vague bad thing that could happen at any time, whether that's five minutes or five years from now. It's this constant buzzing sense that something's not right. If I pay too much attention to it, the buzzing gets stronger and my thoughts get trapped in the what-ifs. Dr. Hymans, the therapist I go to sometimes, calls that an anxiety spiral. It's like I've stuck my finger in a light socket. I get captured by the current as the worrying zaps me: sometimes small zaps that make my day just a little harder, and sometimes big ones that make me frantic and unable to sleep.

Medication helps a lot. Therapy has also taught me ways to work through the nervous hum. I tell myself the worrying will pass. I do breathing exercises, stretches, and yoga and also listen to music, almost anything to convince my brain that, oh yeah, this really is just a regular Monday and nothing awful is waiting to happen. These days, anxiety is mostly just an annoying part of my life, especially if I can avoid stressful or upsetting things, which is why I'm thinking that taking AP chemistry wasn't my best decision.

I push the book away and pick up my phone. Before I can stop myself, I've opened Xander's Instagram.

Sienna was right, he does have an impressive amount of followers. Many of them seem to be "paranormal investigators" too. There's a lot of debate about how images were captured, what they mean, and what they might be showing of the spirit world. There's also a lot of competitive crotch-grabbing, most of it other guys bragging that they could do better.

Xander answers every comment. Single-word answers: *Nope. Wrong. Lie.* Short answers that put people in their place: *Let me know when you get something better than a lone orb and we can talk.* Long answers that detail his methods, his expertise, and his disdain for anyone who would dare to question him.

I get up to stretch my legs and wander over to the big window that looks out on the street below. I feel like I've figured him out. He's an adrenaline junkie whose high of choice is the rush that comes from creeping around abandoned places and then showing off for other adrenaline junkies online. But there's something else, too. Ever since dinner, I've been flipping back to the photo he sent of me laughing in the parade. I zoom in and study the way my eyes crinkle at the corners, the way my head is thrown back, the way he's captured so many dimensions of happiness in one image. Xander really is an amazing photographer.

"Lainey?" Dad pokes his head into the room. "You busy?"

Startled, I go back to my bed and pull my textbook onto my lap.

"Sort of," I say. "Lots of homework."

"Ah, chemistry." He taps the book as he sits beside me. "You'll want to pay attention in that class. It's a big subject at mortuary school."

"Right. I have a test on Thursday."

"Well, good luck." He shifts uncomfortably. "Don't tell your mom I was asking about this. It's usually her area of expertise, but . . . you know I'm no good with technology and internet and all that stuff, right?"

I smile. "It's not a secret. You always say people put too much of their lives on it for other people to pick apart."

"Well, I still think that's true. But the downside is that I don't know what I'm looking at when I look at things like Tweetbook and whatever else is out there. Tell me the truth. Memories and their website your mom was worried about . . . do they look good?"

This is the first time my dad has included me in something so basic to the business. The kid in me wants to tell him Memories sucks and there's nothing to worry about. But the part of me that's starting to understand things like competition knows he probably wants to hear the truth, even if I don't want to tell it to him.

"Memories' stuff is professionally done," I say. "And someone's obviously in charge of maintaining it. Plus, the MacBook thing at the parade and all the other stuff I've seen . . . they look really good."

He sighs, like I've confirmed his fears.

"It's easier for them because they're a franchise," he says. "Sort of like McDonald's, to use an admittedly weird comparison. They have one owner and they buy out different locations, so they can pool resources."

I've never seen my dad look worried like this. Anxiety flares as, for the first time, I really understand why my parents were so upset when Memories opened.

"Are they going to try and buy us out too?" I ask.

"I'd tell them where to shove it if they did," he says. "But they're already big, and they most likely wouldn't be interested in owning two funeral homes so close together."

"Which means they'll try to put us out of business."

Actually saying it sharpens what, until now, has been something vague into a real possibility. Dad sits up straighter.

"A place like that can't offer what we can—generation after generation of family ownership. But all this new stuff . . . I'm out of my depth with it. And though your mom would rather die than admit it, she is too."

He doesn't say what I know he wants to say: He needs help. And the fact that he doesn't feel like he can come out and ask makes me ten times more anxious. And guilty. Memories is a millennials' mecca—my mom and dad can't compete, but they have me, right? All this time I should have been thinking of ways to use my Gen Z skills for them.

"I bet I can come up with some ideas," I tell him.

The gratitude on his face is almost more than I can take.

"Oh, good. Good. I knew you'd be up for it." He stands to go. But before he does, he leans over to kiss me on the forehead. "Thanks, Lainey. You're the best."

CHAPTER EIGHT

Miles's driving is a lot like Miles's personality: comical, in that you always wonder whether he's playing a joke on you because no one could possibly drive that badly. It's probably one reason why Madison is so obsessed with rules—she probably feels like she's personally responsible for making sure her twin brother follows the speed limit and stops at stop signs.

"This is a no-passing zone!" she tells him as he swerves his truck around a tractor trailer filled with chickens on our way to school. Astrid covers her eyes in the seat next to me, and I swallow a carsick urge to lose my breakfast.

"Maybe you should slow down a little," I tell him. I'm grateful he offered to take us; my car is still in the shop and his truck is a million times better than Dakota's VW, but Astrid is clearly terrified.

"Pssht," Miles says. "I always get everybody where they're supposed to be safely, don't I?"

The answer to that is yes. Yes, he does, and that too is something that can be said of Miles in general. He might be a goof, but underneath is someone who genuinely cares. He fosters orphaned kittens and nurses injured birds. He was the one to tell me in junior high that my constant worrying might be something treatable. Miles is going to make an incredible veterinarian someday. I always know he'll be there for me.

"What are you wearing to the football game?" Madison turns around from the front seat in an obvious attempt to have a conversation that is *not* about Miles's driving.

"It's supposed to get stupid cold," I tell her. "So it probably doesn't matter what I wear since it'll be covered up by my coat anyway."

"Good point," she says. "So which coat, then?"

"I vote for matching full-length furs," Miles chimes in. "We're playing the Timberwolves. We should clothe ourselves in the skins of our enemies."

"How very proto-soul of you," I say, referring to *Dragonfly*'s progression of consciousness theory.

"Don't assume primitive means proto," he shoots back. "All rituals get us closer to the mystery, the paradox of which is that—"

I interrupt him with "Bleep-bloop-scoodly-dooo—"

And Miles answers, "BaZOING!"

It's our own special shorthand for *Here be esoteric mumbo jumbo.* It was born out of the fact that *Dragonfly* has a ton of moments where someone goes on a long speech about quantum entanglement, human frailty, and other super-deep topics, until your brain sort of shorts out, making a sound like "BaZOING!" In real life, we skim over long speeches with "Bleep-bloop-scoodly-dooo" and then finish it off with the sound effect to denote that the topic is too mind-bendy to detail and would likely end with everybody's brains smoking.

Miles is laughing. Madison has had enough.

"Quit it with the secret language." She scowls at him.

"It's only a secret to the unawakened," Miles tells her.

"Well, nobody asked you to butt in in the first place," she informs him. And this is true. Madison was my friend first, along with Sienna, and like most things involving us, it started with music. My old piano teacher, Mrs. Parker, used to have these get-togethers she called "salons," where small groups of her students would play for each other. She also taught voice lessons, which both Sienna and Madison were doing, and at one of the salons Mrs. P had me play while they sang. We were only ten, but it felt so grown-up, especially afterward, when Mrs. Parker served us tea around her dining room table.

"I liked your song," I told Sienna, admiring her dress and long braids. "It was so pretty."

"Thank you," she said. "It's French."

I turned to Madison, who was carefully following the etiquette rules Mrs. Parker had taught us. "Your song was hard. It's cool you can do it so fast."

"It's cool you played it like that with no practicing," she replied. "You're really good."

Mrs. Parker smiled at us and said, "So much talent in such accomplished young ladies. Promise me you'll continue, the three of you."

We promised, and then found one another at school the next day, and from then on we've been inseparable. When Mrs. P died, we even performed at her service.

Miles didn't come into the group until we found out he and I were both *Dragonfly* stans, and then Madison had to share. Most of the time it works, but sometimes she gets irritated.

"You know who really needs awakening?" Miles says. "Nelson.

He's going to ruin DraCon with his garbage. Dude could spew enough crap to pollute all of Lake Michigan."

"I'm sure you could set him straight," I say.

"And now you guys are going to Chicago. Without me." Madison has betrayal written all over her face.

"Unlikely," I reassure her. "I don't have enough money unless I can play a ton more funerals, but business is slow, so—"

"Fine," she says. "Whatever."

She turns back around and starts cracking up at something on her phone screen. I peek over her shoulder to see what's so funny. It's a meme, sent by Sienna. I check my own phone, but there's nothing. I'm sure if I asked Madison why I'm not included she'd say it's only fair if Miles and I are going to leave *her* out. But Miles and I have nothing to hide. How many other conversations are happening between Madison and Sienna that I don't even know about?

"Hey, Elaine," Madison says after a few minutes. "Sienna wants to know if you can practice Friday before the game?"

I sit forward faster than I want to.

"Tell her yes. Sure. No problem."

We pull into the school parking lot and Astrid bolts out of the car. The combination of Miles's driving and my lame attempts at staying relevant to my friends has pushed her over the edge.

"Bye, Astrid," Miles calls as she trots away.

Slinging my backpack over my shoulder, I get out and start trudging toward the building alongside Madison and Miles. Halfway there, another person joins the group.

"Elaine. Hey."

It's him. Xander, wearing nothing but shorts and an old Mizzou hoodie despite the plummeting temperature.

"Hey." I pull my own coat tighter around myself, feeling self-conscious, like maybe he somehow knows I spent most of last night stalking him online. Miles gives him a fist bump. Madison gives him hell for not being sensibly dressed. But it's me he zeroes in on.

"I wanted to apologize again," he says. "I can be a little much when I'm excited about something, and sometimes it takes a smackdown to get me back in the real world. So thank you for that. I'll be more respectful from now on."

Two apologies in two days. I can't imagine any other guy I know doing more than a single sorry, and then only when forced. It's time to put Xander out of his misery.

"You don't have to be *too* respectful," I tell him.

"Oh, good," he says. "Because the invitation still stands for Friday. The homestead. But only if you're comfortable with it. I promise we won't do anything *too* out-there."

His voice holds the slightest hint of a dare, which is how I know I have to do it.

"Fine. But I guarantee all we're going to find is a bunch of stoners."

Xander laughs—a long, low laugh that says *dare accepted*.

"We'll see," he says.

CHAPTER NINE

"'Pirate Jenny' or 'Journey to the Past'?" Sienna considers two pieces of music, then holds them up for Madison and me to see.

"I was thinking about doing 'Once Upon a December,'" Madison says. "Would it be weird if we both did songs from *Anastasia*?"

"Maybe," Sienna says. "'Pirate Jenny' is more Mrs. Lovett anyway."

"And it'll be great for your demo," Madison adds. "Let me get the camera going."

She checks the setup they've arranged on a music stand while Sienna sets her song in front of me at the piano. We've already warmed up, the two of them singing along to my scales and arpeggios. Now it's time to get serious. Musical auditions are coming, and other things too. Madison and Sienna are using this practice session to record video for their college demo reels.

"What do you think?" Sienna asks after her twentieth run-through.

"I think you sound amazing," Madison tells her. "I got at least two good takes. Elaine, I'll send you a copy and you can use it for your demo, too."

When Sienna, Madison, and I talk about the future, we are all at music school together. And even though I don't know whether I really want to study piano, I always like being included in the vision. What we don't talk about very much is the fact that we might not all get into the same school. Right now, the idea of that is stressing Madison out.

"'December' is a good Broadway song, but CCM wants an operatic aria too," she frets. "Like what kind of aria? There are a million styles! Plus, they only have a twenty percent acceptance rate."

"Mads," Sienna says. "I know you've got arias. You know you've got arias. You'll be fine, just focus on this song for now."

The two of them switch places, Sienna at my side to turn pages. Now I'm listening to Madison's beautiful soprano voice, and I like that I'm part of their picture.

What I do not like is the way my phone keeps lighting up with texts from Dakota. Dad's been giving him more responsibility for the business, starting with the O'Reilly viewing tonight. Dakota clearly is not feeling up to it. On my screen is a photo of some flowers.

> Do these look right? Also what folder is the slideshow of family photos stored in?

Sighing, I thumb in a response.

> The PowerPoint is where the PowerPoints always are. And how would I know about the flowers? I wasn't in the meeting with the family.

I'm tempted to ask why he's asking me these things, but I know why: because Dakota enjoys dealing with Disappointed Dad as much as I do. In this case, I'm guessing he'd rather face the wrath of the daughter than the painfully formal silences of the father.

Dakota sends me another photo, from a different angle.

> I'm not sure if it was supposed to be orchids and I don't have it in my notes.

I squint at the flowers, scrolling through my mental files. He's lucky I saw Mom place the order.

> That looks right.

He sends me a praying hands emoji and a thumbs-up.

> Sorry—thanks.

The door cracks open, and Miles comes into the room. He does a ballerina leap over to the piano.

"Football time! The Drummond bus leaves in two minutes. Let's go."

"Yay!" Sienna squeals, throwing up her arms in a cheerleader pose. "I told Jaxon we'd be in the eleventh row, since he's number eleven. I can't wait to watch him."

And now it feels like the weekend can finally start. Between stressing over my chem test and worrying about my friends doing friend things without me, this week has been one massive grind. I follow them into the hall, only to fall behind when my phone buzzes with a new text. This time it's Dad.

Hey, Lainey—Dakota's coming to get you. Could really use your help. O'Reilly family starting at 6:30 and with Astrid cheering the game we're feeling shorthanded.

I stop walking. Dakota's been texting all afternoon, not even considering that I might have other things to do like, oh, pay attention in school. He assumes I'm available whenever he has a question. And now he's on his way to get me because my dad assumes I have nothing better to do than help with a visitation.

They always assume, and I'm always changing my plans.

Assumptions suck.

Except they need me. Mom's sick. Astrid's cheering. Dakota's already on the way. I should go home.

"Elaine, are you coming?" Sienna calls.

I start shuffling forward, thumbs poised over my phone screen, trying to decide what to do.

Another text hits.

Before you come home can you also stop by the drugstore and grab some cold & flu medicine? Mom's run out.

Madison pushes open the door at the end of the hall. Sunshine hits my eyes, blinding me for a second. When I can see again, Xander is leaning against Miles's truck in the almost-deserted parking lot.

I don't want to help my parents. I want to go watch football with this new boy. I told him I'd go out to the homestead after. I can't back out now.

Before I can lose my nerve, I text my dad back.

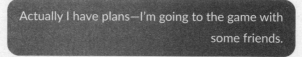

Actually I have plans—I'm going to the game with some friends.

I watch dots blink in and out under my text while Miles and Madison and Xander and Sienna climb into the truck.

I've never refused to help before. I've never told my parents no about anything.

My phone pings again.

It would have been nice if you'd let us know earlier.

For a minute, guilt washes over me. Then I remember.

I did let you know—at breakfast.

Either they weren't listening or they forgot or maybe they just don't care.

Miles rolls down his window.

"We can stop at your house first if you need."

I quickly survey what I've got on. Sweater and jeans—check. Boots—check. Heavy coat—check. I should get the medicine for Mom and drop it off, but if we go to my house, I know what will happen: I'll walk in; Mom will look sick; Dad will look disappointed; there will be a ton of people filling up the visitation rooms; and I will get guilted into staying.

"I don't need to go home," I say.

Once I get in the truck, it will be too late to change my mind.

Dad's response comes as I'm hoisting myself into the back seat.

Okay.

I stare at the screen, unsure how to read that one short word. Is he mad at me? Am I now going to be facing days or even weeks of Disappointed Dad?

Madison moves over to make room, while Xander smiles from the passenger seat.

"Are you sure it's all right if you come?" he says. "You sort of seem like you have somewhere else to be."

I settle in, hoping he can't see how fast I'm breathing, how light my head feels.

"It's fine," I tell him. "They can handle it without me. Let's go."

CHAPTER TEN

"Look at Jaxon!" Sienna points out at the field, where number 11 is setting up at the line of scrimmage. "He didn't think he was going to start tonight, but Coach can't deny how amazing he is."

Everybody makes admiring noises, because Sienna has actual hearts in her eyes. She and Jaxon aren't 100 percent official just yet, and I know she's hoping it won't be long now. She's definitely loving the chance to root for one of the star players on a night that feels made for romance.

"Cuddle close," says Miles. "It's cold as eff out here."

He unfolds the blanket we brought from his house, and everyone crowds underneath it. It's only October, but for some reason—probably the same reason there are tornados in California now and hurricanes in Colorado—it is beyond freezing outside.

Football games are usually a blast when it's not so cold. Mom never misses one. She says it's the best place in town to network. Not to mention if you aren't into high school football where we live, then you probably aren't a real American, and God forbid we appear anything less than flag-waving patriots out here in the heartland. "Our biggest asset is our reputation," Dad likes to say. "Little things matter."

Tonight, Mom's patriotism is on hold because of the O'Reilly visitation, and I'm trying not to feel like it's my fault she's working while she's sick. I tuck my phone into my coat pocket, telling myself the best way to avoid fixating on what I am not doing is to pay attention to what I *am* doing, right here, right now.

Right now, I am sandwiched between Sienna and Miles on the stadium bleachers, watching the Clark County Cougars chew up the Shasta Falls Timberwolves while the sun setting over the visitors section paints the sky firebird red. Madison has her arms around Sienna's shoulders, shivering, and Xander sits on Miles's other side, talking to some guys in the next row.

Miles takes his hat off and fits it on my head. He takes my bare hands, breathes on them, then folds them between his own gloved ones.

"I have news that I believe will be of interest," he says.

"Oh yes?" I lower my voice to match the secretive look in his eyes.

"Yeeesss . . . So. You know all this talking about DraCon?"

"Yes," I say. "So much talking."

"Well, I did a thing today."

"A DraCon thing?"

"Yes. I registered us. Both of us. You and me."

My jaw drops—as in, my mouth literally falls wide-open.

"No way! You didn't!"

"I did. Is that okay?" He looks suddenly uncertain. "I thought about asking you first, but I thought it would be a cool surprise."

Surprise is an understatement. Even with Magnus Tiedemann going, I still fully expected Miles to let the whole thing fizzle out. This is totally unlike him.

"It's amazing," I say. "But the tickets are so expensive. And that's not even considering gas, hotel—"

"I took care of the tickets," he says. "And we can talk about the other stuff later. Pay me back whenever you have money. Is that cool?"

"It's more than cool, it's amazing." Chicago is an adventure—something to look forward to. "So, we're doing it? We're really going to DraCon?"

"Looks like we really are!"

"I love you." Grabbing his shoulders, I plant a big kiss on his cheek. "Thank you for this!"

Splotches of red rise under the place where my lips were; Miles's ginger complexion has always given away exactly what he's feeling. I use my fingers to rub the kiss away until he's squirming and laughing and no longer mortified by my spontaneous display of affection.

"Hey," he says. "Who's that with Astrid?"

Down on the field, by the sign advertising Gillies Family Funeral Home as a proud sponsor of the Cougar Den, my sister performs with the rest of the junior high pom squad. I've always loved watching Astrid dance; where she got her grace and coordination is a total mystery. I can barely take two steps without tripping over my own feet.

They're in between routines now, and a boy is with her. She smiles shyly. He shoves his hands into his pockets, peering at her from under the brim of his baseball cap. The body language is unmistakable, and when he pulls her close, folding her into his coat for warmth, there's not much doubt what's going on.

Then the boy turns so I can see his face, and I feel a little queasy.

"I think that's Quinn Hofstetter."

"Interesting," says Miles.

"Very," I say back.

There's nothing wrong with Quinn, per se. He skateboards and plays guitar in a band that's always performing at school events. Quinn is cool, except he's a sophomore.

The way our school is set up, with junior high through senior year in one building, has raised eyebrows in the past because it puts such a big age range together. A few years ago, an eighth grader got pregnant with a junior. It caused a big enough scandal that plans were drawn up for a new, separate middle school. But when people had to actually put their money where their mouths were, they didn't want to pay any more taxes. So an abstinence unit got added to our health classes, and everyone sort of forgot about the whole thing.

"What are you thinking?" Miles asks me.

"I don't even know," I say, still watching my sister on the field. "If Astrid had a boyfriend, I used to think she'd tell me about it. But lately she doesn't tell me anything."

"Sometimes siblings have secrets," he says.

"Yeah, but we never used to."

Sighing, I let Miles scootch in closer. On his other side, I can see Xander fidgeting. There's something heavy in the way he's sitting, with an expression that looks dark and restless. Suddenly he stands.

"I'm going to get food," he announces. "Anybody want anything? Elaine?"

The sound of my name jolts me upright; Miles jumps in before I can answer.

"How can you be hungry?" he asks. "I personally saw you eat two of my dad's gut-buster burgers."

"Actually, it was three," Xander says. "But I heard student council fundraiser hot dogs are the best hot dogs, and my butt is numb, so figured I'd go see if it's true."

Madison makes a face. "Those things are food poisoning on a bun."

"True," Miles agrees. "Elaine doesn't want to be throwing up all night."

"But maybe she can get us gum," Sienna chimes in. "We all need it after those gut-busters."

She raises her eyebrows at me in a silent signal: She's noticed my fascination with Xander and is making it her romantic mission to put us together.

"Gum. Right. Nobody move, I'll get some." I spring to my feet, getting tangled in the blanket. I teeter, and Miles grabs my waist to steady me. Xander reaches out. I take his steady hand, feeling Miles's grip tighten ever so slightly before I pop free.

I inch past Sienna and Madison to the aisle; then Xander and I make our way down to the stadium concourse. People say hi as we pass. They reach out to high-five Xander for his now-legendary quarry jump. He blows it off like it was no big deal, but I'm grateful for all the attention he's getting because it keeps us from having a conversation, which is good because I'm not sure exactly what to say.

Under the bleachers, the pep band's drums sound like muffled heartbeats. We get in line at the snack bar, and my hand creeps toward my coat pocket, fingers feeling for my phone. What if Dad or Dakota are texting from the visitation? What if they need something?

Stop. You're only going to go down an anxiety spiral if you start obsessing about home. You're here. So be here.

But Xander also seems somewhere else. His head's over his phone, and when I sneak a peek at his screen, I see *Mom* at the top. Xander's face is stormy, his jaw clenching as his thumbs fly over the keyboard.

He scrubs his hand over his face, then puts the phone in his coat pocket.

"So, I've been feeling like we got started all wrong," he says. "Actually, I know we did, and now I'm pretty sure you're thinking all sorts of things about me that probably aren't true."

"Oh?" This is intriguing. "What am I thinking?"

His answer has to wait because we've reached the front of the line. He orders a hot dog and a pack of Twizzlers. When he takes out his wallet, I see why his fingers felt so rough when he shook my hand at the parade. The nails are bitten ragged.

Before I started anxiety medication, I used to bite my nails raw. I still chew the inside of my lip. I wonder if Xander ever feels that buzzing dread, and if he's ever thought about talking with someone about it.

After he's paid, he turns back to me and says, "You're thinking I'm an adrenaline junkie who's addicted to ghost hunting."

"Wow. That's actually pretty accurate," I reply. "So you're not? Addicted, I mean."

"I do like to shake things up, don't get me wrong. But mostly I'm trying to show things other people don't see. Maybe they aren't looking hard enough, or maybe they aren't looking the right way, but I feel like there's so much going on *underneath*. I don't want to miss it." He takes his food, then tells the lady at the register, "I'll get whatever she's having, too."

"You don't have to do that."

"I know. I just wanted to start over with a better impression."

He seems much lighter now, like he's set aside whatever upset him earlier. I order some popcorn—oh, and gum. I almost forgot the gum. Then we attempt to leave the counter. It's hard because there are so many people around.

"Just a minute." He stops at the condiments, and I wait while he puts mustard on his hot dog—an alarmingly overwhelming amount of mustard.

"Isn't your dad a chef?" I ask him. "I would have thought you'd have better taste."

"I have excellent taste," he says. "Which is why I'm trying to not taste this hot dog. And before you say it, I know I heard student council hot dogs were the best, but now I'm starting to think that was fake news."

I laugh, feeling my shoulders relax. My grip loosens on the phone in my pocket. Xander's sweet side is steadily winning me over, but something still pricks at me; it has been all week.

"Can I ask you something?"

"Sure." He takes a bite of hot dog, makes a face, then turns to a nearby wastebasket to shake off several layers of mustard.

"That picture of me—the one you sent the other night. You took it at the parade, but *when*?"

"What do you mean?"

"I mean what was going on when you took it?" It's a weird question, I know. But I feel like I need the answer. "It wasn't when I almost ran over you, because I don't look like I'm terrified for my life. So when was it?"

"It was the first time I saw you," he says. "We were walking, and I was shooting photos for the paper, and everything stopped. There was some kind of backup. We were standing around, waiting to get moving again, and I hadn't really noticed you yet. But then I looked over, and the whole thing was just so amazing I had to get a picture."

"Because it was an old hearse?"

"At first, yeah. But then you were having such a great time. It was this incredible contrast: this girl, dressed for death, laughing her head off."

I can hear my dad's voice in the back of my head: *It's the juxta-position of the universe.* And I'm blushing again. I've looked at that photo so many times that I have every detail memorized. The person in that picture doesn't look like me. Or not like the me I think I look like.

"I guess it's just weird," I say as we find our row and sit back down. The photo is beautiful and disturbing and flattering, and I'm still trying to explain to myself how I feel about it. "I don't even know what I was laughing at when you took it."

"You don't remember? You were right in the middle of the whole thing."

Then it hits me. "Oh my God. The dogs."

Dodson's stupidly overpriced orthodontist, Dr. Boley, had dressed up his ridiculously huge labradoodle in a clown costume and was walking him through the little ballerinas and karate kickers when someone on the sidelines lost hold of their puggle. The smaller dog ran into the street, and the two dogs started doing it right in the middle of everything. Parents went nuts as their kids stopped and stared, while both dog owners struggled to pull them apart. I had a bird's-eye view of the action from my perch on top of the hearse. I have to bite my cheek to keep from cracking up all over again.

"The dogs," Xander says.

"You should have gotten pictures of that instead."

"I was trying to get more of *you*. But I could barely keep up, and then I almost got run over like an idiot."

I eat my popcorn, trying to put my finger on what it all means. The me Xander captured is so different from the me I know. The Elaine I know is busy all the time. She has a sense of humor but mostly saves it for her best friends, and even they're prepared for her to drop the funny stuff when duty calls. I've always been the girl who plays hymns at your grandparents' services. The girl who helps whenever she's asked. No matter how anxious or angry or hungry I am for something different, I keep things going. I do what's needed.

"You can delete the picture if you want," Xander tells me. "And here. Let me offer you some Twizzlers as penance for getting off to a bad start."

"Twizzlers are my favorite." I take one and nibble the end as Madison offers the blanket and I settle in once more. I like the warmth of Xander's shoulder against mine. I like how he reaches across himself to offer more candy, so he doesn't have to move the arm touching me. And I like the way his cheeks are turning red in the cold air. Now that I've spent more time with him, I see that there's nothing particularly special about the way he looks on the surface; he's just a sandy-haired boy with ragged fingernails and a mole on his cheek. But there's something extraordinary underneath. In his eyes I see the promise of adventure.

And what about me? Sitting here next to this new boy in a crowded row of the student section at a Friday night football game, I'm the fun girl, not just the funeral girl. I never saw myself that way before. Maybe all I needed was someone to show me a different view.

CHAPTER ELEVEN

"This game is so boring—when can we go to the homestead?" Madison pushes the blanket away and stands up, bouncing impatiently. "Miles, let's go!"

"Hold up," he says, laughing. "Don't you want to see the fireworks at the end?"

"They're boring too," she says, which is true. The fireworks that celebrate every Clark County win aren't much better than what anybody could do in their own backyard after a trip to the Route 8 Fireworks Emporium.

Sienna returns from the bottom of the bleachers, where she's been talking over the railing to Jaxon.

"He can't come with us," she says, and pouts. "Coach called a team meeting."

"We can take him the next time we go," Xander tells her.

Mom texts me just as the Timberwolves kicker goes for a Hail Mary field goal.

> Is the game almost over?

The ball sails about a mile to the side of the goalpost, and the stadium explodes in cheers.

Just ended, I tell her.

"Homestead!" says Madison.

Mom texts back.

> Thank God—the O'Reillys refuse to go home. SOS!!!

I frown as I read her text. I can see where this is going.

"Who's that?" Sienna looks over my shoulder at my phone screen.

"My mom," I tell her. "She's sick."

"And . . . what?" Sienna's face twists into a not-again look. "Oh no. Seriously?"

"What?" says Xander.

"Elaine is flaking out on us," Madison announces.

The back of my neck goes hot. My friends get annoyed when I have to cancel plans sometimes, but they've never called me out like this before.

"It's cool," Miles tells me. "We'll take you home."

"No, it's okay." I don't want to be a burden on top of being a flake. "I can get a ride with whoever's driving Astrid. You guys go on without me."

I turn and start searching the rapidly emptying field. I don't see anyone in a pom uniform.

"Looks like they're gone," Miles says. "That means you're coming with us."

"But Dodson is nowhere near where you're going."

"You're kidding, right?" He gives me a look that tells me this isn't up for debate. "We aren't leaving you here. We'll go to the homestead after we drop you off."

I smile at him, grateful, and say, "Thanks."

I text Mom that I'm on the way, and then anxiety starts sparking inside of me, because getting out of the parking lot takes forever. Miles's truck crawls for eleven minutes before reaching the main road. But soon, thank God, we're flying.

The roads are pretty straight out here in the country, except for a stretch called Devil's Backbone that veers without warning through a hilly jumble of farms. The truck careens around the curves, making my stomach fly with every bump.

"Miles, slow down!" Madison shouts. Up ahead, a string of red taillights stretches as far as we can see. Emergency lights flash on the horizon.

"Looks like an accident at the market stand," Miles says as he rolls to the back of the line.

"Is it someone we know?" Sienna gets on her phone to see if she can find out.

Worried, I check the app Dad made Astrid and me install that shows our locations in real time. We call it the stalker app, but tonight I'm glad I have it. Turns out Astrid is almost to Dodson. She must have been through here before the accident happened.

"When are they going to put a stoplight out here?" says Madison. "There's a crash every other week."

The adrenaline high I was riding as the truck sped down the road turns into a sinking feeling. I check the time, then call Mom. She sounds like death when she answers.

"There's a wreck at the Backbone," I tell her. "We're stuck in traffic."

"Ugh . . ." She lets out a racking cough. "The O'Reillys are turning this visitation into an honest-to-God wake. They're determined to stay all night! Even after we told them it was time to go home, they've been saying goodbye for the past hour."

"I'm sorry."

"And then we still have to get ready for the Kern service tomorrow morning. Are you sure you can't get here any sooner?"

"I will if they clear the road fast enough. Won't Astrid be home in a little bit?"

"Don't get me started on her. She's supposed to be coming home with Sophia, but when I called to check on that, she was surly and disrespectful. What is wrong with her?"

An image flashes through my mind: Astrid and Quinn on the sidelines at the game. I'd bet anything Astrid isn't with Sophia at all, but I'm not about to tell Mom that until I have more information.

"She's a kid," I say instead.

"You're a kid and you don't give us this kind of trouble. Honestly, I try not to compare the two of you, but I'd be grateful if she showed just a fraction of your consideration. I'll be there in a minute!" she shouts. "I need to go. Your father's patience is wearing thin, and I'm about to keel over from exhaustion."

"I'll be there as soon as I can."

The truck creeps forward a few more feet. Then it stops, this time what feels like for good.

Miles checks his phone to see what people farther up are saying. "They've got both lanes blocked, and it doesn't look like they'll be clearing off anytime soon."

"The police scanner says no fatalities," says Sienna. "And it doesn't sound like anybody we know. Everybody they're dealing with up there is, like, thirty."

"That's a relief," says Miles.

"What did you say this place is called?" Xander asks.

"Devil's Backbone," Madison tells him. "It's a blind intersection because of the cornfields and the curves, and people don't seem to know what a stop sign means on top of that. I'm serious when I say people crash out here all the time."

"The whole place is lined with crosses for people who got killed," says Sienna.

Xander sits still for a minute, then he opens his door and hops out onto the side of the road.

"Dude, what are you doing?" Miles shouts.

"I'll bet you anything there are spirits out here." Xander reaches back into the car and opens a black bag on the floor, pulling out a camera and what looks like a small recorder. "I just want to look around with the infrared, maybe see if I can get some EVPs."

Sienna unhooks her seat belt. "I'm going too."

"Pretty sure that's against the law!" Madison says.

"Honestly, Mads, if you follow the rules all the time, you're never going to have any fun," Sienna tells her. "Plus, it's beautiful outside."

This either makes sense to Madison or she doesn't want her friend doing something without her. She slides across the back seat to join Sienna and Xander in the cold night air.

They don't invite me to come along. I'm sure they're assuming I wouldn't go anyway, and normally I wouldn't, but something inside is tugging at me, telling me to quit worrying and just go.

Before Madison can slam the door shut, I slide out after her.

"Seriously?" Miles says. "What if traffic starts moving again?"

"Just honk," Xander tells him. "We'll run right back."

"Not if I leave your ass," says Miles. With the others already up the berm, he looks out at me, almost pleading. "I thought you thought this ghost-hunting stuff was BS."

"I'm just in it for the told-you-sos," I tell him. "We'll be back before you know it. I promise."

Miles turns up the music and starts a game on his phone, which I take as permission to go. Xander, Madison, and Sienna are already halfway into a row of cornstalks, and I scurry to keep up. Xander turns on the camera he's carrying. Through the screen on the back we can see the area in front of us in eerie reds and black. He scans it around as he walks, then turns back and goes to the front of the field, scanning down the side of the road.

"I think I'm getting something up ahead."

He takes off running. We run alongside him, past the other idling cars, and the cold starts to fade as the blood pumps through my body. Madison and Sienna are giggling next to me, some inside joke, but right now I don't care. The sky is deeper and blacker than I've ever seen it—or maybe I just haven't taken the time to look up at the sky from the middle of a cornfield before. Everything inside me feels awake and alive. I forget about the O'Reillys, about Mom, and about the anxious voice telling me I need to get home. Turns out this is exactly the kind of adventure I've been craving.

We stop as we near the accident, not wanting to get too close. Xander plunges back into the corn, handing the small recording device to Sienna.

"Let that run and try not to brush it against your clothes," he instructs. "You want to hold it up and away from your body."

We walk some more, Xander scanning and Sienna recording.

"How do you know if you've got anything?" Madison asks.

"You don't until you listen back through it," he replies. "Sometimes if you get something, it's really faint. I have software that amplifies and isolates so you can hear better."

We go back to the berm, then head through the corn once more. Always just a few steps ahead of us, Xander scans his camera back and forth, up and down the rows. I wonder what it's picking up. And for some reason, I'm almost warm.

Sienna, on the other hand, shivers as she gives the recorder back to Xander.

"I think I'm out," she says. "My ass is freezing."

"Me too." Madison rubs her mittened hands together. "Let's go back to the car."

"I want to try a couple more areas," Xander calls after them. He holds out the recorder to me. "Will you do the honors? Or are you freezing too?"

"I can stand it a little longer." I reach out to take the device and my fingers skim his. A fiery jolt travels up my arm, landing with a twinge in my chest. I glance up and find him looking at me with a mix of heat and surprise.

Sienna starts giggling again as she and Madison trudge off.

When Xander and I are alone, I hold up my phone for light as I examine the thing in my hand. What if there's something on it—some message from the other side waiting for us to hear it?

"Can I listen to what we've recorded so far?" I ask.

"Sure," he says. "You're looking for anything that isn't normal for out here—voices that don't belong to any of us."

I put the recorder to my ear. I hear the sounds of our feet tramping through the corn, hear our voices replaying the small talk we just made, hear the wind in the cornstalks. Right before Sienna says she's cold, I hear the shortest, quietest sound, like a moan that cuts off before it can even get started.

My heart starts thumping.

"Hey, Xander. Is this something?"

We listen, heads bent over the recorder, which allows me to study his profile in the moonlight. His nose turns up, just the littlest bit. His hair curls at his ears, and he has nice long lashes that are easy to overlook because they match the color of his hair.

"There," I say when the sound comes again. "Did you hear it?"

"Maybe," he says. "It's really faint, though. I'll have to listen at home with my laptop to know for sure."

His response surprises me. "I thought you'd be excited."

"You have to go in assuming everything can be explained by something other than the paranormal," he explains. "When you can't find any other reason for a phenomenon, that's when you know you've got something." He turns off the camera. "Doesn't look like there's much activity. Not tonight at least."

"Maybe it's the ambulances," I suggest. "They're scaring the ghosts away."

"Wait a minute," he teases. "Are you actually getting into this? I thought you didn't believe this stuff."

Now that I've had a taste of ghost hunting—excuse me, *paranormal investigating*—I might be hooked. Just a little. I'm not ready to admit that, though.

"I didn't say I didn't believe," I say. "I said I thought ghost hunting was BS. But it's better than choking on exhaust fumes in Miles's truck."

We start walking back, past the other cars. People look at us oddly, which makes everything feel even more exciting. I've driven down this road, past these cornfields, hundreds of times, but I've never seen them from this vantage point.

Xander takes the recorder from me, bumping against my arm as he does.

"So, when I said I wanted to start over, that includes doing what I should have started out doing," he says. "My dad's been working on some new recipes, and he'd love to try them out on someone who's not seventy plus. You'd get to eat some really amazing food."

Now my heart's thumping for a whole other reason.

"Are you asking me on a date? At a nursing home?"

Around us, cars are starting to move. From down the road we can hear Miles honking his horn.

"Yeah," Xander says. "And you don't have to say yes right this second—"

"I can go."

"You can?" He seems startled. "That's great. I didn't know if you'd need to get permission or something."

"I don't always have to drop everything when my family calls," I tell him, realizing before the words have even left my mouth how not-true that is. Dropping everything is exactly what I've done every other time, but I'm not letting that happen now.

"Cool," he says. "It's an official date. I'll text you the details once I talk to Dad."

Miles honks again, two short, one long, and we start running. The truck is already starting to roll as we clamber into it.

"We almost left you," Miles informs us. In the rearview mirror, I see him eyeing me—a look I can't quite interpret. Is he mad that I left? Or is he just annoyed that we made him honk twice? I smile a sorry-please-forgive-me? smile. Tomorrow when we watch *Dragonfly*, I'll smooth it all over.

"So?" Madison nudges me. "You guys were out there a long time."

"Yeah," says Sienna in her dreamy voice. "Did you find anything, just the two of you?"

Xander and I both answer at the exact same time.

"Maybe."

❧

When I finally get home, I tiptoe up the back steps. Light spills under the door at the top of the staircase, but everything is quiet—a natural, nighttime quiet, not the quiet Dad and Mom demand during the day. When services are going on, especially, there can be no TV, no music except on earphones, no conversation above a murmur, and as little walking around as possible to avoid the sound of footfalls overhead.

Now it's nothing but silence. And I hope the light is just to keep me from banging into the kitchen island as I tiptoe toward the steps to my room. As quietly as possible, I open the door.

Dad is sitting at the table with a mug of herbal tea.

"Hey," I say, putting my key on its hook. He usually goes to bed early; seeing him around the house after nine is like spotting a rare mythical beast.

"Good evening." He pushes a mug toward me with a tea bag already in it. "I waited up."

Uh-oh. The formality of that greeting tells me he's angry I'm late. He's angry I went to the game in the first place. He's Disappointed Dad with a double-capital D.

"There was an accident at Devil's Backbone," I tell him. "That's why I didn't get here earlier."

"That's what your mom said." He stands to get the kettle and motions with his head for me to sit.

For all my bragging to Xander about how I don't have to drop everything for my family, I'm ashamed of how small my voice sounds as I say, "Do you need help setting up for the Kerns? I can do that before I go to bed."

"We'll do it tomorrow first thing. And we do need you for the service since Dakota will be at the church for the O'Reilly funeral and burial. You're set to play piano. You don't have any other plans, do you?"

"No."

"Good." He pours the water, then sits across from me. "So . . . you were out with friends?"

"Just Sienna and Madison and Miles." I tug the string of my tea bag, watching brown ribbons billow through the water. "And another guy, his name is Xander. He's on the cross-country team with Miles."

Dad raises his eyebrows at Xander's name. "Did he behave?"

So far, I've been the dutiful daughter, but now dutiful turns defensive.

"*Behave?* Why? He's not a little kid."

"Believe me, I am well aware that none of you are little kids anymore." Dad gives me a steady look and says, "One of the perks of my job, if you can call it a perk, is that I'm in a position to hear things around the community. Let's just say I've heard a few things about a new runner named Xander. The talk is that he's got a wild streak."

I roll my eyes as I take a sip of tea. "Small towns have stupid gossip. That doesn't mean we have to believe it."

"Right or wrong, sometimes talk and truth are the same thing."

His look grows more pointed, and I want to tell him exactly where he can shove this "talk" he's been hearing. Instead, I say, "Xander was fine. We just went to the game and came home."

"Good. Good," he says. "I don't want to be hearing *your* name around town, okay?"

"Dad, when have I ever gotten in trouble?"

"You're right. You've never given me a reason not to trust you." He gets up and comes around to where I'm sitting. "I know I can always count on you, and I appreciate that."

He kisses the top of my head, then he switches off the main light, leaving just the glow of the lamp from the den.

"Good night, Lainey."

He leaves to go to bed and I finish my tea, feeling relieved and a little freaked out—it's a strange mix of emotions for a conversation that only lasted five minutes. But bigger than all that is an almost absurd sense of exhilaration. My clothes smell like an autumn night. When I close my eyes, I see a sky full of stars, and my right arm still feels the weight of a boy pressed against it—a boy who does daring, dangerous things and who notices things in me that no one else sees.

I put my mug in the dishwasher, then climb the narrow steps to my third-floor room. The rest of our living quarters have been modernized, but this part still has that old-house feel, with worn wood floors, cracks in the plaster ceiling, and a slightly musty smell that never seems to go away, even when I use perfume or burn candles. Mom helped me paint the walls a light blue when I moved up here, back in seventh grade. She offered to take out the old furniture and replace it with newer stuff, but I told her no. I like the spindle bed and the 1940s dresser and the desk that looks like it came from a flea market. The writing surface is a hodgepodge of papers and photos and scraps of things that go back years and years, all preserved under a layer of varnish, like someone gathered up mementoes from all the people who've lived in this room and arranged them into a desktop collage. It's become so much a part of my life that I've explored it all and yet have no real idea what's there. It's just a cool piece of history that I live with.

But my favorite part of the room is the big window.

Moonlight pours through it, beckoning me to look out at my street and the horizon beyond. I grew up in this house, on this street, in this town. To me, they're ordinary. Small. Predictable. But now standing here, seeing the stars in their black night cushion, remembering the sound of something that could have been a voice out in the middle of a cornfield, I feel it for the very first time: There's something more here. Something more in this house. Something more in me.

CHAPTER TWELVE

It's probably safe to say Mrs. Rosalie Kern's funeral service is on track to win the award for Best-Attended Local Senior Citizens' Event this week. Mr. Kern is one of the retired dudes who meet for coffee at Hardee's every morning, so all the other retired dudes are coming to give him moral support. Mrs. Kern was big into quilting, so quilting clubs from at least five different churches will be in attendance, plus a whole vanload of people from Meadowlark Retirement Village (where Xander's dad works—not that that fact caught my attention or anything). The crowd is going to be so big we've had to open both our visitation rooms to make space. And Mrs. Kern is ready, looking pretty in her pink suit and lavender casket.

It's the living who can't seem to get themselves together. Dakota forgot to deliver some paperwork to the cemetery, so Dad's racing to make sure Mrs. Kern will have a final resting place to go to when her party is over. Meanwhile, Astrid and Mom have been arguing for the past half hour. Astrid wants to meet her friends in Shelbyville. I can hear them out in the foyer as I set up chairs.

"Everybody is going," she says. "We're supposed to be having lunch."

"They can have it without you," Mom tells her. "Your attitude has been terrible lately, and I'm tempted to forbid you to go anywhere until you improve it."

"What am I supposed to do, then?"

"Stay and help your sister. You can do the guest book during the service. At the moment, we need more chairs set out, and the programs need to be stuffed."

Astrid shuffles into the room, looking murderous. I keep quiet as she runs down the clock, fiddling with the flowers while I do all the work arranging chairs in perfect rows. She's not the only one who wants to be someplace else. Yet here I am in my navy-blue dress with a full face of makeup, ready to play piano for all Mrs. Kern's friends.

My sister, on the other hand, is sulking in leggings and a T-shirt with her hair in a messy bun, sending a clear signal that she has no intention of working the actual service. We finish the chairs, then I go to the office to get the programs and the smaller box of prayer cards that go inside them. I bring them to the table near the doorway, and we begin to stuff.

We're going to be here awhile, which means this is probably my best chance to ask about last night.

I clear my throat. "So, what's up with you and Quinn Hofstetter?"

She looks up, her face suddenly white.

"Nothing!" she says. "Where did you hear that?"

"I didn't hear it; I saw you guys at the game."

She grabs a stack of programs and starts tapping them against the table to straighten them. *Tap, tap, tap.*

"Nothing is going on," she says. *Tap, tap, TAP* . . . "We're not together if that's what you mean."

"Really?" I take the programs and put them aside. "Because it sure looked like you were together to me. Why didn't you tell me about it?"

"Because I knew you'd make it into a big deal."

She's right, I probably would have—first boyfriends are a big deal in general. But an eighth grader with a sophomore could be an even bigger deal, if only because the chances are really good for Astrid to get her heart broken. There was a time, not long ago, when she would have told me everything and trusted my advice. It hurts that she's been keeping something this important a secret.

I'm still her big sister, though. And I do have advice, whether she wants to hear it or not.

"He's sort of old for you, isn't he?"

"Not if he's just a friend," she snaps. "What are you, jealous?"

"No." But the truth is that I might be. A little. I haven't heard from Xander, which I tell myself doesn't mean anything because it's not even midmorning, and he's probably still in bed. I tell myself it's fine, don't obsess. Which I realize is actually obsessing. I pull out another stack of programs and try to put my attention where it belongs.

"It's just that you've been acting sort of weird," I tell her. "If something's going on, you can talk to me about it."

She rolls her eyes.

"Nothing is going on, I just don't need any more Mom and Dad drama. And if you think I'm acting weird, I'm not the one who got home at one in the morning and left everybody hanging last night. I helped clean up when all those people left. You were—"

"Stuck behind a traffic accident."

94

"Right. So how come Agnes Roell put up a video of you and some guy running through a cornfield? Doesn't look like you were stuck to me."

"We *were* stuck, along with everybody else. We were just . . ." How do I describe last night without looking totally bonkers? "We were just passing time."

"Okay, so then you wouldn't care if I showed the video to Mom and Dad? They stayed up late waiting for you."

I stop stuffing, barely recognizing the person in front of me.

"Why would you show that to Mom and Dad? That really sucks."

"I don't know." She shrugs, her mouth a tight, defensive line. "Maybe instead of constantly being mad at me, they could let you have a turn for once."

"Are you threatening me?"

"I'm just saying, maybe pay attention to your own business instead of messing with mine. These are the wrong prayer cards."

She tosses the program she was stuffing onto the table, then flounces out of the room. I check the name on the cards, and she's right—these are for the Flannery service next week. As I unstuff the programs and pack the cards back in their box, I mentally kick myself for not paying closer attention. Not only would it have been painful for the Kerns to see someone else's name at their service, it would have made Gillies look bad. In this business, little details count.

Mom comes down five minutes later, finds Astrid gone, and throws up her hands.

"That child is giving me gray hairs faster than I can cover them," she says.

I bring out the box of correct cards, and Mom picks up where Astrid left off.

"How was the game last night?" she asks as she stuffs. She sounds better today, not so sick, and it feels nice having someone not hostile to make conversation with.

"Sort of boring but still fun," I tell her. "We won."

"That's nice."

But she's not really listening. She's trying to get things done because people will be here soon. From his frame across the foyer, Great-Great-Great-Grandfather Leathan gives me a stern hurry-up look. I put my head down and stuff faster.

Xander texts just as the guests start arriving.

> Dinner tonight—7?

Normally I wouldn't have my phone with me during a service. It's a rule nobody's ever had to lay down because it goes without saying: Being on screens while people are paying their last respects to a loved one is extremely rude.

But then I've never had anyone text who I wanted to answer back immediately. I duck into the casket showroom and try to be fast.

> 7 works—do I come out there?

> That'd be great.

I emerge with a silly grin on my face in time for the service to start, and now I feel like I should apologize to Mrs. Kern, because I have been personally responsible for almost ruining her funeral at least three more times today. My brain is a merry-go-round of things that clamor for my attention as I attempt to play the piano: *Oh, look, it's my sister's threat to tell on me for ghost hunting with Xander . . . Does Xander asking me to dinner mean I have a boyfriend? . . . Speaking of boy-friends, what is my sister doing with Quinn and why is she threatening me? Holy crap, it's time to play "The Old Rugged Cross"!*

I've hit so many wrong notes you would think I was playing with oven mitts on. When the final hymn rolls around, I almost play "O Little Town of Bethlehem" instead of "It Is Well with My Soul." Dad catches my eye and frowns like *What on earth is the matter?* and I'm glad I caught myself because I'm pretty sure Christmas carols are a) premature since it's October, and b) not appropriate for this particular occasion.

As soon as the service ends, I scurry over to the guest book, where people are leaving parting messages for the Kern family. This job is easier. All I have to do is smile and turn pages when they get filled up.

As people file past, I recognize many of them from visitations and services past. It seems like when you get to be old, funerals turn into a big part of your social life, and while some are really difficult, often I'm surprised how *not sad* people seem. They do a lot of laugh-ing. They talk and reminisce. Family members will cry, but when the deceased is an older person, their friends are more likely to treat funerals like real celebrations of life.

Ms. Walter stops as she passes, arm in arm, with her friend Mrs. Sedlacek.

"Such beautiful music," she says as she takes my hand. "Thank you for sharing your gift with us, dear."

"It's my pleasure," I reply, opting not to point out how badly I mangled "My Jesus I Love Thee."

"You have such beautiful manners," Mrs. Sedlacek chimes in. "And your family is always so respectful and kind. I was just saying I'm glad Alan decided to bring Rosalie here. I told him the new place wouldn't have that personal touch."

"Oh yes, the new place," Ms. Walter says. "What is their name? It's something ridiculous, like Moments or Memento."

"Memories," I tell her.

"Oh yes. I saw one of their commercials on TV this morning. They certainly seem to be gaining a following; I've been to two services there this month already."

"But they aren't anywhere near as nice as Gillies," Mrs. Sedlacek assures me. "Some people may be drawn to the modern ways of doing things, but more will be loyal to you. Don't worry."

Suddenly I am worried, though. I honestly haven't thought about Memories since I talked with Dad days ago. And after today's service, I don't think the funeral home has anything else on the schedule besides the Flannerys. If more and more people are going to Memories, does that mean we're going to see even less from now on?

"Are you feeling all right, dear?" says Mrs. Sedlacek.

I pull myself together, wishing the anxiety buzzing underneath my skin would buzz off.

"Yes, sorry!" I say. "Thank you so much for coming."

I force myself to focus for the rest of the visitation, being extra nice and professional to everyone just in case they're thinking about going to Memories too, when the time comes. I can't help feeling like it's my fault so many people are choosing them. I promised I'd find ways to promote our funeral home, and I haven't done anything at all.

When everybody's left, I go up to my room to figure out what to do. The more I think about it, the more I realize I have three problems.

Problem 1: I've completely neglected the marketing stuff for Mom and Dad.

Problem 2: I've got a date tonight, but it's hard to justify going out two nights in a row when I haven't done anything to address problem number 1.

And problem 3: My date is with a guy who's on Dad's radar thanks to stupid small-town gossip. Best-case scenario, Dad will give me grief about it. Worst-case, he won't let me go at all.

The clock on my desk says it's two-thirty. I've got a little more than three hours to solve as many problems as I can. First, I take my laptop to the kitchen table. When my parents come up after accompanying the Kerns to the cemetery, I'm hard at work.

"Hey, Mom," I call out as soon as she steps into the kitchen. "Can we hire someone to create a new website for us? Having something professionally done will help us look better next to Memories."

She looks impressed. She turns to Dad.

"I don't see why not," he says. "As long as you hire someone from this area. We support local businesses."

"Got it. I also set up automatic tweets for whenever we post obits."

"I didn't know we even had a Twitter account," says Mom.

"Surprise—we do!" I leave out the fact that the account hasn't had a post since 2019, when I first set it up. As of today, it'll be more active, starting with the obituary of Mrs. Rosalie Kern.

Thanks, Mrs. Kern. Sorry again for almost messing up your funeral.

"I knew you'd be a natural at this." Dad gives my shoulders a rub, and I feel another shot of guilt: I've done nothing more than the bare minimum. For now, though, it will have to do.

"Hey." I push the computer away and rub my eyes like they're worn out from staring at the screen. "Would it be okay if I have dinner out tonight? I sort of have a date."

Mom's eyes light up. "A date? Who's it with?"

"I don't think you know him. He's new at school. His name is Xander and his dad is the chef at the nursing home in Philipsburg and he's making dinner for us with a bunch of new recipes he wants to try out."

I say it really fast, hoping Xander's name will get swallowed up in the other details. But Dad has a good ear.

"Is this the same Xander as last night?" he asks.

"Yes . . . What?"

"You know what."

"What?" says Mom, looking from Dad to me, then back to Dad. "Is something wrong?"

So far, I've masterfully handled the first two problems on my list. Problem number 3 is the trickiest. We're talking Mom here, so being direct is probably best.

"Dad thinks Xander has a wild streak because of some stuff he heard from the guys at Hardee's."

"Oh goodness," she says, laughing. "What would those old farts know?"

Touchdown! I never thought my mom could be as cool as she is right now.

"Exactly," I say. "Someone should tell those guys to mind their own business."

"It's not just that," Dad says. "What do you really know about this boy, Elaine? Have you met his family?"

"I'm meeting his dad tonight."

"Is he coming to pick you up so we can meet him?"

"I'm driving out there. He doesn't have a car."

"I actually like that idea," Mom chimes in. "It means Lainey can be home promptly by ten."

"Wait a minute, what?" I feel like I have whiplash. "Ten?"

"Yes. You were out late last night. You should be home early tonight."

Dad's nodding now, picking up her strategy and getting on board.

"Less time out means less time to get into trouble," he says.

What? No. First, why are they assuming there'll be trouble at all? And second, how did I fall into this parental tag-team trap?

"There's no way we could get in trouble because we'll be eating with a bunch of grandmas and grandpas," I tell them. "It'll be the best-chaperoned dinner date in the history of dinner dates."

"Wonderful," says Dad. "Then I hope you have fun. And bring us back a doggie bag."

CHAPTER THIRTEEN

The drive to Philipsburg isn't long. You get on the highway just past Dodson and drive for about fifteen minutes until you see the new megachurch, then get off at the next exit and you're there—in the middle of a small and depressing main street with a bunch of other streets that branch out until they all peter off into fields and pastures. The biggest things in Philipsburg are the bank, the second-hand shop, the nursing home, and—the crown jewel of the shiny, new development taking shape just outside of town—that church.

Oh, and Memories. Of course.

But I don't want to think about them anymore today. I'm escaping—going someplace where the only things I have to worry about are what delicious dish is in front of me and what I'm going to talk about with this new boy who's asked me out.

And Dragonfly.

I slam on my brakes.

"Crap!" I pull over and scramble to FaceTime Miles. "Crapcrap-crapcrap . . . hi!"

"Hi!" he says, laughing. He peers into the camera. "You're in the car? I was just getting ready to text you and ask, *my place or yours?* But it looks like you're already on your way, so all good!"

Inwardly, I cringe. Outwardly, I put on my I've-got-some-bad-news-but-it'll-be-okay smile.

"I'm actually in Philipsburg. I'm going to see Xander. His dad is cooking us dinner."

Miles frowns. "But *Dragonfly* starts in an hour."

Another cringe. This is the first time in probably forever that we haven't watched together. I should have thought about that when I told Xander I could come; the fact that I didn't makes me feel like the crappiest of crappy friends. But it's Saturday night. If I'm always doing *Dragonfly* with Miles, what does that leave for things like dates with new boys?

"I'm going to watch it as soon as I get home," I tell him. "I've got a strict curfew, so I won't be late. Ten-thirty, I promise. Do you want to still watch it together online? We totally can."

Miles does not look like he thinks this is an acceptable alternative.

"You could have told me earlier," he says.

"I know." I let out a huge sigh, hoping he can see how much of a weight I've had on my shoulders. "It's been a really hectic day. I had to work at a service, then I had to help my mom and dad with some advertising stuff."

"And now you have a dinner date."

The way he says it drips irritability, which I can understand, but there's something else, too. Bitterness creeps just under the surface—a tone I've never heard from Miles before.

"I'm so sorry," I tell him. "If you don't want to wait up for me, I totally understand . . ."

"Why don't we watch it tomorrow?" he suggests. "You don't have a date then, do you?"

"No! And yes! Watching tomorrow sounds great. I'll be at your place at one."

"Okay."

I wait for him to say something else—crack a joke, lighten things up, give me a bit of *Dragonfly*-speak to banter off—but that's all he says: *okay.*

"Okay, well . . ." I check my rearview mirror and roll my shoulders, trying to ease the tightness. "I'm already late so I'm going to go. But I promise I won't sneak any peeks later on tonight. And if you do, keep it quiet. No spoilers!"

"Okay," he says again. "Say hi to Xander for me."

❧

When I pull up to Meadowlark Retirement Village, Xander is waiting in the circle drive. He directs me to one of the visitor spaces, then opens my door to let me out.

"You look really pretty," he says, admiring my new sweater. I put it on with a skirt, tights, and boots because it was cozy but also because I wasn't sure what the appropriate attire was for visiting a nursing home. I figured it was a little more casual than what I'd wear for a funeral service but not as casual as what I'd wear to school. Hence the skirt. But it's a corduroy skirt, so not too dressy. And the boots make it more outdoorsy, instead of school-ish so . . . yeah. Clearly I overthought it.

"You look nice too," I tell him, and mean it. He's wearing a plaid button-down and dark jeans that look new. His hair is slicked back a little, but not enough to stop it from curling in all the right places. The only thing that's not on point are his ratty sneakers, but they complete the look by adding just the right amount of *don't care.*

"Would you like to start with the grand tour?" he offers as he leads me through the sliding front doors. "I've been talking you up, so people are excited to meet you."

"I'm flattered, I think. Or should I be nervous?"

"You should definitely be flattered," he says. "When I showed your picture to Mr. Ford, he said you looked like a young Olivia de Havilland."

"Wow, that is the compliment to end all compliments."

"I'm impressed you know who Olivia de Havilland is."

"My mom's into old movies—*The Heiress* is my favorite. They tried to make her look plain in it, but she was still so beautiful."

"Well, Mr. Ford is a known ladies' man, but I do think he has a point."

Inside is like every nursing home I've ever visited. People sit in armchairs and wheelchairs in the common area, reading and playing cards. One woman plays the piano. Another works on a cross-stitch. They smile and wave as we go past.

"Mr. Kiradjieff's family invented Cincinnati-style chili," Xander tells me, giving one of the men a high five. "His son brings it when he comes to visit and it's amazing. And that's Mrs. Kemper. She's teaching me German. Guten Tag, Frau Kemper."

I do my best to mute my smile so as not to show how adorable I think this is. He's like a little kid introducing me to his favorite grandparents, and the way they look at him so affectionately, you can tell they think he's adorable too.

"How do you know all these people?" I ask.

"Well, my dad's here all the time," he says. "Which means my house is empty all the time. I like to be alone, but not constantly, you know?"

"I can imagine." Although to me it sounds kind of nice. With three other people in my family and a business running downstairs, I'm never alone for long.

"The administrators let me do my homework here. They say it's good for the residents, and I've gotten some pretty stellar math tutoring from Mrs. Van Whye." He waves to a smart-looking woman with cropped hair and glasses. Then he leads me into a side room where chairs are arranged around a giant TV. "Here's where I hang out when I'm not doing school stuff."

The room is packed, the TV tuned to a show that looks like it's from the 1970s—lots of big hair and wakka-wakka music.

"I've turned into a huge *Sanford and Son* fan," he tells me. "And have you ever seen *M.A.S.H.*? It's a classic."

"I have not seen *M.A.S.H.*, no."

"That's right, you and Miles are into *Dragonfly*. That show is intense."

"Yes, but not the way we treat it. Miles and I think the whole point of liking it is not taking it too seriously."

"There's no shame in being a fan, though," Xander says. "I've got everybody here hooked on *Spirit Seekers*."

I glance at him, surprised; this is a new development.

"Didn't you say TV ghost hunters were douchebags?"

"Most are," he says. "But the guys on *Spirit Seekers* are legit. I've followed them for years and can find no flaws in their methods."

We leave the TV room and go back through the lobby. Looking around, I spot a stack of brochures on one of the tables and recognize the logo immediately. Memories.

I snag one as we walk by. It's just what I'd expect: smiling people hugging each other and touchy-feely language that reads like it could be from a commercial for tea or yoga pants or an Instagram about living your best life. And brochures aren't the only thing Memories has left. There are little cardboard tents on the tables with inspirational quotes. On the wall next to the reception desk sits a banner announcing a Memories-sponsored trivia night.

"What's that?" Xander asks.

I hand him the brochure. "They're a competing funeral home."

"Oh, seriously? I thought they were some kind of photography studio."

I would laugh at his confusion, but it's really not that funny because it just shows how fabulously different Memories is from our super-traditional business.

"They're turning into our arch-nemesis," I say. "Making us look dumpy and old-fashioned. It's a whole thing with my parents."

He's quiet for a minute. "I'm glad I know that. Now."

"It's cool," I say. "Well, actually it's not, but you aren't responsible for their cringey advertising, so don't worry about it."

"Right." He still sounds nervous. "Except my dad's been getting calls to do catering jobs, and this might be the place that's been calling."

He makes a *yikes* face. I *yikes* back. What really bothers me, though, is an idea that's been bugging me for the past few weeks—my family's business has become too comfortable. Even though Mom does all that community networking, even though we sponsor things like the new city hall auditorium and the high school football team, we haven't done enough.

I'm going to change that. As soon as this evening is over, I'm going to throw myself into marketing with so many new ideas that

Memories won't be able to see straight, let alone compete. We were here first, and we'll be here long after they've decided to move on and make money somewhere else. All these sweet people around me, when their time comes, they deserve a family touch.

Xander stops to read a text.

"That's my dad. Dinner's ready. You up for some amazing food?"

"Absolutely," I reply. "I skipped lunch so I'd have extra room."

Xander leads me into the dining hall, where residents are eating at cozy round tables. It's nothing like the big-city restaurants I've always dreamed of visiting; still, it's oddly exotic in its own way.

"I know this is a little strange," Xander says. "But I tried to make it special."

He's put a trellis around a table in the corner, creating our own isolated nook. A man appears wearing an apron and a black cap. He's an older version of Xander—same espresso eyes, same sandy hair—and he smiles as he pulls out my chair.

"You must be Elaine. I'm Mr. Nicholas, and it's an honor to serve you. Do you like scallops?"

"Have I ever had scallops?" I say, mostly to myself because I honestly don't think I have. Mom and Dad are good cooks, but seafood isn't a regular part of their rotation, and the fanciest foods most restaurants around here serve are steak and shrimp.

"You're not allergic to shellfish, are you?" Xander says. "I should have asked."

"Oh no, I'm not!" I put on a smile that says *Not only am I not allergic, but I promise I'm not a hick who won't try new things.* "I'm sure I'll love them. Thank you!"

That is the cue for the food to start coming out. We begin with salad, then a cheese-and-sausage board that I'm grateful I know is called charcuterie. Then soup, then the scallops, which turn out to be tender buttons of heaven in a red pepper cream sauce. We finish off with crème brûlée and raspberries. Xander and I are so busy eating that we barely talk while we shovel food into our faces.

"So?" his dad says when he comes to clear the dishes. "What did you think?"

"Amazing!" I'm almost drunk with the deliciousness of it all. "The people here are lucky to get this kind of thing every day."

"I wish the residents were that adventurous. For them, the blander the better." He grins, obviously thrilled we're enjoying the meal. "If you're planning to stay and chat, I'll go put on coffee."

"Your dad's an incredible chef," I tell Xander when we're alone again. "How come he's doing this and not someplace cooler with his own restaurant?"

"He did have a restaurant in Springfield," Xander replies. "But that business is brutal. When it tanked, my mom was a real dick about it. So when he got this offer from my uncle, I don't think he felt he could turn it down."

I flash back to the football game, how sullen Xander was, and the word *Mom* on his phone screen.

"Where is she?" I ask.

"Still there." A shadow falls over his expression as he takes his napkin out of his lap and starts folding it into a fan. "She's supposed to come out here at some point. But since she works for the zoo, it's hard to see what kind of a job she's going to find."

I want to know more about his mom, but it feels too much like prying. So I say, "What about you? Didn't you have friends in Springfield? Why would you leave all that to come to Philipsburg?"

"When my dad lost his job, most of my friends bailed on me because I couldn't afford to go everywhere and do everything with them," he says. "You don't realize how much of a big deal it is to have twenty bucks for a movie or pizza until you don't have it anymore."

"Actually, I do. I get paid to play piano at the funeral home, but business has been slow. And my friends . . ." I find myself searching for a way to describe the feeling of watching Sienna and Madison go off without me. It's not so much about money, but it still sucks. "Let's just say it can be complicated."

"So you get it," he says.

"Yeah, I do." But there's more. I know there is. And now is my chance to dig as deep as I can. "I also heard . . . well, Madison and Sienna said . . . you got kicked out of school?"

He looks up from his napkin folding, and I can see the sadness that's becoming so familiar in his eyes, plus a glint of something darker.

"Let's just say when you go investigating for the ghost of an old janitor, but you end up finding the principal's stash of white supremacy propaganda, it's a little tough not to share that around. One benefit of having tons of followers is you can really get the word out."

"They kicked you out of school for that?"

"Not immediately, and not exactly for that. They made it about me being there in the first place, at night, in a building that just happened to have a really badly secured service door, but whatever. We could all see where it was heading, and then my dad got this job. When I got a chance to escape, I took it."

Mr. Nicholas comes back carrying a silver tray with a coffeepot and a pair of delicate china cups on it.

"I figured I'd bring out the good stuff to top off what I hope has been a good evening," he says.

"It's been great," I tell him with a special smile for Xander. "I've been needing some escape too."

"Funeral business not exciting enough for you?" Xander's dad chuckles. "I'm surprised this guy hasn't showed up on your doorstep with his ghost-hunting stuff yet."

"It's not ghost hunting," Xander says. "It's paranormal investigation."

His dad shakes his head as he pours the coffee; I can tell he's heard all this before.

"I hope this doesn't sound insensitive," I say, "but people die every day in nursing homes. Wouldn't that make this a great place to investigate?"

"You would think so," Xander answers. "But pretty much everyone here has led a long and full life. When they go, they don't stick around. Plus practicalities—there are people here twenty-four seven. Nurses and families and other residents. They probably wouldn't approve of me poking around with cameras and recording equipment."

"Also I need to keep my job," his dad says on his way back to the kitchen. "I don't know why Xander is so preoccupied with that stuff, but I guess we all have hobbies, right?"

"It's not a hobby!" Xander calls.

"Whatever, son!" his dad calls back. "Let me know if you want more coffee."

Xander slouches. "He doesn't get it."

"Relatable," I tell him, both to lighten the mood and because it totally is. "My parents don't get most of the stuff I'm interested in either. If it's not funerals, then it doesn't register with them."

"My dad's always telling me how *impractical* investigating is. Like, I'm sorry he chose a tough career and he's miserable, but that doesn't mean it's going to happen to me, too."

"I think that's my biggest fear about the whole grown-up thing," I say.

"Being trapped in a job you hate?"

"Yes, or stuck in a town where everybody only knows you as one thing. This is going to sound terrible—I know it really sucks that your dad's restaurant failed and he's unhappy—but I sort of envy you. At least no one's expecting you to take over the family business someday. As far as everybody here is concerned, I'm the next funeral director at Gillies."

"You can't even hang out with your friends without them bugging you," Xander agrees. He looks into my eyes with such intense sympathy that I feel it all the way in the pit of my stomach. "I wonder why that doesn't make you mad."

If he only knew—how I've strangled my anger all these years, how it's simply assumed now that I'll be the calm and compliant one.

"I don't think I'm allowed to be mad," I tell him. "Or if I am, I can't let my parents know. They need me."

"Well, I'd be straight-up pissed. Feeling trapped is the worst. That's why I want to travel—see the world."

"Me too!" I'm laughing now because it feels so good to have someone understand so much. "We never get to go anywhere because my dad's always on call. Dying people don't care if you've got a Hawaiian vacation planned. Sometimes I think they pick holidays to croak just so we can't leave town."

He snorts, spitting coffee back into his cup.

"Well, I'm planning to chase the dead in my travels," he says. "I don't mean prisons and hotels and all the quote-unquote haunted places that have been done to death. I'm talking obscure places only the locals know about."

"Like the homestead?"

"Yeah, if I can ever get there. Last night it was too late by the time we got around the wreck."

And now I feel bad again, because my getting back to my family's business kept him from getting where he wanted to be.

"That was my fault," I say. "I'm sorry."

"Don't be. It gave me a chance to show you how investigating works—at least a little. There's a ton more to it, but that moan-type sound we recorded last night, for example, there was too much other noise around to tell what it really was. You have to be in a place where there aren't so many distractions."

An idea comes to me—or maybe it's been forming these past couple of days, waiting until the right time to surface.

"What if I had someplace nice and quiet where you could show me more of how it all works?" I ask.

His eyes go wide as he realizes what I mean.

"Are you saying what I think you're saying?"

I know it's ridiculously risky. My heart is racing and my shoulders tingle, but not in that awful way they sometimes do when anxiety takes over. This sensation is new and delicious—I'm standing at the edge of the quarry pit, holding the rope, daring myself to swing.

"I'm not saying you'll find anything at my house, but even if there's nothing—"

"It could still be amazing." Excitement lights up his face, then he catches himself and switches to a more *respectful* tone. "But only if you're cool with it, though."

A week ago, I was certain he only wanted material to impress the guys who crowd his social media with competitive mansplaining crap. But Xander's not the spotlight-hungry adrenaline junkie I thought he was. He's passionate about something. He knows what he wants, and maybe he can help me figure out what I want too.

"There would have to be rules," I tell him. "My parents are never going to agree—I already know that. So we'd have to do it at night when everybody's asleep."

"One hundred percent," he says. "Nighttime is perfect."

"If I say stop, we stop. If I say leave, you have to leave."

"Absolutely," he says. "You would be completely in charge."

I'm almost there; my toes peek over the ledge. All I have to do is be brave enough to step off.

"And it has to be a group thing," I add. "If we get caught, it'll be easier to explain what I'm doing with a bunch of friends instead of just one guy."

"Totally get that. Totally agree." He's nodding, getting caught up. "Plus, more people bring more energy."

His eyes are so big and brown, and they're staring right into mine with so much gratitude and excitement that I feel like I should look away. I don't want to look away, though. I want to stay here looking into those eyes forever. Except if I'm not home soon, forever is how long I'll be grounded.

I let out a long breath and say, "I can't believe I'm saying this, but okay."

A massive grin spreads across his face.

"Wow!" he says. "I can't believe you're serious. Wow!"

For a moment, it looks like he might be about to jump out of his seat and hug me, which I would definitely not hate. Then I see what time it is.

"We can plan the details later," I tell him. "But right now, I have to go. I'm supposed to be home by ten."

"Oh." He looks disappointed. "Okay, come on, then. I'll walk you out."

We say good night to his dad, then make our way back through the main room. People smile as we pass—knowing smiles that bring the blood to my cheeks. Xander glances shyly at me, and I can tell he's thinking the same thing: We look like a couple.

"Thank you," I say when we get to my car. "For getting me out of Dodson and getting me to try new food and introducing me to all your senior citizen friends. They're sweet."

"They like you too," he says. "Mr. Ford gave me a thumbs-up behind your back."

I realize I'm using my genuine smile, the one I don't even have to think about because it just spreads wide and natural across my face. And then he leans over and brushes his lips against mine. It's light and off-center, and my eyes flutter closed. When they open again, he's still there. Just as he's moving closer, the door to the nursing home slides open and a lady comes onto the sidewalk, talking loudly on her phone.

We each take a step backward and I feel it almost physically, leaving that super-charged space that had begun to materialize between us. Xander looks at his sneakers, running a hand through his hair.

"So, um . . . when can we do it?" he says. "I mean, not do it, obviously. God that's embarrassing. I mean investigate. At the funeral home?"

Smiling, I think about it, then offer, "Next Saturday? My parents go to bed early, and Astrid's usually at some sleepover. So . . . eleven-ish?"

He nods. "That's perfect."

"Oh, and don't tell anyone yet. Madison or Sienna or Miles—especially not Miles. Let me set it up, okay?"

He grins, the mole on his cheek quirking up so adorably I have to stop myself from grabbing his face and kissing it.

"No worries," he tells me. "I'll be as quiet as a ghost."

He opens the car door. I get in, and before he shuts it, he kisses me again, a true kiss this time that scrambles me up like a smoothie.

"See you Monday?" he says.

"Yes," I say back, and I have to get it together as I drive back through Philipsburg because my senses are all jumbled and jangled and swoony. A week ago my life was boring and predictable. Now there's a boy in it—a boy who twists up my insides in the most thrilling way and who makes me want to do things I've never imagined doing before. Like me, he wants to explore the world, and we'll start in my own backyard.

I can't wait.

CHAPTER FOURTEEN

"Hello! I'm here!"

I never ring the doorbell at Miles and Madison's house. Their parents told me years ago I was welcome to walk in, and usually one or both of my friends are right there to greet me when I do.

This time the foyer is empty.

"Miles?" We're supposed to watch *Dragonfly*; I'm here right on time. Instead, it's Madison who bounds down the hallway from her room.

"Oh my God, how was last night?" she asks. "Was it amazing? Why didn't you tell us about it?"

"Yesterday was a blur," I say. "I didn't have time to tell anyone."

"You have time now, right?" She starts tugging me toward her room. "Come on and tell me everything."

"Actually . . ." I hate to do it, but I hang back. "I'm here to see Miles. We missed *Dragonfly* last night."

"Oh." The anticipation in her face dissolves into disappointment. "He didn't say you were coming."

"Weird. Maybe I got the time wrong."

"He's in the den. If you remember, you can tell me about your date after your show."

"I will," I tell her. "I promise."

"Uh-huh." She looks like she doesn't believe me as she shuffles out of the hall.

Hurrying into the TV room, I find Miles playing *Call of Duty* and tap him on the shoulder. He lifts his headset and says, "Oh, you're here."

"Exactly when I said I'd be. Did you get my texts last night?"

"Yes," he answers.

"You didn't text back."

"I was mad at you. We've never missed an episode."

"And I *didn't* miss it. I'm here, right now."

"I know," he says.

"So come on, you're still mad?"

His iciness starts to thaw; he moves over so I can sit next to him. His old golden retriever Baggins squeezes in next to me and gives my cheek a slurpy kiss.

"Are you sure nothing else is wrong?" I ask.

"Just farm stuff with my mom," he says. "You'll probably think it's stupid."

"Why don't you try me and see?"

"Okay. Well, the sow at the Schmidts' is looking like she'll deliver any day, but it's too soon, and basically I'm worried about a pregnant pig."

"Totally not stupid," I say. "If you weren't worried, it would mean you weren't Miles."

"I guess that's a compliment," he says as he reaches behind me to scratch Baggins's ears. "So, how was X?"

"Good. Dinner was incredible."

I'm getting ready to tell him about ghost hunting when he says, "But seriously, though . . . you might want to be careful with him."

The smile on my face falls; I can feel my eyes narrowing.

"Have you been having coffee with the old dudes at Hardee's? My dad's been getting Xander warnings ever since Harvest Home."

"You know I'm always and forever a Dunkin' boy," he says. "And I don't have a problem with X. He's just super fixated on his followers and being some kind of paranormal expert. Makes you wonder how far he'll go for likes and clout and whatever."

"Investigating is what he's passionate about. Back up and take out the parsley."

It's what Miles and I say when a conversation is going in a direction it doesn't need to go. It's like how restaurants are always putting in parsley and other things that most of the time are just extra stuff nobody needs: When somebody's throwing in things that don't add anything to the big picture, we say, *"Take out the parsley."*

"Fine with me," says Miles. "I'd actually love to not be thinking about Xander. But this is your thing; do you want to watch *Dragonfly* or do you want to talk about your date?"

"Dragonfly," I say, feeling sour. The past two minutes have squashed my desire to tell him about the ghost hunting that we agreed on last night.

Miles hits Play, we settle in, and then *Dragonfly* turns out to be a total letdown. It's really badly written, and there's this twist where Skye learns that the runes in her palms match other people's too, not just the seal over Pax's heart. It's probably the worst episode in *Dragonfly* history.

At least Miles and I are experiencing it together. Sitting here with him, picking the whole thing apart, laughing at the same places, getting mad at the same things—even the most terrible episode can't be that terrible when the two of us are watching as a team.

"People are going apeshit about this," Miles says as he checks the fan boards. "They're saying it's, quote, a total betrayal of the characters' story arcs."

"It's definitely going to mess things up," I say. "Pax is going to kill her now."

"Pax would never do that."

"Why not?"

"Because he loves Skye."

I play with the floof around Baggins's collar as I consider this. "Sometimes I wonder, though: Does Pax love her, or is he just stuck with her?"

Miles shakes his head, certainty written all over his face.

"They're the alpha and omega," he says. "They're endgame."

"But we don't know what the endgame looks like. And maybe this twist means he's not the only one. Maybe there are others she fits with too."

"Maybe," he says. "But at the end of the day, he's the one she was meant to be with."

We fall silent, each of us reading fan comments on our phones. Miles seems convinced this is just a blip in the story, but I'm pretty sure it's going to cause some major changes.

After a few minutes, I lean in and bump his shoulder with mine. "Am I forgiven for last night?"

"Yes," he says. "Sorry for being a crappy friend."

I reach over and give him a hug, which Baggins takes as a cue to start licking us both.

"You're not a crappy friend," I tell him. "You're my best friend. Please don't ever change."

CHAPTER FIFTEEN

I wake up on Monday with my anxiety revving like the engine in Dakota's old VW, and at first I have no idea why.

Then I remember: ghost hunting. I haven't told my friends yet. Saturday night and Sunday, when I felt brave and full of possibilities, the whole thing sounded easy and fun. But now the week has started. Now it feels like an actual countdown. And now that I'm heading back into the reality of my regular life, I can't believe I ever agreed to sneak someone into my house and let them poke around for spirits.

Xander meets me before school in the parking lot. There's something almost shy about the way he nudges me with his elbow. It's the first time I've seen him in person since that kiss.

"So you know I love *Spirit Seekers*, right?" he says. "Well, when they start an investigation, they always do research. So I went over to the *Daily* and looked through their archives, but I didn't find anything about the Gillies Ghost."

I push aside my mushy kissing thoughts and try to get on his level.

"Not surprising," I say. "The *Daily* is always trying to include us in stories about local hauntings, but my parents tell them no. They say they're fine if people want to talk about it, but putting stuff like that in print gives it too much credibility."

He makes a little sound, like he thinks my mom and dad are being dumb.

"I would disagree, but whatever. After searching for *Gillies Ghost*, I went really far back, to when the funeral home got started."

"You can go back that far?" I had no idea the *Daily* was even around in 1878.

"Yeah, it's all digitized. I searched a ton of variations on Gillies and Funeral Home with *suicide* and *jump* and even *murder* and got nothing there, either."

"So maybe it really is just a story." I feel sort of vindicated. The Gillies Ghost has always felt like something somebody would make up about a place people already find kind of scary—a funeral home seems sad, so why not add suicide and make it even sadder?

"But it's still worth investigating, right?" Xander says. "You're not changing your mind?"

He's looking at me with those dark eyes that right now seem almost desperate, and I don't want to lose the chance to look into them more. There's also a part of me—a big part that craves the exhilaration I felt on Devil's Backbone—that does want to do the investigation. Maybe we won't find anything, but it still sounds like fun.

"I'm not changing my mind," I say. "I'll tell everybody at lunch."

"Baby pigs! Baby pigs!" Miles runs up to our table with his phone out and sheer joy on his face. He shows us a photo of a massive sow next to three little pink blobs.

"Mama's in labor," he tells us. "And so far, it's going great."

"That's amazing," I tell him as Madison and Sienna *ooh* and *aah* over the other photos Miles's mom has sent from the Schmidts' farm. A couple are really graphic and gross, but he's so happy that nobody mentions it.

"Mom thinks there are eight more coming," he says. "I asked if I could get out of school to help, but she told me no."

"You have an econ test," Madison reminds him.

"Thanks, non-Mom," he replies.

Xander arrives while the two of them are bickering. He sits down, shoots me an expectant glance, and I tap Madison on the shoulder to interrupt.

"I have some news too."

And then I tell them the plan, because once I've said it, I can't take it back. It's like ripping off a Band-Aid—best to do it fast.

"You're really going to do a ghost hunt at your house?" Madison says. Her eyes are saucers of disbelief.

"It's an investigation," I correct her.

"That sounds so romantic," says Sienna.

But Madison is still crabby.

"Wow, who *are* you?" she says.

"Yeah, who are you?" Miles is suddenly on his twin sister's team. "Last week you were all adamant that ghost hunting was a crock. Now you're ready to strap on the proton pack."

"This isn't *Ghostbusters*," Xander corrects him. "We aren't trying to capture ghosts, just find them. Besides, the proton pack was a dumb idea, anyway, because ghosts use energy, they aren't actually energy, so you can't suck them up and catch them."

Miles squints at Xander, like he can't decide whether to keep joking or be pissed off at getting mansplained. I jump in to smooth things over.

"But there's no *Dragonfly* this week, so we don't have to worry about messing that up. I figured Saturday was the perfect time to do it."

"Do your parents know?" asks Madison. "Did they give permission?"

"No, it's got to be top secret, after they're in bed."

"What if we attract an evil spirit?" says Sienna. "If there's a Ouija board, then it's a hard pass from me. I don't mess with demonic stuff."

"I never use those kinds of tools," Xander assures her. "We want to contact and document but keep a safe distance. Just in case, though, I'll bring some sage to burn."

"No one's burning anything," I tell them. "It's going to be as low impact as possible. You know how my dad is."

"Yeah, I do," says Miles. "Which is why I hope we only contact the nice spirits. What if the Gillies Ghost tells your dad on us, and you get in trouble on both sides of the veil? Or what if you get possessed and we have to find an exorcist? I'm not sure Reverend Gammill at the Methodist church is going to be up for that job."

Before Xander can launch into a lesson on Possession 101, I assure Miles that I'll wear my anti-possession panties, which makes him laugh and restores balance to our group vibe. I hate it when everyone's tense.

And so starts the countdown to Saturday. As the days go by, my anxiety gets worse, the voice in my mind telling me I'm going to get caught, going to freak out my dad, going to screw things up with Xander.

Weirdly enough, the thing that calms me the most is funeral-home marketing.

First, I start on the new website. I look around and land on a one-man agency in Shasta Falls called Artichoke. (*Why Artichoke?* you may ask. To which I would answer, *Exactly.*) The man behind Artichoke is Randall, a dude-bro operating out of his parents' basement who spends most of our meeting talking about his "theory of engagement" while asking barely anything about what we do. The concepts he shows me for Gillies range from ultra-minimalistic ("Very European—very now") to haunted-house gothic ("Trust me, irony is the way to go").

Since Randall is useless, I decide to do things myself. I find a better template than my mom's and get started on an aesthetic that plays up our heritage. I spend most of Friday afternoon and evening putting candles in mason jars and taking photos of funeral programs stacked next to antique books, then testing out filters so our Victorian décor appears lived-in in a trendy sort of way. When Mom looks at it Saturday morning, she declares it "nice." Dad asks if we are going to have to have "twinkle lights" up in the foyer all the time now, and whether I could move the reclaimed wood I'd arranged on the front porch by the time the Reillman visitation starts.

I finally make it to evening, and I'm almost too exhausted for an investigation. But Madison and Sienna are coming over soon and it'll be too late to back out. I distract myself while I wait by scrolling through the *Dragonfly* fan sites. There's no episode tonight because supposedly a big bombshell is coming next week. Everybody's speculating about what it could be, and everybody thinks it has something to do with Pax.

Miles will love that. One more thing he can ask Magnus about when we go to Chicago.

"Wow, what a day." Mom sinks into the chair next to the couch where I'm curled up, a glass of wine in her hand. "What are you up to?" she asks me. "Sienna and Madison are coming over?"

I yawn and stretch, bigger than necessary, just to make clear how not-exciting of a night it's going to be.

"We're just watching movies," I tell her. "Pretty boring."

"Boring sounds nice," she says. "I can definitely get on board with that."

"Knock-knock!" My heart jumps into my throat as Sienna's voice comes over the intercom. Dad presses the button to unlock the back door, and we can hear footsteps coming up the stairs. Sienna and Madison emerge in the kitchen as Astrid comes out with her overnight bag.

"I'm going now," Astrid announces.

"Make good choices," says Mom. She opens the window over the couch and waves at Sophia's mom on the curb below. "I'll pick her up at ten tomorrow," she calls. Then she sits back in her chair while Dad puts a bag of popcorn in the microwave.

"Is it okay if we hang out with you girls?" she asks. "Dad and I haven't watched a movie in ages."

Sienna and Madison look at me with thinly veiled panic in their eyes. Miles and Xander are coming at eleven. I'd counted on my parents being in bed long before that. If they watch the movie, we'll be cutting it super close.

But what are we going to do, say no?

"Sure thing," says Madison.

"Totally," says Sienna as I scroll through Netflix looking for the cringiest rom-com with the shortest running time that I can find.

Mercifully, Dad starts nodding off less than forty-five minutes in. Mom loses interest and starts playing on her phone. They've both shuffled to their bedroom by the time the lead couple discovers they were perfect for each other all along, and Sienna, Madison, and I let out a sigh of relief.

"Are you ready?" Sienna asks me.

"Are we really doing this?" Madison asks both of us.

I stand, stretching my arms over my head, willing myself to be calm. Be zen. Be brave.

"We're doing this," I tell them. "Let's go."

CHAPTER SIXTEEN

Madison, Sienna, and I creep down the back stairs and wait for the boys to arrive.

Xander steps through the door first with his black bag. Miles comes in after. Xander smiles when our eyes meet, and my stomach does an actual somersault. I put my hand against the wall. Are my knees really wobbly? Every fiber of my being is awake and buzzing. I can't believe I'm doing this.

As soon as everyone's gathered on the landing, I motion for them to pay attention.

"So here are the ground rules. First, obviously, be quiet. And nobody goes off by themselves, no exceptions. Got it?"

"What if we have to pee?" asks Sienna.

"Hold it."

"What if Xander can't stop farting?" says Miles. "He was ripping some silent-but-deadlies in the car."

"Gross," says Madison. "Miles, you are disgusting."

"What?" Miles nudges Xander, who doesn't look all that amused. "Our friend is stinky. There's no shame in it."

I want to be diplomatic, let Miles be his usual jokey self, but the longer we stand here, the more my nerves are fraying.

"If anybody has a question that has anything to do with anything below your waist, then put a plug in it," I tell them. "Yes, Miles, I know what I just said, and you know what I meant."

"We should get started," Xander says. "Miles has to be back at one and he's taking me home, so . . ."

"Fine. Okay." I shake out my arms, crack my neck, bounce on the balls of my feet. If I'm really going to do this, now's the moment. Holding my finger to my lips, I motion for them to follow me into the foyer.

"Daaaaamn," says Xander, while Miles and Madison and Sienna look around with silent wonder. Everything that has always been so familiar about my house looks new and mysterious. The furniture casts weird shadows, and the ornate wallpaper looks vaguely sinister. My friends' eyes are skeleton holes under the night-lights my parents keep on when the business is closed. You can see enough to get around, but not much more.

"You know what would be romantic?" Sienna says. "If we lit candles."

"Burning this place down is probably not a good idea," I counter.

Xander takes a flashlight out of his bag and turns it on. He sweeps the beam around the space, landing on the portrait of my great-great-great-grandfather.

"This looks like someone important," he says.

"That's the original Gillies. The literal OG," I tell him.

"Right," says Xander. "I read about him in the *Daily*. Let's start here. If anybody knows the Gillies Ghost, it'd probably be him."

Xander rummages in his bag. He pulls out the EVP recorder, turns it on, and places it on the table underneath the portrait.

"Is there anybody here?" he asks. "If any spirits are around, I want to assure you we aren't here to harm you in any way. Make a sound if you can—knock or move something. Or speak into this recorder."

We listen. Something clanks in the walls, and everyone tenses. I motion for calm.

"It's just the heater kicking on."

"Hey, I've got some activity," Xander whispers. He's holding up a device I haven't seen before.

"What is that thing?" asks Miles.

"An EMF reader. It measures electromagnetic fields. It just spiked off the charts. Right here."

He holds it up again, and Sienna gasps as the needle jerks to the right. The closer it gets to the portrait, the more the needle moves.

"Hello?" Xander says. "Is there anyone here?"

Silence.

"Is this the ghost of Leathan Gillies? Leathan Gillies, are you with us?"

More silence.

"Speak into this recorder if you can, Mr. Gillies. Or make a noise. We'll be quiet and listen."

He gives the recorder to Sienna, then pulls out another device that he hands to me. He turns it on, and it fills the area around us with a grid of little green projected dots. To Miles he gives a small video recorder.

"We'll let the EVP recorder run for a while. I'm going to take some photographs. You guys go back in that room and get a good view of the entire space. Elaine, you hold the grid projector and,

Miles, you film. You're looking for anything that moves and disturbs the grid."

Miles and I go sit on the love seat at the opposite end of the visitation room, allowing the device to cover the entire space in green dots. Meanwhile, Sienna and Xander and Madison are by the portrait with the EVP recorder and EMF reader. Occasionally Sienna will ask the questions because Xander wants to see if the "spirit" responds better to a male or female voice.

"So"—I gaze out at the green-dotted room—"is this like some low-budget version of the Quantum Corridor?"

Miles snorts at the *Dragonfly* reference.

"After last week's episode I'm starting to wonder if all their money is going to the Night Queen's eyelash extensions."

"Right?" I say. "What was that crappy thing? Someday when they rank episodes from best to worst, that one won't even be on the list."

He sighs as he surveys the room. "Somehow this isn't as exciting as it looks on TV."

I have to agree. As thrilling as the cornfields were, I was expecting tonight to be at least similar. So far, it's a lot of nothing.

"I'm pretty sure those ghost-hunter shows edit all their stuff so you don't see the downtime," I reason. "But I still don't think ghosts operate like this. Why would they just hang around when they could be doing something useful?"

"Like what, fold the laundry? How could a ghost be useful?"

"I don't know. This kind of thing is just not what I've experienced."

He squints at me. "What *have* you experienced?"

I take a moment to consider whether I really want to talk about this. I haven't told anyone about it, not even my parents. I know it happened. I don't want anybody trying to talk me out of it or telling me I'm imagining things.

"No laughing. If I tell you, you have to take it seriously."

"I promise," he says. And I believe him. When it really counts, Miles knows when to listen.

"Okay, so . . . remember that little boy who died of cancer a few years ago? They did all those fundraisers around town and he went to Disney with Make-A-Wish?"

"Yeah. They thought he might get better, then he didn't. That was really sad."

"Well, they had this entire visitation room filled with stuffed animals and balloons and photographs for him. It was really beautiful. Mom sent me down to check on something about an hour before his service was supposed to start, and the whole time I was there this woman was standing by the casket. She was quiet, just looking at the boy, and I didn't want to bother her because she was clearly someone who had meant a lot to him. I finally did ask if there was anything she needed. She smiled at me and said, 'No thank you, dear.' I went back upstairs and told my dad people had started arriving. I didn't see her later at the visitation, but people are always coming and going at those things. Then later, as I was helping the little boy's aunt gather up all the stuff, I saw two photos with that lady in them. I told the aunt that I'd met her earlier and how nice she'd been. And the aunt said that was impossible because the lady had died four months earlier. She was the little boy's grandmother."

"No way," says Miles. "That really happened?"

"I swear to God."

"Was she wearing all white? Did she have an angelic glow?"

"No. She had on pants and a sweater. I remember her turquoise earrings. She was as real as you are."

"That's so weird and amazing and I think I might cry." He takes a shallow breath, and my heart pangs because weepy Miles is a rare thing to see.

"Hey, are you okay?" I put my hand on his hand.

"Yeah, it's just been a weird week," he says. "Animals getting born, animals getting sick . . . Four of those new piglets died, Mom just diagnosed a whole litter of kittens with panleuk, and someone dumped off a dog that's so neglected and skinny you can see every one of its backbones. I'm not even the one taking care of them and it's . . . a lot."

He leans into me, just the slightest bit, but it creates a little bubble—a space of comfort and caring. He tips his head down, wipes his eyes, then looks up at me with an embarrassed laugh. I squeeze his hand, and in the green-dot darkness, we are quietly bonded.

"So, not much is happening out here," Xander says as he comes out of the hallway with Sienna and Madison. "Can we try some other places?"

I give Miles's hand one last squeeze, then I get up and shake out my legs. They're sore from sitting.

"Maybe this way?" The four of them follow me to the inner hallway.

"It's like a maze in here," says Sienna.

She's right. The house is even bigger than it looks from outside. Down a short corridor sits the casket showroom in a wing that was added sometime during the 1920s—close enough for easy access, but not right in your face since families often find this part the hardest.

Xander sweeps his flashlight beam across the space, and I realize I'm chewing my lip. Even though there aren't any windows in here, I think surely Dakota will see the lights and come bust us. For a long minute, no one says anything, they just look around at the caskets.

Pretty soon they start to wander, running their fingers along the smooth finishes, feeling the cushions inside, while Xander snaps photo after photo of the space with his traditional camera.

"Looking at these is making me claustrophobic," says Madison.

"If you were in one of these, you wouldn't be alive," Miles tells her. "So, you wouldn't even know."

"Hello, is anyone with us?" Xander says to the air. "We're looking for a person who people say they've seen in the window upstairs. Is there someone here who might have done something to hurt themselves? Maybe you jumped from that window?"

I suddenly feel like I need to add my own voice.

"We're not judging if you did," I say. "You must have really felt helpless. We just want to know more about your story. Maybe we can help?"

"Can you maybe tell us your name?" Madison asks.

The silence stretches out, then Xander suddenly turns his head.

"I thought I saw something move," he says. "Out the corner of my eye. You don't have a cat, do you?"

I shake my head. "We aren't allowed to have pets. If there's movement, it's probably my dad or our intern, Dakota." So far, I've been pretty calm. But now anxiety is flooding in. "We should probably stop. I'm worried we're going to wake up someone, and not from the afterlife."

"Let's listen to the recorder first," says Sienna. "Maybe there's something on it."

Xander looks to me for permission, and I give in. I'm not in a hurry to see him go, plus I'm curious what we might have captured too.

We settle in a circle on the floor, heads bent over the device. Listening to it is like the other night in the cornfield, only odder, being inside my own home. Hearing our voices, the stuff we said and did just a few minutes ago, everything feels turned on its side, like I'm watching a movie and in it at the same time.

Nothing happens when Xander addresses Great-Great-Great-Grandfather Leathan. Nothing happens until we're in the casket room. We're listening to Madison complain about being claustrophobic when we hear the sound.

"What was that?" says Madison.

Xander hits Replay. It's a voice. It sounds like a woman, but we can't make out any clear words. There's nothing else until Madison asks for a name, then the voice comes again.

It's staticky and a little garbled, but it sounds like two syllables—a word ending in an "ee" sound.

"No freaking way," says Miles.

"Is it the Gillies Ghost?" says Sienna.

My heart does a double-skip. I've always hated that story. I've fought it because I've found no evidence of it in my everyday life. So why does hearing this voice make my pulse race like this? And why does that feel *not bad*?

"What is it saying?" asks Madison.

Xander plays the recording over and over. Now that our ears are used to it, we can make it out clearer each time.

"I think it said Flossie," says Xander.

"Is that a name, though?" asks Sienna.

"Pretty sure it's from an old song." Madison hums a couple of bars. "You know, by—who was that lady from that band named after peas? 'Fergalicious'?"

"Why would a ghost listen to the Black Eyed Peas?" sniffs Sienna.

"Maybe it was their favorite song," Madison snaps back. "I mean, you still like Justin Bieber, so—"

"Maybe Elaine knows someone named Flossie," Xander suggests.

My first reaction is to feel totally overwhelmed.

"Thousands of people have been through this place—dead and alive," I tell him. "If one of them was named Flossie, I'd have no way of knowing."

Xander rewinds, he adjusts the volume settings, and now we can hear it almost as clearly as if it was one of us speaking.

"This is . . . wow." Xander stands up and starts running his hands through his hair in disbelief. "Okay. Wow. I've never heard an EVP like this before. And it's answering us, which means it's intelligent! This is huge."

He turns, tugs me to my feet, and kisses me. A real kiss, right in front of everyone. When he lets me go, I literally see stars.

An awkward interval passes, everybody trying not to stare. Then the business phone rings.

Immediately, my head clears. The warp speed of my ability to go from Swoony Elaine to Responsible Elaine surprises even me.

"You've got to go," I tell them. "Now."

I thumb in the alarm deactivation code to open the front door instead of the back since Dakota will probably come in that way. They slip out, then I scurry to hide in the darkest corner of the visitation room as Dad goes out to the garage for the van. Through the front window I see Miles's truck pulling away from the curb just as Dad backs out of the drive.

Now that I've successfully evacuated everyone, Swoony Elaine comes back with a vengeance. I can't stop giggling. I can still feel Xander's lips on mine, the sensation of everything suspended in surprise, in shock, in service to one short, perfect kiss.

Thanks, Flossie, whoever you are.

CHAPTER SEVENTEEN

No matter what I may have experienced of dead grandmothers in turquoise earrings, no matter what stories other people have told about my world, I've always told myself that spirits who whisper cryptic things to teenagers in the dead of night aren't real.

Except that voice. I heard it so clearly.

I wake up on Sunday morning buzzing, not just from kissing Xander but with curiosity. Who is this Flossie, and what is she doing in my house?

I could check the records to see if we've ever cared for a person with that name, but I wouldn't know where to start considering how long we've been in business. And even if I knew where the old record books were, I wouldn't be up for going through every single one.

I reach for my phone and use it to find the *Daily*'s digital archives. I search *Flossie* with *Gillies* and *Funeral Home* and *Leathan Gillies*. Nothing.

Frustrated, I study the window across my room—the one I like to look out when I'm sad or bored or just trying to figure out life. Did somebody really jump from there?

I throw off the covers and haul myself to my feet. If there's one thing I've learned experiencing grief up close, it's that things like this are deeply private. If somebody did end their life here, they don't need strangers gossiping about it, even if it's hundreds of years later.

Still, that voice. We all heard it. And whether it's connected to some old local legend or not, it's clear that there's something—or someone—here. *Why* are they here? And what do they want?

I head downstairs to find my dad making pancakes for Astrid, who just got back from her sleepover.

"Lainey," he says. "We had a death call last night and you didn't make coffee. I almost wondered if you were even up in your room."

I freeze, dreading what he'll say next. Does he know I wasn't there? Did he hear us ghost hunting downstairs? Is this his lead-in to the biggest punishment in the history of parental punishments?

"I didn't hear the phone," I say. "I'm sorry."

He winks at me, amused.

"Don't sound so guilty! I certainly never *expect* you to make coffee, I've just gotten so used to it that I missed seeing your face. Dakota and I went through the McDonald's drive-through on our way to the pickup." He holds up a spatula on which balance two perfectly round pancakes. "You want a couple of these?"

"Yes! Please!" I suddenly feel so light that I almost bounce over to the island. Looks like today I'm getting Whimsically Fun Dad, not Disappointed Dad.

I drizzle syrup over the pancakes and take a big bite. Turns out investigating the paranormal builds up an appetite.

"Astrid and I were talking about going to the Sauers' orchard later," he says. "Do you want to go with?"

I glance over at my sister to see how she feels about me tagging along. She smiles, one of those smiles from before she stopped wanting to talk all the time. A connection passes between us, and I smile back.

"Maybe," I say. "I have a ton of homework, and more stuff to do on the new website. I accidentally hit Publish before it was ready, so right now it's one big marketing fail."

"I know you're doing your best," Dad says. "Like always."

"Actually . . ." I have an idea. "Some guy from one of the churches called, and their genealogy club is doing a book on Dodson history. I told him I'd talk to you since the book's a fundraiser. I know we don't publicize it, but he was asking about the Gillies Ghost."

"That old story again?" Dad chuckles as he heats oil for more pancakes. "Talk about something that refuses to die, no pun intended."

My parents have always been breezily dismissive of the Gillies Ghost, but now I'm wondering: Dad grew up in this house too. Maybe there are things he's not telling us.

"Have you ever seen anything?" I ask. "Or maybe heard anything around the house?"

He flips a pancake into the air, watching with satisfaction as it lands back in the pan.

"I've experienced a lot of strange things over the years, but I can't say I've ever seen a ghost," he says. "Did the man have new information, or was he just looking for family folklore?"

"He didn't seem to have much. Except he did say her name might have been Flossie."

"I don't think so."

Wait a minute. He shot that down way too fast.

"Why?" I ask. "Do you know that name?"

He slides another pancake onto my plate and says, "That's another old family story, but this one is true. I'd say I'm surprised anyone else would know about it, but the whole thing was supposedly a big scandal when it happened. Maybe there's a record somewhere that I don't know about."

"When *what* happened?"

"Your great-great-grandad Francis had a sister, Florence. Her dad, your great-great-great-grandfather Leathan, called her Flossie."

My heart's pounding again, so hard I'm afraid I'll pass out. I grip the seat of my barstool as Dad goes on.

"The story goes that she was a talented embalmer, so she was supposed to play a big role in carrying on the family business."

"Supposed to? What happened? Did she kill herself?"

Dad laughs. "Oh no. I was always told she fell in love with some man and ran off."

"That's it?" says Astrid. "That was the scandal?"

"At that time, a young woman running away from her family would have absolutely been scandalous," Dad says. "Especially one who was such a pillar of the community. People said it broke her father's heart. He never fully recovered."

I pull in a deep breath, willing my heartbeat to slow down. It's too much of a coincidence. Maybe the Gillies Ghost *is* real, but not like everyone thinks.

"So, what did happen to Flossie?" I ask.

"I don't think anybody knows," Dad replies. "We might have had some old letters I could dig up to see if she kept in touch, but a lot of those family records were damaged when our storage unit flooded. If you find out anything, let me know. I'm curious how that story ended myself."

I swallow my last bite of pancake, turning this information over in my mind. Flossie was a real person—someone my great-great-great-grandfather loved and lost. Now her name is being whispered by a ghostly voice almost 150 years later. There's no way it could be fake; of all the names in the world, who would have ever known to utter that one?

I give my dad my empty plate and try to sound casual as I ask, "Do we have any pictures of her?"

"The album in the foyer downstairs has photos going back to the start of the business," he says. "She'd be in there for sure."

"Good to know. I might check it out."

And then, I have to force myself to walk to the stairs instead of bolting.

The table in the grand foyer has two levels: the top, which always holds a vase of fresh flowers, and a lower shelf suspended between the legs. On that shelf sits an album with a red leather cover and GILLIES across the front in gold script. Anybody who's interested can look at it, perhaps while they're waiting to meet with Dad or searching for something to take their mind off a long visitation. But the ones who should be the most interested in the book—those who might know about and actually be related to the people in the photographs—pretty much ignore it. I've spent my whole life in this house, and I don't think I've cracked it open once.

I pull out the book and take it to the staircase, where I sit and flip through the first few pages, past stern-faced Leathan posing in front of what is now our guesthouse, Leathan shaking hands with some important-looking person, and Leathan standing by the frame of this house as it's being built. I flip and flip until I find her.

The girl stands outdoors next to the buggy, dressed all in black, a single braid falling over her shoulder. Even if her name wasn't written below the photo, I'd know her by the expression on her face.

She looks dutiful and dignified, but something in her eyes betrays a current of restlessness. It could be nothing more than irritation with the photographer. Or it could be dissatisfaction with her life. It could even be anxiety, like mine. But the sight of her makes me gasp. She gazes at the camera with her hands folded in front of her.

She looks just like me.

CHAPTER EIGHTEEN

"Xander." I almost drop the album as I try to hold my phone up for video chat. I called him immediately, but I'm so stunned I can barely keep my grip on anything. "You are not going to believe this."

"What?" he says.

His brown eyes are adorably sleepy. I force myself to not think about them and stay on topic.

"Flossie. I know who she is."

He suddenly looks 100 percent awake.

"You do?"

"Yes! My great-great-great-grandfather Leathan—the one in the painting—she's his daughter."

"How do you know?"

"That's what my dad said."

Xander's face goes pale. "You didn't tell him about last night, did you?"

"No, are you kidding? There's no way I would ever tell him

about that. I approached it delicately. But it turns out my grand-father Leathan—"

"The OG?"

"Yes. Right. He had a daughter named Flossie. But get this: She didn't kill herself. She ran off with a guy."

I wait to see how he'll react to this twist in the story. He nods and says, "Wow. That's amazing evidence—it proves that what we captured is a real spirit."

"Can you come over?" I ask. "I want to try and find out more."

"Dad has the car; I don't have any way to get there."

I could offer to go pick him up—I want to. But by the time I drive out to Philipsburg and back twice, most of the day will be gone. Plus, something tells me Dad wouldn't be thrilled at me having Xander over, the boy with the wild streak.

"I can research on my own," I tell him. "I'll let you know what I find out."

"Great. Last night was incredible."

"It was," I say, and I'm not really talking about the paranormal investigating.

But I need to share this with someone. I need to be reassured that this is real and not some weird coincidence. So I call the person I share everything with: Miles.

"Wouldn't you rather have your boyfriend help you?" he asks when I invite him over.

"Xander isn't my boyfriend."

Yet. I don't say this to Miles because I don't know how weird it would be to have a romance in our friend group. None of us has had a serious relationship at all before, besides Sienna's new thing with Jaxon. Xander and I together could upset everything.

"You know my family better anyway," I tell Miles. "I thought it would be fun."

"No, fine. You're right," he says. "I'll be there in ten minutes."

And then he shows up in five.

Technically the funeral home isn't open on Sundays. We do services and viewings and meetings with families when needed. But the doors aren't open for people to just walk in, and when I check the schedule, it looks like Dad's meeting with the family of the person they picked up last night isn't until four. I don't want to take Miles upstairs because my parents might ask what we're doing, so we sit in the front visitation room, on the love seat where we sat last night, and I open the album to see if we can find any more photos of Flossie.

"I don't want to freak you out," Miles says when I show him the first one. "But she looks a lot like you."

"Too late. I've been freaking out ever since I saw it."

I flip a couple more pages, until we see her again. This time, Flossie is standing by an open casket. Inside lies a man in a uniform that must be from the Civil War. A huge wreath with a black banner reading VETERAN is propped against the bier. Flossie's expression in this photo is one of pride.

"My dad said she was talented at embalming," I tell Miles. "Maybe they took this picture to show off her work."

There are two more photos of Flossie in the album. The first shows her on the front porch of the house arm in arm with another girl, who looks about the same age. The girl is wearing a maid's uniform, and the handwritten caption under the photo reads *Florence Gillies and Margaret Beatrice Wright*. Both girls are smiling, wider than you usually see in these old pictures. In fact, of all the photos in the album, this is the only one where someone has a genuine smile on their face.

Finally, there's Flossie in a gown with a plaid sash running over her shoulder and down to her waist, fastened by a Celtic knot brooch.

The photo is in black and white, but I think I recognize the plaid pattern. Dad has a kilt like that; he wears it every year when the Caledonian Society has their winter feast.

"That's the Gillies tartan," I tell Miles. "Leathan came here from Scotland."

After that, there's nothing else. There are a ton of photos of Francis, her brother, who took over the business after Leathan Gillies. But no more Flossie.

Closing the book, I chew the inside of my lip. "It's like she disappeared. Where did she go?"

"Your dad said she ran away," says Miles. "So why?"

"Isn't it obvious? She was in love."

I can imagine it all so clearly—Flossie feeling restless with her responsibilities, an intriguing stranger coming into her life, the two of them escaping together.

"You don't have anywhere else we can look?" Miles asks as he puts the album away.

Then I remember—the *Daily*. When I first searched the archives, I was looking for a Flossie. It's possible I missed something because I didn't search the right name.

I search again and find three articles that mention Florence Gillies.

DODSON STUDENTS WIN
AGRICULTURAL AWARD

Miss Florence I. Gillies, daughter of Mr. Leathan Gillies, proprietor of Gillies Funeral Parlor and Chapel, and Mr.

Noah J. Kahnwald, son of Mr. Bjorn Kahnwald, local farmer, have been honored by the Agriculture Society for their work on a device which helps obtain milk more efficiently and with greater sanitation from dairy cattle. The device was developed as part of their studies in lifestyle and scientific inquiry at Dodson Senior High School, where both are students. Each will receive a $20 award and certificate of achievement.

"Flossie was into cows," says Miles. "She's my kind of girl."

"Okay . . ." I mull this over. "So not only was she an embalmer, she was also some kind of inventor."

The second article is about Florence Gillies hosting an evening of music at the funeral home to raise money for the First Presbyterian Church. Not much stands out, except for this sentence: *Proprietor Leathan Gillies expressed pride in his daughter's efforts, saying, "Our Florence is a steadfast and dedicated member of the family who can always be relied upon to help our business and community."*

Finally, we find this.

Mrs. Dorothy Gillies, wife of Mr. Leathan Gillies, proprietor of Gillies Funeral Parlor and Chapel, is pleased to announce the engagement of her daughter, Florence Irene, to Mr. Charles Clarence Graham, Esq., partner in training at Graham and Mossell, Practitioners of Law. The couple are to be married May 11 in the Willow Lyceum garden. They will honeymoon in Chicago before returning to make their home in Dodson.

"She was getting married?" I drop my chin into my hands, confused.

"But then there's nothing else," Miles says after searching on his own phone. "If she was a big enough deal to have her engagement announced, they should have said something about the wedding too. There's nothing about a Florence Graham, no birth announcements if she had kids, and no obituary either."

I push all of these puzzle pieces around in my mind until a picture starts to take shape—spotty at first, but clearer the more I put it all together.

"I bet I know what happened," I say. "It's a classic story. Flossie was expected to marry some upstanding guy from some upstanding local family. Ugh, *Charles*. Even the name sounds boring. She was supposed to come back and stay here, but she couldn't take it and left."

"I sort of feel bad for the upstanding local family guy," Miles says.

"Oh, I'm sure he was fine. I bet if you keep searching, you'll find he ended up with someone who didn't mind sticking around Dodson for the rest of her life."

I read back through the news stories, and while they don't answer all my questions, they do hint at something I feel like I already know, deep in my soul: Flossie wanted more.

And that is something I can 100 percent relate to.

CHAPTER NINETEEN

Monday at lunch, I show everything to Madison and Sienna. They bend their heads over my phone as I flip through the photos I snapped of the family album, the screengrabs of the old newspaper articles.

"So Flossie was a real person," says Madison. "And she broke her father's heart."

"She did it for love," says Sienna. "But who did she run off with?"

That's the one question I don't have a theory about yet. Nothing I've found gives any hints of a tempting other suitor, but maybe that's the point: If he was some secret stranger, there wouldn't be any articles or photos.

"Maybe it was somebody new in town," I say. "Someone her parents didn't like."

"Miles says he thinks it's probably never going to be solved," Madison says.

"Where *is* Miles?" I ask, realizing our group isn't complete. I'd thought he'd be at our table by now.

"I'm here."

Miles slumps next to me, setting down a plate with one sad-looking burrito on it. When he sees the concern on our faces, he attempts a smile.

"Sorry, I was up all night. The panleuk kittens are getting sicker, and the piglets aren't nursing. I went out with Mom to start bottle-feeding."

We're all giving hugs and support when Xander slides into the table too.

"You okay, bruh?" he says. "You sort of look like your dog died."

"Close, but not exactly," Miles answers. He pulls himself up straighter and tries on a bigger smile. "Let's just say farm animals don't respect business hours when they decide to get sick."

"That sucks," says Xander. "But maybe some good news will cheer things up? I found another EVP."

The mood at the table definitely shifts as everyone waits to hear about this new development.

"I ran the audio we captured through my software," Xander explains. "I cleaned it up, and check this out."

We huddle over the device until we hear it—a near whisper, but pretty clearly an actual word. It sounds like "Kaahhhh" and something else, but none of us can make it out fully, even after replaying it twenty times.

"Sounds like someone trying to take a dump," says Miles. Normally I'd mock-scold him for turning everything into a bathroom joke, but he's obviously operating on tons of stress combined with not much sleep.

Plus, I'm getting frustrated too.

"What is it with this one-word-here-and-one-word-there stuff? If

I had some sort of message from the afterlife, I'd make damn sure people could understand it."

"You might not be able to because it would take so much energy," Xander tells me. "Just making the slightest sound takes a ton. Were you expecting something like a full sentence?"

"Wouldn't you want something like that too?" I fold my arms over my chest, annoyed that Xander isn't being more encouraging. "You spend all this time investigating, don't you want to dig any deeper?"

"Just finding evidence is enough for me," he says.

"Not for me." Now that I've heard Flossie, now that I'm *aware* of her, I want to know everything—who she really is, and why, of all the places she could go in the world, she's still here.

Xander plays the EVP one more time, then says, "If we want to know more, we have to investigate again. As soon as possible. Saturday night?"

Miles starts humming the *Dragonfly* theme song under his breath, reminding me I've promised Saturday to him.

"It has to be late," I say. "Miles and I are watching *Dragonfly* at my place."

"Actually . . . ." Miles pushes his burrito away and gets up. "I'm staying in Saturday night. You can text with me while you watch and still make your date . . . er, investigation."

"I thought you'd want to see it together—in person. It's supposed to be some big bombshell."

"Well, then . . . Boom!" He smiles again, which I guess is supposed to make everything lighter, but just feels off.

"So you don't want to help investigate?" I ask.

"If I change my mind I'll let you know, but right now I'm thinking I'd just be a third wheel."

"Okay," I say. The whole thing is weird, which sort of sets the tone for the rest of the week.

Wednesday, Sierra and Madison aren't at school. I don't find out why until Madison posts a photo of the two of them at Indiana University in Bloomington. She's captioned it, COLLEGE VISIT! LOOKING TO THE FUTURE WITH MY BESTIE.

Thanks for inviting me along, I text her.

The musical theater program is totally different from the music school, she responds. **This tour is just for theater people.**

What I want to text back: *You could have at least told me you were going.*

What I really text back: **K.**

Thursday, when the two of them return, all they want to talk about is their trip and I feel shut out. Finally, Friday arrives and Xander asks if I'll take him to the Sunset Diner because he heard they have great apple pie. I've been crafting a list of other local attractions I could introduce him to, including the Point, which is where people go to make out in their cars. But just as the last bell of the school week chimes freedom, my mom texts that the Whitmans have just dropped off a huge box of family photos.

> The visitation's @ 6:30! Can you scan and put in a PowerPoint? As many as possible before people start arriving—I'll pay you extra!

"Let me guess," Xander says when he sees my face. "You have to work."

"This just came up and it has to be done by tonight," I tell him.

"Or you could blow it off. Let somebody else do it."

"I can't. My parents are useless with PowerPoint."

He gives me a look that says *Really?*

"You take all this so seriously," he says, as if it's a bad thing.

"It's a grieving family who wants to remember their loved one," I shoot back. "I'm not sure how much more serious it gets than that."

"Fine," he says, holding up his hands. "Then I guess I'll see you tomorrow."

When I get home, I scan and upload photos for the Whitmans until my eyes see a white glare around everything. Then I go upstairs to change my clothes; might as well help with the actual visitation since I have no evening plans now.

At the landing, I pause by the little door that leads to the other attic room. I open it and stoop through into the dim, musty space, mentally kicking myself that I didn't have this idea sooner.

Immediately it's obvious that this won't be like one of those movies where I discover a treasure trove of diaries from the past. A few years ago, Mom did a major clean-out; now everything is stacked in plastic bins with labels like GIRLS' SCHOOL ART and CHRISTMAS DECORATIONS. The only thing close to what I'm looking for is BUSINESS RECORDS, which is just folder after folder of numbers, and legal documents, which don't go back any further than the 1950s.

I open a bin labeled YEARBOOKS AND ANNUALS because the old books are cool and the hairstyles are funny. I find Mom and Dad with their big '80s mullets. I find my grandparents with their 1960s coifs. In the back of the bin, I find older books. And at the very back is a thin, yellowed booklet titled THE EAGLE—DODSON SENIOR HIGH SCHOOL ANNUAL 1896.

Is this what I think it is?

Hands shaking, I flip the pages, looking at the old-fashioned printing and flowery script. There weren't many students at Dodson in 1896 so it's easy to spot Flossie. She's in a photo of eight stiffly posed people. Everyone else is staring with bland, almost stern, expressions. But Flossie smiles widely, her attention seemingly caught by something outside the frame.

On the opposite page is a list of "Senior Superlatives"—things like "Most Refined" and "Most Amiable." Again, I find her right away.

"Most Intrepid—Florence (Flossie) Gillies"

Intrepid. I look again at the photo, putting this together with the tiny bit I know, and it makes sense. A girl who would run away from home would have to be adventurous. She'd have to be fearless to leave behind the people who loved and counted on her. She looks strong and confident, like someone you'd want for a friend.

Maybe she wants to be my friend.

Looking at her face, I feel like there's a reason we're now starting to hear from Flossie. Maybe she's ready to be seen. Maybe she's ready to be heard. Maybe she was waiting for someone who would listen. And maybe that person is me.

CHAPTER TWENTY

By Saturday night, I've got my Flossie-hunting kit ready.

Item 1: Photo album

Item 2: My dad's kilt in the Gillies tartan

Item 3: Flossie's high school yearbook

And then, because I've heard spirits can be summoned by things like smell, I went to the drugstore and got the most flowery rose-scented perfume I could find because when I looked up Flossie's name, I found that *Florence* means "blossoming."

As soon as my parents go to bed, I sneak down the back stairs and spritz perfume everywhere. Minutes later my friends are stepping through the door: Madison first, then Sienna, then Xander, red cheeked and smelling like campfire smoke.

And then, it's Miles.

"Hey," I say. "You're here."

"I guess I am," he says. "*Dragonfly* was such a dud, I needed something else to give me my Saturday night thrills."

"I know! What is the deal with all these constant letdowns?" I'm so glad I have him to banter with again. That bombshell everybody's been predicting didn't happen. And texting about it wasn't any fun either, because how many times can you write a variation on *This is boring*?

"Why does it smell like roses?" asks Madison.

"Better than smelling like Xander's ass," Miles says, and everybody laughs because it's nice to have Joking Miles back, even if the joke feels a little extra jabby at Xander.

Xander doesn't seem to notice. He heads straight for the foyer.

"I want to start here again," he tells us. "Since that's where everything happened last week."

We venture in, sticking close to each other. Xander sets everything up, giving Madison the grid projector and asking Sienna to film anything that disturbs it. He gives Miles the infrared camera, turns on the EMF reader, and starts the EVP recorder.

I call out. "Flossie? I've been learning about you ever since we heard you last week. Were you supposed to get married? To a guy named Charles?"

The space is quiet. Completely still.

"Did you love Charles? Or not? Did you run away? Maybe with someone else?"

No response, but that's okay. I've got plenty of tools in my box. Pulling out the yearbook, I open it to her class photo.

"You'd have to be brave to do something like that, right? Is that why they called you intrepid?"

"I heard something." Xander's whisper pierces the quiet.

"I heard it too," says Madison from over on the love seat.

"Footsteps," says Sienna. "Somebody was walking down the stairs."

"Keep the grid up," Xander tells them. "Don't move it."

I put down the yearbook and pick up Dad's kilt.

"Do you know what this is?" I ask. "It's the Gillies family tartan. I saw you wearing the same one in your picture. Does it mean anything to you?"

Miles gestures for me to stop whispering. "Look!"

Something is disturbing the green dots. We all gasp in unison as the dots ripple, disappear, then reappear as whatever it is—a shadow, maybe?—passes by the wall.

Xander snaps a ton of photos, until the movement stops as whatever it is goes through the door that leads to the second visitation room.

"You got all that on video, right?" Xander takes the recorder from Madison and we review the footage. It's even eerier on playback, the way the dots skim over the shadowy moving thing.

"That's creepy," says Madison.

"Let's look at your camera," I tell Xander. "Maybe there are orbs or something."

Xander opens his view screen, and we gather around it. He flips photo after photo, until . . .

A figure stands by the door of the visitation room—a girl in an old-fashioned dress with a single braid falling over her shoulder. She's made of mist, but she is unmistakably there, hands folded in front of herself. The detail is so crisp, it's almost like someone superimposed an old photo onto the modern background.

"No freaking way!" says Xander.

"It's her," I say. "It's Flossie."

If I look close enough I can almost make out her features—the expression on her face. A shiver ripples down my back as that looking-in-the-mirror sensation I had the first time I saw her returns.

"Are you sure it's real?" says Miles.

"It's not fake if that's what you mean," Xander says. "There's no way anybody here could have planted that."

"But if someone like *this* was around, wouldn't we have seen it?"

"There's a lot happening all the time that people don't see." Xander turns the camera this way and that, looking at the image from as many angles as possible. "This is the most amazing apparition I've ever seen." He turns on the EVP recorder again. "Flossie, are you here? Obviously, you are; can you speak to us?"

We wait. We listen. We ask again. We listen again. For more than an hour we try everything in Xander's repertoire, but Flossie doesn't speak or show herself again.

"She's not a trained dog doing tricks," I remind everyone. "She probably figures she's given us enough for one night."

Reluctantly, Xander starts shutting down his equipment and the others start getting ready to leave, everyone shocked at what we've seen and processing what it could mean.

I, for one, feel both thrilled and more than a little terrified. The night may be ending, but things are just getting started. We've not only heard Flossie, we've seen her now. And I can't help feeling like that will change everything.

CHAPTER TWENTY-ONE

Video chat chimes me out of bed early the next morning. I open it to see Xander looking almost feverish.

"I can't stop thinking about last night," he tells me. "I didn't sleep at all."

"Me either." I pull myself to my feet and start pacing my room, trying to burn off the leftover adrenaline. "I can't believe we actually got a picture of her."

"It looks even more amazing when I sharpen the image. Look at this." My phone vibrates and I see that he's sent me an even crisper version of the photo. Flossie's eyes are dark, piercing shadows, and her brow appears almost knitted. In the blurry, misty soup of pixels, she looks impatient.

Xander runs a hand through his hair, leaving it sticking up in a million adorable directions.

"This is the best apparition I've ever seen," he says. "Better than anything on *Spirit Seekers*. When people see this, they are going to freak out."

Wait a minute. I stop pacing and hold the phone closer to my face.

"What do you mean, when people see it?"

"This is huge," he says. "Something like this is too good to keep a secret."

A bolt of terror shoots through me. I look again at the photo he texted and realize it's actually a link. When I follow it, I find not just the photo but the video and the EVP too.

"Xander." I'm almost afraid to ask. "Why is all this online?"

"I post all my investigations," he says. "Well, not all of them, just the stuff that's really good."

"You never asked if you could post *this*. This is my home. It's my family's business."

"When you look at the pictures, you can't tell where it is."

I clench my free hand into a fist. He's not getting it.

"But I can tell. Anybody who's spent any time here could tell. And what happens when your followers start asking where this was taken? There are already rumors about my house being haunted. People are going to lose their minds."

He's silent.

"Xander?"

"I won't give any identifying details," he says. "I'll just say it's a funeral home and leave it at that."

"No." This is all wrong. It's like someone took me, all warm and tingly and full of excitement about new discoveries, and doused me with cold water. Posting online was not part of the deal. And his promises are too thin. Xander can't guarantee people won't figure out where the evidence was captured. If they do, all the care my parents have taken to be respectful about the Gillies Ghost will go out the window. We'll have ghost followers camped out on our sidewalk 24/7. Worst of all, Dad will know it was all because of me.

Xander has no idea how much damage this could do.

"Take it down," I say.

"What?"

"Take it down," I repeat. "Please."

"Wait a minute." He squints into the webcam. "Are you mad at me?"

"I'm just . . ." What *am* I actually? Not mad; it's deeper than that. I'm confused and hurt that someone I thought I knew could violate my trust like this.

"It's too much," I say. "I didn't know you were going to post this online. I kind of can't believe you did. Especially without asking me."

His forehead wrinkles, like it's just now hitting him that what he did was wrong.

"I'm sorry," he says. "I got caught up in the excitement. I didn't think."

"That's probably the worst part. I took a big risk letting you into my house."

"I know."

"And it's like you didn't care."

"You're right." He looks embarrassed. "I got carried away. I'll take it down." He goes silent for a minute then says, "It's done."

I open the link again to check; it goes to nothing.

"Are we okay now?" he says. "Elaine?"

I swallow hard against the things I want to say—how I only just found out my house is haunted by the spirit of a family member, and rather than thinking about what that might mean, all he thought about was impressing his fans. I want him to understand how much I'd love a message—some sort of guide from somebody who's been where I've been, someone who struggled with big decisions about who they are and what they want to be. This is bigger than a paranormal investigation, it's a link to my past, and maybe my future too.

I've never fought with a boyfriend, or a maybe boyfriend, or whatever Xander is after everything that's happened. Does fighting mean breaking up? And is there anything to break up if I'm not sure I can trust him? Now that my anxiety has kicked in, I'm a wound-up mess. So I do what I always do: I keep everything inside.

"We're okay," I tell him. "I have to go help Madison and Sienna. It's our last practice before musical auditions."

"But I'll see you tomorrow?" he asks.

I already know I'll be avoiding him. I've been this way since grade school, when I found that fighting back against my Funeral Girl tormentors only made them torment me more. Since I realized I'd rather bite my lip and help out at home than deal with Disappointed Dad. I put my head down, keep things neutral, dodge the discomfort. I hate that I do this, and yet I will continue to do it, starting tomorrow at school.

"Yes," I tell Xander. "I'll see you."

Then I turn off my phone and try to put him out of my mind.

"Where've you been? I was trying to get hold of you all morning." Sienna opens the door to her house and raises her eyebrows suggestively. "Were you with Xander?"

"No," I say. "About that . . ."

She lets me in, and I go straight to the piano in her living room.

Madison comes in from the kitchen with two glasses of water. She hands one to Sienna and keeps the other for herself.

"Elaine," she says. "Why aren't you returning texts?"

I haven't returned texts because I've been quietly freaking out ever since I said goodbye to Xander. I'm actually not done freaking out, but I hoped music would take my mind off it.

I try to look breezy. "Oh, I locked my phone in my dad's office so I could get some studying done."

Madison gives me a knowing look. "Are you *sure* you weren't with Xander?"

I can't blame them for jumping straight to the juicy stuff. Even so many days later I can still feel the shock of his mouth, the warmth of his body pressed against mine, the stars when he released me, and the realization that the kiss was happening in front of my friends. Of course they want details about what's going on. It's just that the details have taken a nosedive into a sea of suck.

"I wasn't with Xander," I assure Madison. "I was by myself. No other human contact."

"So, you didn't see that picture he posted?" she asks. "Of Flossie last night?"

"I saw it," Sienna says. "But just for a minute. When I went to find it again, it was gone."

"I got a screen capture." Madison takes out her phone, pulls up the photo of Flossie, and my world tilts. There is the image I made Xander delete, still out in the world. How much good did it do for him to take it down if people can still get at it?

"Erase it." I snatch her phone away. "Erase anything you have from last night."

"Ow!" Madison brings her hands to her chest. "That hurt."

"Jeez, what's the big deal?" says Sienna.

I try to soften my voice. The anxiety is now making me physically dizzy.

"It's just, if my dad saw any of this, he'd flip out. Whatever we heard and saw last night, posting pictures of it online was not cool."

"So it's against the rules," says Madison. "Fine. But that doesn't mean you have to treat us like crap. We didn't know it was wrong."

"We were just trying to help," says Sienna.

"I don't need help," I tell them. "I just kind of need to take a break."

"Wait a minute. So now you and Xander *aren't* together?" Sienna looks genuinely disappointed. "We've been watching this thing develop between you guys, and then just when it looks like it's officially a thing, it's *not* a thing anymore."

Before I can stop myself, I'm snapping at her. "Look, I'm sorry this isn't all fitting into your perfect-romance-novel ideal. But it's more complicated than falling in love with the star football player at some stupid festival. This could really screw up my life."

I wait for Sienna to respond with hurt. Instead, she squares her shoulders and says, "Well, maybe that's your fault. If you don't want us to get involved, then fine. We won't. Right, Mads?"

"Right," says Madison. "Are we practicing or not?"

I wanted to drop the subject, but not with them simply dismissing me. No talking it out, no smoothing hurt feelings, no chance to clarify, just me playing, them singing, and icicles in the air.

A lump feels permanently lodged in my throat. This thing I've been watching happen subtly for the past few months is happening in the open now. No matter what was going on in our lives, music used to be the thing that bound Madison and Sienna and me together. Now even with music, we're growing apart.

And I have no idea how to stop it.

CHAPTER TWENTY-TWO

"Hey. There you are."

Miles stands in the door of the deserted choir room. Lunch has just started on this rainy Monday; I can hear people in the halls on their way to the cafeteria.

"I couldn't face everybody," I tell him. "So I'm hiding out here."

"Mind if I join you?"

He climbs the risers and sits next to me on the back row. In his hands are two Dr Peppers and a bag of the one thing our cafeteria makes that I can never resist.

"I knew it had to be serious if you were missing Saratoga chip day," he says while I dig in.

"I don't deserve you," I tell him through a salty mouthful. I open the soda and take a swig, letting the sugary goodness overwhelm me for one heavenly moment. When the moment's over, I sigh. "I'm sorry. My life's just a mess right now. Madison and Sienna aren't speaking to me and I'm barely speaking to Xander. I figured I'd spare everybody some awkwardness and take myself out of the equation, at least for lunch."

"But me minus you equals sad."

"You plus me right now probably won't equal much better."

"Well, if nobody's talking, then this is nicer anyway."

I lift another chip to my mouth, then lower it as humiliation depresses my appetite.

"I was so excited. I made something happen with Flossie. I made *contact*. And then Xander ruined everything by putting it online. And before you say you warned me about him, you have to admit that we wouldn't have even known about Flossie without him. It's like Xander came here for a reason. I let him in and we found all this incredible stuff, but then it all went out of control, and now I don't know what to do."

Miles munches on a chip, considering.

"And you think Flossie has some kind of message from beyond?"

"I'm the one who said ghosts show up to be useful. Maybe she's telling me to get myself together and not make the same mistakes she did."

"What mistake, though? Hurting her father?"

"Or getting engaged? Maybe she regretted tying herself to this place. Maybe her leaving wouldn't have been so heartbreaking if she hadn't been such a 'steadfast' and 'dedicated' daughter to begin with."

Miles takes another chip, but instead of popping it into his mouth, he starts breaking it into ever-smaller bits.

"All you know so far is pieces of family stories and some local legends that are sounding more and more like they're not true," he says. "Maybe Flossie was perfectly happy with her life here."

"Then why would she leave? I can totally see why she wouldn't want to stay in boring old Dodson, doing the same thing every day for the rest of her life."

Miles's voice grows quieter. "Don't be so hard on Dodson. There's a lot about this place that's great too."

"You're a homebody," I say. "Plus you want to help with your mom's business, and she's cool about it; she's not expecting anything else. Meanwhile, my dad is practically posting a business succession plan on our kitchen fridge. He wants to start visiting mortuary schools, and I have no idea if that's what I want to do. What if I want to try something else? You're happy staying here, but I don't think I would be."

"Bleep-bloop-scoodly . . ."

"No, this isn't parsley, Miles. Who I am and what I want to do with my life are main ingredients."

"But sometimes you can go too far with main ingredients," he says. "Sometimes you can put in so many that they basically become parsley."

"Why are we fighting about herbs in the first place?"

"Because it made you smile?"

He laughs, and I look around the room, at the rows of chairs and the piano and the podium where Mr. F directs the choir—everything I've known for the past four and a half years with people I've known for even longer. The reality that this will all end soon, all of us leaving for college, maybe leaving each other behind forever, settles on me like a heavy blanket.

"Things are just so much more complicated now. I knew I'd have to think about all this stuff eventually, but it was always far off. Until it wasn't. One minute we were little kids, and then we were . . . this."

"Ah, being little . . . ," says Miles. "Those were the days."

"My biggest worry back then was just staying away from Ella Schmidt."

"Yeah, she was the queen of all that Funeral Girl crap. Remember Halloween when you went as Maleficent and Ella was Cinderella, and you told her you were going to turn her into a lizard if she didn't leave you alone?"

"Oh my God." I crack up at the memory. "I think that was the last time I ever stood up to anybody."

"It was also the last time you came trick-or-treating."

Ugh, no. Miles has just reminded me that Halloween is this weekend. Everybody's excited about that but me.

"I hate Halloween," I say. "Every dork in the state seems to think it's their free pass to act like an even bigger dork, creeping around my house and leaving things for the Gillies Ghost. Also sorry, but slasher stuff isn't cool, and jokes about murder aren't funny."

"Trick-or-treating isn't about murder jokes," he tells me. "It's dressing up in costumes. It's free candy."

I put another chip in my mouth and wash it down with another mouthful of soda. "Free candy does sound pretty great."

"So, come with Mads and me. We'll forget about the future and just be kids—like we used to. It'll be fun, I promise."

He drops his head and locks eyes with mine. His are blue and clear—in them, I see the boy he used to be and the man he's turning into. Then he waggles his eyebrows, and it's my turn to laugh.

"Okay, fine, but only if we get to go as Pax and Skye."

"I'm way ahead of you," he says. "I've already started on my costume."

CHAPTER TWENTY-THREE

Skye is a pretty easy look to pull off—if you've got a certain kind of wardrobe, which I do not. Ripped jeans aren't a problem, I do have those. And a white T-shirt is a fashion basic, so I can check that off my list too. But black combat boots? Nope. Battered army jacket? Nope again. And pink hair? Very funny. First of all, my hair is so dark that it would take hours of bleaching and coloring, not to mention tons of money, not to mention I have no idea what salon in town even does that kind of thing. I'll need a wig, and even if I could find a place that sells wigs here, I'm pretty sure their regular inventory wouldn't include pink.

A more intrepid girl might not find this a hard costume. Me? Thank goodness for Amazon.

Once I've ordered everything, I should start on homework. I can't bring myself to open my chemistry book, though. Instead, I Google *how to communicate with spirits*.

I don't fully realize what I'm planning until I'm halfway through my third article on the topic. Who says I need Xander to contact

Flossie? According to the internet, I can reach out to ghosts on my own. All I have to do is follow some basic steps:

Step 1: Quiet your mind. Ha-ha, right. Whoever wrote this obviously didn't have anxiety.

Step 2: Concentrate on a single entity. This I can do. I know exactly who I want to reach.

Step 3: Use something to focus your energy. Also doable. I find a candle, set it on my desk, and sit in front of it. I light the wick, watch the flame start to dance, and let out a long, controlled breath.

"Flossie . . . ," I whisper.

A voice answers. It's not a girl from the past, it's my dad.

I spring to my feet.

"What are you doing?" he asks. He's standing in the door of my room with the mail in his hands and a look of amusement on his face.

I lean against the desk, attempting to appear innocent and unbothered.

"Just trying out a new meditation technique. It's supposed to be calming."

"Oh," he says. "Well, be careful you don't burn the house down."

"Okay."

An awkward beat passes, until he remembers the envelopes he's holding.

"I came up to bring you these." He pulls out two booklets and a brochure, which he passes to me. "I reached out to some colleges with good mortuary programs, and a few things started coming today. Thought you might like to look them over."

The materials are slick, promising *A career of caring* and *Your opportunity to make a difference.* They make me instantly furious. Did my father really take it upon himself to research colleges for me? I'd been hoping he'd forget about mortuary schools.

I don't tell him I'm furious. I tell him, "Thank you."

"I also got hold of Kevin Berland. Turns out he's on the board of the Cincinnati College of Mortuary Science, and he'd be happy to show you around when we go for a visit."

"Great," I say.

"Great," he says back. He spots the chemistry book on my bed. "Oh! How did you do on that test by the way?"

I feel myself grimace—I got a C-minus. "Maybe we shouldn't talk about that."

He nods as he turns to go. "Well, whatever you can do to keep that grade up, you'll want to do it. And next year you should plan on taking advanced biology. That's a requirement at some of these schools. If you score well on the AP test, you might be able to get out of that class for freshman year. Night, Lainey!"

"Good night," I say. Then I wait until I hear the door latch behind him to throw the brochures onto my desk. The sound of them hitting the antique wood is like the sound of a starter pistol going off. Once I start visiting mortuary schools with Dad, it'll be harder if I decide I don't want to go.

I knew this pressure would be coming, but now that it's real, I can feel the worries starting to spiral.

You'll have to decide soon. If you want to explore other things, you have to do it now. But where are you even going to start?

The candle still flickers on my desk. I go to blow it out. As I do, a drop of wax falls on the varnished surface and starts to harden. I scratch at it with my thumbnail, which gets me to notice the scrap of paper captured underneath the varnish. It's one of the oldest things in the weird collage on the desktop, and parts of it are covered by other, newer scraps. But I can tell it's a ticket—or a receipt for a ticket. It looks like it's for a ship voyage, and I can just make out the name *Florence Gil*... Much clearer is the destination: *Port of Glasgow*.

I look up, half expecting to see a ghostly figure in the room with me. This clue is almost like an apparition; I never would have noticed it if I wasn't already searching for Flossie. And now I know— she traveled to Scotland, or she had plans to. Is that where she went when she ran away?

Dad's kilt still sits on top of my dresser, the bright yellow bands through the green, red, and blue panes winking like a beacon. I don't know what it means, but I know I have to keep digging, because more and more I'm starting to think Flossie has something to say to me.

With or without Xander, I'm going to find out what it is.

🌿

"Elaine, honey." Mom pokes her head into the bathroom, where I'm attempting to transform myself into Skye with the help of an eyeliner pen. "Something's happened with Grandma. We think she may have had a stroke."

"Oh no." I lower the pen and turn my black-rimmed eyes to her. "Is she going to be okay?"

Mom reaches up to try and wipe away some of the liner that's fallen onto my cheek, frowning when it refuses to budge. She looks worried, which worries me. Her mom's health has been pretty bad lately, and we were planning to see her at Thanksgiving because it's been too long. The idea that we might have waited too, *too* long smacks me in the gut.

"Grandpa's trying to sound brave, like he always does," Mom says. "But I think it's best if I go there. Dad's going to drive me to Quincy. There's no way I'd be able to concentrate on the road. He'll get me settled, then he'll drive back tomorrow so he's home in time for Mr. Bohmer's service."

"Okay," I say. It's Saturday afternoon and Quincy is three hours away. They'll need to leave soon if they want to get there before dark.

"Dakota's in charge of the business while we're gone," Mom continues. "But I'll need you to help with things up here."

I nod. I can do that.

"Will you give Grandma a hug for me?"

"Of course." She pulls me in for a squeeze. "I need to get ready, and your dad went to get new tires put on the car. Thanks for holding down the fort."

She leaves, while the anxiety buzzing just under my skin gets more intense. I tell myself not to worry. It's Halloween, Miles will be here in a few hours, and I'm excited to spend an evening having fun. My parents will take care of Grandma. It'll be okay.

I pick up the liner pen and try to focus on my eyes again. Skye has this really smoky look, almost like she slept in her makeup and it's smudged but it looks great that way, because she is the kind of girl who can wear day-old smudged eyeliner and still look amazing. I, on the other hand, look like a raccoon.

The doorbell rings. I give up and pull out a gray shadow. This works a little better; not so harsh.

The doorbell rings a second time; Mom shouts from her room.

"Elaine, can you get that? I'm trying to pack!"

"Sorry, yes!" I shout back and rush down the front steps.

A box sits on the porch. I carry it into the office and open it to find the programs for tomorrow's funeral. Usually we like to have them two days in advance so we can correct any errors, but the new printing company we've been using has been running down to the wire.

I pull out the program on top, just as I hear the back door open. "Dakota!"

He comes in with his lab coat open, a wrinkled dress shirt underneath.

"What's up?" he says.

"The Bohmers wanted a sunset on the cover," I tell him. "Not a farm scene."

Humming under his breath, he peers over my shoulder at the programs.

"Mrs. Bohmer told me farm. She said Mr. Bohmer grew up on one."

I circle around to the desk, wake up the computer, and pull up the meeting notes. "It says sunset, right here. Did you send her a mock-up to proof?"

"I think so?"

"God, Dakota, that's a basic requirement." I go back to the box and start rifling through, hoping there might be just a few incorrect ones on top. But no. Every single one has a farmscape on it. "Great. It's too late to reorder now."

Dakota puts down his coffee mug and crosses his arms.

"You know what, Elaine? You're not helping anyone with your constant negativity."

"I'm not being negative," I tell him. "I'm doing my job—and everyone else's too like usual."

He sighs as he picks up the office phone. "Hold on. I'll figure it out."

He calls Mrs. Bohmer and explains the situation. He puts her on speaker as she's saying she liked both the farm scene and the sunset equally and can't remember which one she chose, and she's sure that whatever we've selected will be beautiful.

"Thanks for letting us double-check," Dakota tells her. "We'll see you tomorrow, and please don't hesitate to let us know if you need anything else."

He glares at me as he hangs up. I glare back, feeling defensive now, and ashamed.

"Okay," I say. "So maybe it wasn't that big a deal."

"I told you it wasn't. I'm learning, but I'm not as stupid as you seem to think I am."

"I don't think you're stupid." I have to look away. Hearing him say it out loud is even worse.

"Then why are you so critical?" he says. "You act like you're the only person who knows how to do anything around here."

Anger starts sprouting again, pushing words into my mouth that I'm afraid to say. I settle for, "Yeah, well, sometimes I feel that way."

"Well, maybe take a look at why that is. I'm not your punching bag."

And now I feel like a jerk. Yes, I get angry and no, I don't feel like I can let my parents know about it, so yes, I do sometimes take it out on Dakota. That's not cool. But it's also not cool that I'm never able to say no.

"I don't need a punching bag," I tell him as I close the box of programs. "I just need people to stop putting things on me all the time."

"You were the one who opened the programs and went through them," he says. "You say you want people to leave you alone, then you go looking for more work. How about thinking about what you really want here?"

"Fine. What I *want* is to not be thinking about this at all. I'm going back upstairs."

The voicemail light is flashing on the office phone, but I don't point it out as I head for the door. If I'm done doing everybody else's job, then it starts now.

Still, Dakota's voice sticks in my head. *Critical. Negative.* I'm not a critical person. But sometimes I feel like I don't have a choice. I get put in situations where I have to hold everything together, and that would make anyone feel negative, wouldn't it?

The worst part is that there's nobody who truly gets it. The only person who might understand isn't even a person, at least not anymore. Flossie must have something to say—something that could help me figure out what to do.

If only I could get hold of her again.

🪰

Miles comes for me at five-thirty sharp. I've just finished helping my parents lug their suitcases into the kitchen when he bursts in singing the *Dragonfly* theme song at the top of his lungs.

His red hair is spiked straight up and tipped in electric blue. His eyes are lined in smudgy black. Around his neck hangs a replica of the spectacles Pax wears that allow him to see dimensions layered on dimensions. Over ripped jeans and a white T-shirt he wears a long black trench coat. He looks like a badass.

An extremely *hot* badass.

I have to take a minute to make sure my mouth isn't hanging open.

"Hey, Miles!" says Dad. "It's been a while since we've seen you around here."

A secret look passes between the two of us. If my parents only knew how many times Miles has actually been here and what we've uncovered during those late-night visits, they'd probably never let me socialize with anyone ever again.

Miles lifts his spectacles and peers through them at my parents.

"Mr. and Mrs. Gillies. You're not doing Halloween?"

"No, sadly," Mom says as she slips a crossword puzzle book into her bag. "We've never missed, but my mom is sick, so they'll have to do it without us this year. Maybe we should stop by city hall," she says to my dad. "Make sure they have enough candy?"

Just because I hate Halloween doesn't mean the rest of my family does. We can't exactly decorate the funeral home in cobwebs and dripping blood, but every year Mom dresses up like a witch and hands out treats from the back of her car at the annual Trunk-or-Treat community celebration. If Dad's not busy tending real dead bodies, he puts on his Victorian undertaker's outfit and joins her. He loves to entertain the little kids with magic tricks he taught himself using the costume's top hat. My parents even laugh at the ridiculous Gillies Ghost stuff that people do—the way they leave offerings by the sign out front and take photos of my third-story window. One year, Dad wanted to prank everybody by putting a mannequin up there. I shot that idea down quick.

"Are you here to watch your show with Lainey?" Dad asks Miles. "Saturday is *Dragonfly* night, right?"

"I'm actually dragging Elaine out for trick-or-treating if you can believe it. We'll watch *Dragonfly* tomorrow." Miles looks me up and down. "Or maybe Elaine is standing me up again. Pax is here, where is Skye?"

I've been waiting to put on the whole costume, nervous what my parents would say seeing me in something so different from my usual look. But now it's time to be *intrepid*—that's my new favorite word.

"I just have to do the finishing touches," I say. "Back in a minute."

I duck into my room and take a couple of deep breaths, still trying to get my brain around how stupidly *hot* Miles looks in his costume. Once my pulse has stopped pounding, I put on the pink wig, letting it cascade over my right eye in a mysterious, Skye-esque way. I slip the army jacket over my ripped jeans and T-shirt, then step into the combat boots. Finally, I draw the water lily runes on my hands that match the seal over Pax's heart.

Before I go back downstairs, I take a quick look out my window. So far nobody's showed up to leave anything for the Gillies Ghost, but it's not dark yet; the night is still young.

"Why would you cover your face like that, Lainey?" Mom asks when I come back to the kitchen. "You're so pretty. Why hide it?"

"Elaine looks as beautiful as ever," Dad says. "And I'm glad to see her wearing something sensible."

As usual, there's a whole other set of words under the ones he actually says. Because Astrid just left in a minidress cut up to her thighs, her hair pulled back in an old-school Ariana Grande ponytail. And when I looked out the window to see who she was trick-or-treating with, there were three girls on the sidewalk dressed like a sexy astronaut, a sexy chemist, and a sexy Alice in Wonderland. When I mentioned how problematic it is that costume companies make everything sexy instead of just letting girls dress up like regular scientists or Disney characters, Astrid told me to shut up and mind my own business.

So much for that connection we had the other day.

I know my dad knows it's slut shaming to say a girl can't dress however she wants. But he's old-fashioned at heart. He nods approvingly at my jeans and boots. And when Miles goes to the bathroom, he reaches out to tickle me.

"So . . . Is this a new development? Boy next door versus wild new kid—I like this choice much better."

"What, Miles?" My cheeks are suddenly on fire. "No! This isn't a date. He just came to get me because Madison wasn't ready yet. We're meeting up with Sienna and her boyfriend. It's a group thing."

"Oh." A mixture of amusement and disappointment plays across his face. "My mistake, then! A group thing sounds like fun too."

He goes back to making a to-do list for Dakota, and again, his silence says more than his words. He's glad I'm not going out with Xander. He's curious what *is* going on with Xander. I don't tell him we broke up, or whatever it is we did, since I'm not 100 percent sure we were officially dating in the first place.

It's confusing, which is why I pounce when Miles comes out of the bathroom.

"Let's go! Bye, Mom, bye, Dad, drive safe and tell Grandma and Grandpa I'll send pictures—I know Grandma loves that."

Before I can hustle Miles down the stairs, Dad stops me.

"Oh, Lainey, I almost forgot. I heard back from Kevin. He's got a free weekend coming up, and I made arrangements for us to visit Cincinnati. He can walk you around the mortuary program, maybe even arrange for some of the students to meet for lunch and answer questions." He gets out his phone. "I'm putting it on the family calendar."

My phone buzzes as the notification goes through. Miles glances at me like *uh-oh.* I widen my eyes. The what's-Elaine-going-to-do-with-her-life? train is leaving the station, and it doesn't matter whether I'm on it or not. If I'm not, I'll just get dragged along.

Time is running out.

"Dang, you weren't kidding," Miles says once we're safely in his truck. "Your dad is all about getting you to funeral director's school."

"Yep, without even asking how I feel about it." I purposefully avoid looking at the calendar notification he sent, like maybe not looking will make it disappear.

"Well, he was right about something too," Miles says. "You do look beautiful."

I pull the wig farther over my eye and stare at him through the veil of pink hair.

"It's a glamour to hide the evil underneath, mwa-ha-ha-haaaa!"

The humor is a shield, and I am totally aware that I'm using it because ever since Miles walked into my kitchen, and especially since my dad suggested some "new development" between us, I have felt an odd sort of woozy discomfort, and discomfort is something I've never associated with Miles before.

"Maybe I like the evil underneath," Miles replies, which makes the discomfort even more discomforting.

Still, from a fangirlish standpoint, I do have to admire his Pax-esque transformation.

"Well, you look one hundred percent on point," I tell him. "We should wear this to Chicago."

"I'm down for that," he says. "We need to make plans! Since the panel is Sunday morning, we'll probably need to get a hotel room. Not, I mean, one room for both of us. But hotel *rooms*—plural."

"I knew what you meant."

He's blushing. Bringing my hands to my cheeks, I'm surprised how hot mine feel too. *This is Miles,* I tell myself. *Just because your dad thought he saw something, there's no reason for* you *to freak out. It's just Miles. Calm down.*

"Okay," I tell myself.

"What?" says Miles. "Were you talking to me?"

"No," I tell him. "I was talking to myself."

"Oh, her," he says as he starts the drive back to his house. "That girl is pretty cool. Tell her I said hi."

CHAPTER TWENTY-FOUR

"This is it, the holy grail of trick-or-treating!"

Jaxon makes an arc with the arm that isn't draped around Sienna, encompassing the vista of McMansions before us. We've all met up at Dodson's newest, shiniest neighborhood with our pillowcases ready.

Sienna, dressed to perfection as Dionne from *Clueless,* snuggles into Jaxon's side.

"I heard they give full-sized candy bars up here," she says.

"I heard some of them even give out money," adds Madison. But Sienna's too entranced with Jaxon to respond. Jaxon slings his pillowcase over the shoulder of his *Umbrella Academy* uniform and reaches for her hand. They lead the way and we follow, trudging up the hill toward the rows of perfectly manicured lawns.

The night is crisp as the sun rolls away over the houses. A few people have firepits going, and the smell of wood smoke tickles my nose. Little kids and their parents have taken over the street; I can see the silhouettes of small bodies everywhere.

"Are you sure we aren't too old for this?" I ask Miles. "Don't people look down on high schoolers trick-or-treating?"

"It's fine as long as we're not acting like idiots," he tells me. "And if somebody doesn't want to give us anything, that says more about them than it does about us, right?"

We reach the first house and follow a group of grade schoolers to the front door. I'm ready for the woman who answers to tell us to get off her porch. But she just plops a giant Snickers into each of our pillowcases and tells us, "Happy Halloween!"

It's like that everywhere. People are either too busy handing out candy or too much in the holiday spirit to be judgy. One dad even makes some *Dragonfly*-savvy comments about Miles's and my costumes.

Looking at the little kids in their princess and superhero outfits, I see it in a way that I don't when I'm holed up in my room avoiding the gawkers gathered underneath my window. No one's trying to be disrespectful, they're just out for candy.

"Hey, Sienna," Madison calls, tottering on her *Breakfast at Tiffany's* heels. "Maybe slow down a second."

Miles and I stop while she takes off her shoes.

"Of course Mads has a pair of sneakers in her bag," he says.

"Madison's always prepared," says Sienna, who's come back to see what the holdup is.

"There's prepared and then there's . . . this." Miles pokes his sister's tote, which has compartments for candy, extra shoes, even a first aid kit. "I know you're the mom of the group, Mads, but did you have to bring an actual diaper bag?"

It's such a mean-brother thing to say, but it's also funny, especially when Miles reminds Madison that he *is* potty trained. I can't help laughing.

Madison glares at him and changes the subject.

"Hey, Elaine. Did you get on the IU email list?" she asks. "I think there's a visit day for the music school coming up."

"Not yet," I tell her. Honestly, the thought of looking at colleges—any college—has me paralyzed.

"Well, Jaxon's been talking to Coach," Sienna cuts in. "He doesn't know if he can get a football scholarship to IU, and I don't want to be long-distance."

"So, no IU now?" Madison makes a face. "You don't want to follow some guy to college."

"I'm just saying." Sienna shrugs. "If we're in love, it's something to consider."

"Are you guys official now?" I ask.

"Hello!" she says. "Where have you been?" And I resist the urge to say, *I've been frozen out, Sienna,* because I'm not sure how she'd take it. Time has worn down the edginess between the three of us— each day taking a little off the prickly distance until it is now a nub that we don't talk about. The unspoken agreement is that it's easier to simply move on and pick up where we left off.

Jaxon runs behind us and gooses Sienna, who grabs my arms to use me as a shield. When Madison tries to rescue me, Jaxon goes in for the tickle, which is Madison's kryptonite. She takes off squealing with Sienna and Jaxon in pursuit.

"See?" Miles says, nudging me with his shoulder. "I told you trick-or-treating was fun."

"It's definitely better than sitting at home, getting ding-dong dashed." I look around, at the kids, the big sky, the firepits glowing in the dark, and say, "I don't want things to change."

"That makes me selfishly happy," he replies. "The last I remember, you were all about getting out of here."

"I want to go new places," I clarify. "But then I also want all this to still be here, just the way it is now."

"You want a lot," he tells me.

"I know."

Searching for Madison and Sienna up ahead, I see a girl in a white minidress and high ponytail coming toward us. It's Astrid, hand in hand with a guy in an Iron Man costume. Quinn. The closer she gets, the clearer it becomes that she has no intention of saying hi. Just as I'm resigning myself to getting snubbed again, the voice in my head tells me, *Hell no. Astrid doesn't get to just walk on by like that. Go talk to her.*

I tell Miles, "Hold on." Then I run to catch up with my sister.

Astrid stops, pretending she's surprised to see me.

"Um . . . hey?" I stare at her, realizing I don't know what to say— until I remember I'm supposed to be taking care of things while our parents are gone. "So Mom and Dad never told me what time they wanted you home."

"I'm not going home," she says. "I'm spending the night at Sophia's."

I look around; there's no trace of a sexy astronaut, a sexy chemist, or a sexy Alice in Wonderland.

"I don't see Sophia anyplace. Where are you really going?"

"Where I said I was. It's not your business anyway."

"Except it is. Mom and Dad put me in charge."

Her eyes narrow. "So . . . what? Are you going to make me go home?"

I almost say, *Hell yes.* But something tells me to wait; why do I have to be the bad guy all the time? Dakota said I should figure out what I want, and right now what I *don't* want is to be obsessing about when my sister is going to come home, knowing she'll only be pissy when she does.

"Actually, I'm not going to tell you you have to do anything."

"Really?" she says.

"You seem surprised."

"It's just, you're usually so uptight. I figured you'd try to get me to go home and do something boring like play Scrabble."

Uptight.

Critical.

Boring.

Nobody likes hearing those words said about them. From now on, they won't be said about me.

"I don't think we even have Scrabble," I tell her. "So, you're off the hook."

"Okay . . ." She waits to see if there'll be some kind of catch.

"Okay, then," I say. "Have fun!"

Still side-eyeing me, she turns and runs back to Quinn. I switch my candy-filled pillowcase from one hand to the other, then finally lug it with both hands as Miles and I catch up to the others at the end of the street where it drops off into a vista of downtown.

Sienna and Jaxon are taking advantage of the view to make out. Madison's trying filters on a selfie, and I realize I'm standing really close to Miles. Maybe that's because I don't like heights and the overlook is steep. Or maybe it's just always been so natural to seek out the solid comfort of his body.

So why does it feel so *un*-natural all of a sudden?

I'm hyperaware of how his shoulder is just the right height to rest my head on, and the broadness of his chest beneath his tight white T-shirt under his trench coat, which would be so easy to step inside, wrapping myself in the worn fabric, and in him. His cheeks are ruddy under the stubble he's let grow out to play Pax, and a memory pops into my head—my mom, after a party last Christmas, musing, "The older that Drummond boy gets, the more he looks like a young Prince Harry." I teased her for being obsessed with the royals; I didn't consider whether she had a point. But now I suddenly see it.

When we were kids, Halloween was a time when anything could happen. We were best friends running the streets after dark, dressed as other people, with nothing to think about besides getting as much candy as possible.

Except we're not kids anymore. When Miles looks at me, his kohl-ringed eyes are familiar and yet entirely new.

"I've missed this," he says. "Hanging out, just us."

"It's not just us," I remind him.

"It's the original group, though."

"Right."

"Are you coming over tomorrow?" he asks. "Whatever this big *Dragonfly* bombshell is, if it ever comes, it sort of feels like we should watch it together."

"Yes. I'll be there." I want to hug him, for talking me into coming out and for making this an almost-perfect night. I step closer, knowing in the back of my head that a hug might turn into more and yet, in the weirdest way, not caring.

"Hey! Hello!" Madison interrupts. "Can I just say that it's so much fun being the only person here without a date?"

I step backward. "This isn't a date."

"Good to know," says Madison. She grabs Miles's hand and tugs, pointing at a brightly lit storefront at the bottom of the hill. "Look, Valentino's is open. Let's go get a Coke."

Miles gives me a look that's half relief, half regret.

"I guess trick-or-treating is over," he says.

"Yep," I say. "Back to the real world."

CHAPTER TWENTY-FIVE

Noisy. Muggy. Packed. Everybody we know has chosen Valentino's as their post-trick-or-treat hangout, and now we're stuck in a sea of costumed bodies.

"My feet are killing me," Madison says, pouting. "I need to sit down."

"There's no way we're getting a table," says Sienna.

"Hey, Miles! Elaine!"

Squinting across the room, we see Xander calling to us. He's at a table with Jonas Berk and Tony Reverman from the cross-country team, and he's standing and waving his arms.

"Yeah . . . no," says Miles.

"Why, what's wrong?" I ask. "Are you guys fighting too now?"

"It's just . . . I was sort of enjoying a Xander-less night," he says. "And it sort of seemed like you were too."

At the overlook, Miles told me he'd missed our original group, so I can sort of see why he'd be less than thrilled to see Xander now. But his reaction still feels harsh. Also at the overlook, I told Madison that Miles and I weren't on a date. Now I'm starting to wonder: Was this a date to Miles?

I have no time to process that question, because Madison and Sienna are pulling us over to Xander's table. I'm hurtling toward him, whether I'm ready or not.

Xander wears an old-school Jedi costume, which suits his sandy, scruffy look so perfectly it almost hurts. I can feel my pulse start to race like it always does when I'm around him, and I start to panic. We haven't spoken in a week. What will I say? What will he do?

Xander might be a Jedi, I tell myself. *But you are a time-traveling, quantum-dimension-hopping goddess. You can handle this.*

Tony and Jonas leave to go mingle, freeing up the chairs. Sienna and Jaxon rush to claim seats next to each other. Madison boxes Miles in so he has to take the third seat, which means the only seat left for me is—of course—next to Xander.

Madison surveys the area.

"Where's your candy?" she asks. "You didn't trick-or-treat?"

"We went to the homestead," Xander tells her. "Halloween is prime time for supernatural activity."

Everyone nods at this; it makes sense.

"Well, we hit up Guinevere Heights," Sienna says. "Check this out."

She dumps out her pillowcase. Madison does the same. I decide to go along and let my stash tumble onto the table too.

"Almond Joy!" Xander crows. He reaches out to steal one; I smack his hand.

"Over my dead body!"

"You're kidding," he says. "I don't know anybody else who likes those."

"Coconut is my favorite," I say.

"I thought Twizzlers were your favorite."

"Twizzlers are Elaine's favorite non-candy-bar candy," Miles informs him. "When it comes to candy bar fillings, her number one choice is coconut, followed by toffee as a close second."

He's smiling his trademark smile, going with the flow, but I can hear the edge in his voice. I need a peace offering.

"Speaking of which . . ." I pick out a handful of blue Airheads and slide them across the table. "I'll trade you these for your Heath Bar. Blue candy reminds me of toilet bowl cakes."

"Mm-mmm," says Miles, a genuine smile now stretching across his face. "Toilet bowl cakes are *my* favorite."

Xander scoots his chair closer to mine. His messy hair and little brown mole are so perfect with that costume; he dead-on looks like Luke from Episode IV.

"Hi," he says quietly, so only I can hear.

"Hi," I say back.

"You look great. Skye, right?"

"Yes. You did your homework."

"I've had a lot of time to since you weren't speaking to me."

So. Here we are. I can't hide from this conversation anymore, and it's probably for the best. If Xander's going to be in our group, then we need to come to an understanding.

"You really freaked me out," I tell him.

"I know," he says. "Remember when I said I need a smackdown to realize when I'm going too far sometimes? This was one of those sometimes. I'm sorry and thank you. Again."

"You're welcome, I guess." I'm not sure I like being Smackdown Girl, especially on top of *negative, boring,* and *critical.*

"How's Flossie?" Xander asks. "Have you seen her again?"

"No." I sigh. "I tried, but it wasn't the same."

"Don't get discouraged," he says. "When I started investigating it took me a year before I got anything good."

Except I only have a few months before I have to start making some decisions—at least about what I *don't* want to do. Applications might not start until next fall, but visiting mortuary schools feels like the beginning of the end because it'll crystallize my parents' vision of me as a future funeral director. And maybe it's dumb to think a spirit would have anything to say about it, but Flossie's already given us some pretty incredible things. Maybe I need to open myself up to her even more.

Everyone's hungry despite having piles of candy in front of us, so we order pizza. Just as the waiter is bringing it, a guy comes to our table.

"Hey, you're the ghost hunter. Xander, right? Those pictures you just posted were sick."

"Thanks," Xander says. "The homestead has a lot of potential."

I pull out my phone. Two new photos are posted to his account, time-stamped an hour ago: one of the old barn with a smudge of white mist in the doorway, and one of the tallest cross in the old cemetery surrounded by orbs.

"You going back out tonight?" the guy asks.

"Maybe," Xander says. "The energy is amazing right now. Or maybe I'll hit that party at the warehouse."

"Yes!" Jaxon's been listening in. "Warehouse party. When are we going?"

"You guys might need to find a ride," Miles tells him. "I'm taking Elaine home."

"Why would you take me home?" I ask.

"Because you avoid that party like the plague," he reminds me. "It's a slasher theme this year. Lots of fake guts and *Chainsaw Massacre* movies."

I know what kind of party it is. Every year there's a massive bash at an abandoned warehouse outside of town. It's always been part of my Halloween boycott; except I'm not boycotting Halloween tonight.

"Elaine hates Halloween," Sienna announces, and I feel like I'm headed for a lifetime of being the boring, uptight Smackdown Girl who's so respectable people don't even think about inviting her places.

I need something—a sign—to tell me that's not where I'm going.

Madison, Sienna, Miles, and Jaxon are getting ready to leave. If the idea that just popped into my head is going to happen, I have to speak up now.

"Wait a second."

They stop. I turn to Xander.

"You said Halloween is prime time for ghost communications, right?"

"Definitely," he says.

"Then I have something better than a warehouse party." I've got their full attention now, and I barrel ahead before I can lose my nerve. "My parents are out of town. So how about an investigation right now? If we saw Flossie last time, maybe she'll actually speak to us now that we don't have to be quiet and stick to the front rooms."

Xander looks like I just told him Christmas is coming early.

"You know I'm in," he says.

"Can Jaxon come?" asks Sienna.

I tell her, "Yes." I don't want to be uptight. Sienna trusts Jaxon, so I trust him too.

"Halloween at a funeral home," Jaxon says. "That's a no-brainer. Gotta do it."

"I don't want to do another investigation," Madison cuts in. "If your parents are gone, they're going to be *really* mad."

"They'll never find out," Sienna tells her. "Live a little."

"Well, then how about this?" Madison scowls. "I'm sick of tagging along with *you* guys. At least at the warehouse I won't be a freaking third wheel."

"Come on, Mads," I say. "The warehouse isn't even legal. If it doesn't get busted by the police, then what if there's a fire? You know they aren't following codes there."

This finally gets through to her, though she still doesn't look happy. She picks up her candy bag and starts trudging toward the door.

"Are you serious?" Miles asks me as we follow. "I thought you were done with investigating."

"You heard my dad," I tell him. "I'm on the mortuary school track unless I can find some way to get off. If Flossie can tell me what to do, then I have to let her. And something tells me we're going to find some amazing stuff tonight."

CHAPTER TWENTY-SIX

"Dang, this place is legit," Jaxon says as Miles pulls up to my house. "You guys really do ghost hunts here?"

"They're investigations," we all say together. Then I add, "We're actually past the investigating stage, now we're in the communicating stage. And tonight, I need some specific information from one specific ghost."

The house sits quieter than I've ever seen it; even Dakota's apartment is dark, and I remember I saw him leave earlier wearing Harry Potter robes. Two guys who look like they're old enough to know better are standing on the sidewalk under my window. They run off as our headlights fall on them, leaving a bouquet of grocery store roses and a candle burning in a jar next to our front-yard sign.

I wonder if Flossie sees all those Gillies Ghost people every year. I wonder what she thinks of them. Maybe I'll ask her. And maybe she'll answer. But first, I want to know one thing: Where did she go, and why?

Also, what should I do?

Okay, I realize that's actually three things. Basically, I want a lot from Flossie. I really hope Xander's right and the energy is extra good tonight.

"Park a block up, in the street," I tell Miles. I want some cover in case Dakota comes home. We have an answering service that will call his cell if anyone needs help, so there's always a chance our investigation could be interrupted.

Which is why we need to get going. No time to waste.

"Can we really go anywhere we want?" Xander asks as we walk through the back door.

"Yes," I tell him, funneling everyone up into the kitchen. "And we should because I don't know when we'll ever get a chance like this again."

Xander looks around. "Wow, this is nice. You'd never know you were in a funeral home."

"See?" Sienna says. "We told you."

"It's almost too nice," he adds. "Sometimes it throws spirits off when places have been updated."

"I'm sure Mrs. Gillies would love knowing the spirits don't like her design taste," says Miles.

"It's not taste, it's what's familiar to them," Xander explains, but Miles has already wrapped himself in one of Mom's living room drapes.

"What do you think, Flossie?" he calls out. "Don't you like this pattern or what?"

Madison pulls him away from the window. "Elaine's room hasn't been updated," she says.

"Old attics are so atmospheric," Sienna chimes in. "I bet a ghost would love it up there."

I take everyone up the narrow staircase and try not to be

self-conscious about the clothes lying around, the unmade bed, my desk overflowing with books and dirty dishes from late nights doing homework. Xander opens his bag while Jaxon goes to the window.

"Is this where the Gillies Ghost jumped?" he asks.

"That's what people think," I say. "But we couldn't find any record of anybody falling or killing themselves here."

"Glorifying suicide is—"

"Not cool, we know," says Miles, completing Madison's sentence for her. She glares at him.

The window might have been ruled out as a site of tragedy, but Xander aims his infrared camera at it anyway, and I hold my breath. I'm almost relieved when nothing happens; I don't want to believe Flossie would have felt hopeless enough to hurt herself like that. Xander scans the EMF reader around the room; the needle stays still.

"Flossie?" I speak up. "Are you here? If you're trying to get in touch, then give a sign. Maybe flash the lights?"

We wait. Nothing happens. And I realize that if I want a message, I need to make it easier.

"Let's try a system. Tap once for yes, two times for no. Was this your room?"

We listen, hearing the old furnace through the vents, the cars on the street outside, but nothing that could be considered a tap. I move to the desk and place my fingers on the old steamer ticket under its layer of varnish.

"I found this the other day. Is it yours?"

All I hear are the familiar nighttime sounds of my bedroom. Okay, so Flossie doesn't want to talk up here; I'm not discouraged. This is a big house. We're just getting started.

"Let's go downstairs," I suggest. "That's where all the activity's happened before, so maybe we're supposed to be there."

This time down, we take the main stairs. There's no reason to creep or sneak, but we still fall silent as we descend into the semidarkness. We pass through the foyer, and Great-Great-Great-Grandfather Leathan frowns down at us from his portrait on the wall. I pause, staring up at that face, and feel like I'm seeing it from a whole new angle. Flossie may have broken her father's heart, but didn't he bear some responsibility for that? He probably drove her away with all of his expectations and assumptions.

When the others aren't looking, I stick out my tongue at him.

The main visitation room has already been set up for Mr. Bohmer's service. The empty chairs look ominous, arranged in their perfect lines before the scaffold that will hold the casket. Xander lets Jaxon hold the EMF reader while he scans the room with the infrared. The battery's dead in the grid projector, but I'm not as concerned about that. Tapping is what I'm after now.

"Flossie?" I call. "Did you want to work here? Tap once for yes, twice for no."

I try again: "Did you feel trapped?"

And again: "Were you in love? Did you run away with someone?"

"I just don't understand why everything is so dead tonight," Xander says. He gives his camera a shake.

"Well, technically everything around here is dead," Miles informs him. "So . . ."

Trying not to get frustrated, I take out Dad's kilt.

"What about Scotland?" I ask. "Is that where you ran away to?"

Three sharp raps sound across the room. We all snap to attention before rushing over to where they came from. It's the same spot where Xander captured the image of Flossie last week.

"Did you mean to make three knocks?" I ask. "I said one for yes, two for no. What does three mean?"

Miles tugs my sleeve.

"Could it have come from here?" He points to the nearby window. "You can see the old hearse right there. Maybe she wants us to go outside."

"Right!" I can't believe I didn't think of that sooner. "The photo album has a picture of Flossie with the buggy. Maybe that's where all the clues are."

Everyone follows me out back; Xander points as we pass the guesthouse.

"What's that place?" he asks.

"That's where the original funeral home was," I tell him. "But if ghosts don't like updated places, they really wouldn't like it there. It's where Dakota lives now. He's our intern."

We tiptoe around to the buggy, which sits horseless under its canopy. I stand under the driver's platform and say, "Flossie? What's here that you want me to find?"

We wait. I hold my breath. But all I hear is the wind in the trees.

Sienna and Jaxon are whispering to each other. Madison is fidgeting irritably. Even Xander is starting to look bored. I need to get them interested again, and I think I know what will do it.

"My dad told me Flossie was a talented embalmer. Maybe we should go down to the prep rooms."

"Is that where they work on bodies?" asks Sienna.

"Yes," I tell her. "It's where my dad gets them ready for viewing."

"What if there's someone down there?" says Madison.

"Who would be down there?" I ask. "My parents are out of town."

"I mean *someone* . . . ," she says. "Like somebody dead."

"Oh. Well, there actually is. Mr. Bohmer's funeral is tomorrow. But there's an empty room we can use."

"I don't know . . ." She hangs back.

"You aren't scared, are you?" Miles teases.

"Like being scared isn't natural, jerk." She smacks his arm, which only makes him laugh harder.

"Ow, Mads," he says. "You're fierce when you're frightened."

"It's not scary," I tell her to break up the bickering. "Come on, I'll go down with you."

No one says a word as we descend into the tiled hallway. The lights down here are bright, but I remind myself no one can see.

There are no windows, and Dakota's out anyway. Calm down.

Passing the first prep room, I make sure the door is closed.

"Mr. Bohmer's in there," I tell everyone.

"How did he die?" Sienna asks.

"I don't know . . . old age? Does it matter?"

"I just want to make sure his spirit isn't angry or restless or anything."

"Well, leave him alone and you won't make him angry or restless."

I walk into the second prep room and turn on the light. The six of us fill the space, standing around the table in the center. Sienna wrinkles her nose.

"What is that smell?"

"Embalming fluid," I answer. "I barely notice it anymore."

"So do you really drain out people's blood?" Jaxon asks.

"My dad does. Then he replaces it with a solution of formaldehyde and other things."

"Would you want to be embalmed like that?" Miles asks.

"No." I've actually thought about this a lot. "I want a green burial, somewhere bodies can decompose naturally. Or cremation. You can be more flexible about a funeral that way, and you don't have to have a grave. People can take you with them. Or you can be scattered somewhere."

"My mom has my grandmother on the mantel in Springfield," says Xander. "It's surprisingly not-weird."

"Well, people can do whatever they want with me when I'm dead," Miles announces. "Dress me up in a prom gown, give me a green mohawk, and stand me up with a Monster in my hand."

"Way to set the right mood," says Madison.

"It's exactly the way to set the mood," he shoots back. "I hate it when people are sad."

It's such a Miles thing to say that the investigation fades, and I'm suddenly aware of the humanity of what we're talking about. My father's voice echoes in my mind: *It's joy in the face of sadness—the juxtaposition of the universe.*

"Elaine," Xander interrupts. "Do you want to try making contact again?"

"Yes. Sorry." I blink, coming back to the reason we're here. Xander checks to be sure the EVP recorder is on, then I step forward.

"Flossie? Did your father want you to take over the business? Was that not what you wanted? Were you afraid of disappointing your parents? Tap once for yes, two times for no."

This whole thing is getting way too personal in front of my friends. But I'm starting to get desperate. There's nothing standing in Flossie's way now—at least nothing here in the land of the living—to keep her from communicating. So why is she so quiet?

We wait, staring at one another over the table, hearing our breathing, the pipes clanking through the old house, everything but the ghostly voice we're seeking. We get the same result when we play back the EVP recorder: nothing.

"What are we doing wrong?" says Madison.

"No freaking idea," says Xander. He shuts off the recorder with a resigned *click*.

"I guess the spirits just aren't in the mood tonight?" Miles suggests.

"Well, I'm in the mood," Sienna says as she wraps her arms around Jaxon.

"And we're missing the warehouse party." Madison pouts.

Miles turns to me as we follow everyone up the stairs.

"You okay?" he asks.

I drag my feet, letting my boots bump the stair treads with a loud *thump . . . thump . . .* "I just don't get how we got such amazing stuff those other times, and now there's nothing."

I don't notice Xander's gone until he comes in through the back door carrying a case of beer.

"Don't be mad," he tells me. "Dakota left his place unlocked, and he's got a major stash in there. We can have our own party. What do you think?"

CHAPTER TWENTY-SEVEN

should be furious. But I honestly feel so defeated right now that I can't bring myself to care. I don't usually drink either, but what the hell? I take a beer and chug the whole thing down as fast as I can.

"Whoa," Sienna says. "You might want to pace yourself."

"Is it okay with your parents if we have alcohol?" Madison asks.

"Absolutely not." A beer-fueled laugh bubbles out of me. Her obsessive rule-following is suddenly very funny.

"Don't worry, Madison," says Miles. "If we get caught, everybody'll know *you* followed the rules."

"That's not why I asked," she says.

"Oh yeah?" he shoots back. "I wasn't aware you'd become a completely different person all of a—"

"We aren't getting caught," Xander interrupts. "And even if we did, it'd be worth it. Dakota drinks the good stuff."

He grabs a bottle and pries off the cap. That's the cue for everybody else to take one—including Madison, who chugs hers, too, I guess to make a point. I open another and swallow once, then twice, letting the buzz spread from my stomach to the rest of my body.

"Bruh?" Xander holds a bottle out to Miles, who shakes his head.

"Apparently I'm the designated driver," Miles says. "Yet again."

I jump in to smooth things over.

"And we appreciate it!"

But my appreciation doesn't do much to improve the atmosphere. We sit on the stairs, we drink, and the whole thing feels less like a party and more like something a lot more familiar: a funeral.

Miles finally breaks the silence.

"Here's to my first college brochure coming in the mail." He raises the bottle of Mountain Dew he brought in from his truck. "K-State veterinary school in Man-Happenin', Kansas."

"You didn't tell me about that," I say, surprise mixing with an even more surprising shot of jealousy that he's already getting correspondence from his dream career. "Why K-State?"

"That's where Mom went. But I really want Ohio State. If I don't get serious pretty quick, though, my grades won't be good enough."

"At least you don't have to audition for the stuff you want to do," says Sienna.

"Period," Madison agrees. "Just thinking about *Sweeney Todd* auditions is making me break out in hives." She studies the bottle in her hand, her third by my count, and her words start to slur. "This isn't going to help us be in good vocal shape either."

"Who cares?" Sienna retorts. "I'm drinking as much as I want because I'm sick of thinking about everything and ohmygod sometimes I just caaaaaan't!"

She buries her head in Jaxon's shoulder, almost making him spill his beer, while Madison pulls her knees to her chest and scowls. This makes me want to laugh—or cry, I can't exactly tell which—because the whole idea of trying out for things and applying for college and having to decide what you want to do for the rest of your life in general seems ridiculous when you could be enjoying the simple fact that you exist while everything around you is literally reminding you that someday you won't anymore.

Or something like that.

"Xander." Sienna nudges him with her foot. "What do you want to do when you grow up?"

"Not be a complete failure," he answers.

"Wow," says Jaxon. "That got dark fast."

"Yeah, sorry," Xander says. "Things have been sort of crappy on the home front."

"What happened?" Sienna asks. I know she's dying for the whole story—how Xander got kicked out of school in Springfield, why he's really here in Dodson. I'll admit I'd love to know more too; so much about him is a mystery.

"Nothing happened," he answers. "At least nothing new, which is sort of the problem. You know what? I need some air. Excuse me."

He picks his way over our knees and down the stairs. We hear the back door open and close. I want to follow him, but what if he wants to be alone? What if following him makes everyone think I still like him? What if I maybe still do? Miles is sitting a step up from me, and I remember the tension between us earlier this evening—the uneasy way it made me feel. One thing I do know is that things would be a lot easier if I didn't have to think about it.

Sienna stands and leads Jaxon off upstairs. Miles puts his head against the wall, his eyes drifting shut. Madison is on her phone. I get to my feet.

"I'll be back," I tell them, then head outside. I walk around the house, but Xander is nowhere to be found. I go back inside and wander—down to the prep rooms, and up again to the main floor. I drink as I go, getting woozier with every step, until I reach the front visitation room. I sit against the wall next to the window and rest my cheek against one of the velvet drapes. Before long, my heartbeat calms. My face feels numb. I am wonderfully sleepy.

I have no idea how much time passes, but I open my eyes when I feel a body nudging in next to me. I can sense him more than see him in the dim light. He smells like beer and cinnamon gum. It's Xander.

"I saw you coming in here and thought you looked lonely," he says. "Can I join you?"

"Where are the others?" I ask, stretching.

"Maybe they all fell asleep. If you ask me, everybody could use a nap."

I let my head fall to his shoulder. "That sounds amazing."

The grandfather clock chimes in the hall. We are a cocoon of velvet sleepiness, just the two of us, and right now everything feels right with the world—all except for one thing.

"Where is Flossie?" I moan. "Why isn't she talking to me? Last time we did this we got to see her, and now it's like she was never here."

"Hold on . . ." Xander sits forward. "Maybe she did show herself. I haven't checked my regular camera yet."

He wakes it up, and we look at the screen as he flips through the photos he just took. There's nothing of Flossie, but there are several of me. In most of them, I'm laughing. It's like the photo from the parade, but the person in these images is easier to recognize. I like how Xander captures me.

I don't like how Flossie has decided to go MIA.

"I thought she had a message for me. I thought I'd find out what it is tonight." The more I think about it the more I want to cry. "Maybe Flossie's mad at me. Maybe she's with her dad on the other side, and they both disapprove."

"Why do you care so much, though?" Xander says. "That's what I don't get. You aren't her, and this funeral home isn't your job, even if they try to make you do it. Break free!"

"You don't understand. Everybody wants me to make a commitment. They all think they know me. But *I* don't even know me."

"I was starting to get to know you," Xander says. "Before you ghosted me—literally."

I think back to our dinner at the nursing home. I told him I wanted to escape, and he didn't try to talk me out of it, didn't tell me how great things are in Dodson or remind me of all the history I have here. Xander understood.

"I was scared," I tell him.

"Yeah . . ." He sighs. "I seem to have that effect on people."

"Hey, what's wrong?" His voice has that same darkness it had when we were all on the stairs. "Why were you talking about being a failure back there?"

I feel his shoulder rise and fall under my cheek.

"I guess you could say it's been a bad week. I heard my dad on the phone with my mom, and he was crying. Then she called me and said she's not coming here. She says she can't leave her job in Springfield, but I'm pretty sure there's also some guy she can't leave too."

"Oh, Xander." I reach around and squeeze him to me. "That's awful. But it's not your fault. What goes on between your mom and dad isn't because of you."

"That'd be easier to believe if they didn't have a bunch of crap to nitpick whenever they actually decide to pay attention," he says. "My mom is obsessed with my grades. She flipped out when she got my first-quarter report. Plus, my dad thinks I don't do enough around the house when he's gone, which is pretty much all the time. And don't even get me started on how they feel about my paranormal stuff. You heard what my dad said. The only way I'm ever convincing them I'm serious is if I can do something really big."

"Screw them." I take his hand in mine. "If they can't make more of an effort to be in your life, then they don't have any right to comment on it."

"Maybe you're right." He smiles, and the mole on his cheek does that adorable quirk I love so much. I run my thumb over the ragged edge of his fingernail, lifting it to the night-light to study the damage.

"Is that why you bite your nails like this?" I ask. "There's barely anything left."

"Maybe?" he says. "It's something to do when I'm restless."

"I used to bite my nails too. But I have anxiety. I don't so much now that I take medication."

"I didn't know about that," he says. "You never told me."

"I never got the chance."

He brings my hand to his lips and presses a kiss to the backs of my fingers, raising goose bumps up my arm.

"I was such an idiot," he says. "I know I messed up posting that stuff, and the worst part was, it messed up what I had going with you. That felt really good."

Getting my voice to work takes a second, and I'm not sure if I'm talking about the past or the present when I say, "It did feel good."

"I missed you." His eyes are glinting in the dim light, deep and fiery. I reach up and take his face in my hands.

"I missed you too."

His breath quickens as I pull him in. His mouth is on my mouth, his hands are on my hands and then other places too. I've longed so much for this dizzying, exhilarating sensation; I can totally see why Flossie would want to leave everything behind, break all the rules, and follow this feeling anywhere.

Xander kisses me until my insides are a twirling, twisted swirl, then he pulls away.

"So, it seems like commitments are sort of a negative thing with you right now," he says. "But maybe there's one you'd be cool making?"

The goose bumps I felt earlier are now everywhere, making everything feel alive and tingly, telling me this moment is important; this is one to remember.

"Are you asking me to be your girlfriend?"

"You could call it whatever you want," he replies. "But yeah. That's what I was thinking. Do you want to?"

The question is sort of like an answer in itself. It solves so many problems. Because being Xander's girlfriend means I'm only friends with Miles. Still just friends—the way things have always been. Being Xander's means not messing up the dynamic of our original group, keeping the core intact.

And being with Xander just feels right.

Maybe this is my sign—this boy with me at this very moment. Instead of a ghost, I've got flesh and blood right here, right now. Maybe Flossie's trail has gone cold because it leads to him.

"Yes." I kiss him. "Yes." I kiss him again. He shifts to his knees so he can get closer; now there's no distance between us at all. It is absolute, utter heaven.

Crash!

We freeze. My already-wannabe-gymnast heart does a triple backflip.

I scramble to my feet and bolt for the casket room, which now blazes with light. Sienna stands by the switch, pale, while Jaxon and Miles attempt to set upright the shelf that holds our cremation urns. Madison is crying.

"I didn't touch it," she hiccups. "I promise. Everybody went off and I was looking for you guys, and when I looked in here, it just fell over!"

"How could that happen?" Sienna asks. "That thing looks heavy."

We all look to Xander, who for once appears to have no explanation. Jaxon and Miles get the shelf back up. They all stand back while I replace the urns in their display. Miraculously, none of them are broken.

"It's fine," I tell them. "Not even a dent."

Madison starts sobbing. I put my arm around her. "Hey, don't worry. Everything's okay, see?"

"I want to go home," she says.

"I have to go too," Sienna adds. "Miles, can you take Jaxon with us?"

"I see how it is," Miles says. "Everybody's coming out of their macking sessions to get a ride."

Sienna and Jaxon don't even try to deny what they were up to, while I suddenly can't shut up.

"We weren't doing anything, I was trying to contact Flossie again, and Xander was helping, but we still didn't get anything, which really sucks."

"It's fine," Miles tells me when I stop for breath. "I get it."

He's pulling out his keys just as we hear the back door open. Dakota!

"Go! Out the front!" I whisper through my teeth.

Sienna, Jaxon, Miles, and Madison scurry down the walk, but Xander holds back in the doorway.

"See you tomorrow?" he says. "We have tons of catching up to do."

"I have to work," I tell him. "I'll call you after."

"Okay." He pulls me in and kisses me again—a quick kiss, but intense enough that I feel it all the way to my toes. It takes all my willpower to push him away.

He runs down the steps, turns, waves, starts walking backward, and stumbles. I clamp my hand over my mouth, trying to quiet the laughter. He puts both hands to his mouth, then throws them wide, blowing a kiss as Miles's truck pulls up behind him. Sienna drags him inside, then they glide away down the street.

I turn around and all my warm fluttery feelings vanish when I see beer bottles littering the stairs. I scramble to put them all back in the box. Dakota walks into the foyer just as I'm stashing the box in the office.

"Hey," I say, pulling the door shut. "What are you doing in here?"

"I thought I heard something," he says. "You're still up?"

I force myself to stand still, tell my mouth not to smile too wide and my eyes to focus so he won't know I've been drinking. I wonder if the hallway smells like alcohol.

"I thought I heard the phone."

"The business line rings upstairs too," he says.

"Yeah, but the ringer's been wonky lately, so . . . yeah. I came down. But it was nothing."

"Okay." He looks at me funny. "Everything else all right?"

210

"Yes." I need to get out of here, go upstairs and go to bed, because every second that I stand here, the room gets tilty-er and I get less sure of my ability to speak clearly.

Still, my heart is telling me I can't go until I do one more thing.

"Hey, Dakota, I just want to say you're right. I do use you for a punching bag, a lot. You don't deserve that. I'm sorry."

He looks surprised, then suspicious, then he smiles.

"Thanks for apologizing," he says.

"Cool. No problem." I start up the stairs, beyond ready to throw myself into bed.

"Oh and . . . Elaine?"

I pause. "Yes?"

"Maybe take some aspirin before you go to sleep. It'll help with the hangover in the morning."

211

CHAPTER TWENTY-EIGHT

There's a smile glued to my face when I open my eyes on Sunday. For a minute while I'm waking up, I wonder why I feel so deliciously happy. Then the memories start trickling back.

Some of it is hazy, but the important parts are there. I close my eyes again and feel Xander next to me, the soft of his lips, my fingers twining in his hair. He asked me to be his girlfriend, and I said yes. That, I'm positive, was my message from Flossie. She's not going to give me career advice, she just wants me to follow my heart.

I could stay under the covers reliving it all, but I have a funeral to help with. I drag myself out of bed and immediately feel woozy. I grip the back of my desk chair to steady myself, then stand in the middle of the floor, giggling. It's stupid and sappy, but I cannot stop acting like some character in an old cartoon. I'm pretty sure there are actual hearts and birds flying around my head.

My stomach grumbles. It's almost ten, and I am starving. I check the mirror as I put my hair in a ponytail and nope, no cartoon birds. I wander into the kitchen to find Astrid at the table eating a grapefruit. She looks so young without her Halloween makeup, and guilt wallops me with a solid *whump*. I have no idea when she came home or who brought her. I forgot about her almost completely. If something had happened, I'd never forgive myself.

"Did you have fun last night?" I ask as I fix myself a bowl of granola.

"No," she says.

I have to play this carefully. It's the first time in ages that Astrid has honestly answered a question. If I act too interested, she'll shut down.

I munch on my cereal, keeping things light.

"So what did you end up doing?"

"We went out to the warehouse."

Again, she's being honest. I push back the urge to lecture her about being too young for those kinds of parties, about how she should have at least texted where she was, because I don't want to lose this chance at finding out more about her world.

"Was the party boring or something?"

"It was fine." She gets up to throw away her grapefruit rind. "You know Quinn?"

"Quinn. Right. The guy you're not going out with."

Astrid rolls her eyes, but she keeps talking.

"Quinn and I have been hanging out. And it's fine. It's good. Last night was just . . . not good."

My mind jumps to the worst possible scenario.

"What did he do?"

Defensiveness and fear dart across her face. Immediately I worry my tone was too intense. I can feel her starting to pull away.

"Nothing!" she says. "I'm just sick of people. And I basically just pretty much hate everybody."

She swipes away a tear. I put down my bowl and take a step toward her, feeling like a ranger in a nature show, approaching an animal that might bite any second.

"Maybe I can help?"

"How?" she says.

I pick up the coffeepot and a mug and pour in the remnants of yesterday morning's batch. I won't drink it, but pouring it gives me something to do while I walk this fine line.

"Maybe if you could talk to me. Like we used to. We were really close once."

"Yeah," she says. "But it's different now."

"Why, though? It doesn't have to be. And I'm older, so I know how guys can be. If Quinn's trying to force you to do things you're not ready for—"

"He's not!" She looks horrified. "Is that what you think? Quinn would never."

Crap. I've pushed too far.

"Just forget it," she snaps. "It's fine. *I'm* fine. I can handle it myself."

She pushes past me, and I hear the door to her room slam. I look down at the mug in my hands.

"Ohhhh-K," I say to my silhouette in the cold coffee. "I'd say that was a pretty epic fail, wouldn't you?"

My answer comes in a jolt of panic. The beer bottles from last night. They're still in the office where I put them when everybody left!

"Crapcrapcrapcrap!" I run down the main stairs, ignoring the flashing voicemail light on the office phone, then grab the box of bottles, take it out to my car, and stash it in the trunk. I'll find a dumpster for them later.

Just for a minute, I lean against my car and catch my breath. Nausea is nudging at my stomach, and sparks of pain are pricking behind my eyes. If this is what a hangover feels like, then it just might be pure evil.

The guesthouse sits quiet as I return to the back door. Dakota's probably still asleep. He'll have to get up soon, though; before long it'll be time for the Bohmer service.

I go back upstairs, gulp some aspirin, take a shower, then spend extra time with my makeup—not for Mr. Bohmer, but for the guy I'll be seeing afterward. I won't have much time to hang out with Xander; I've got a ton of homework, and then catching up on *Dragonfly* at Miles's house. Somehow, though, I feel like I can stretch the minutes to make extra. Is this what love feels like? If it is, then it's giving me superpowers.

A half hour later, I hear footsteps on the back stairs. Dad pokes his head into the kitchen and looks around.

"Is everything still in one piece? You girls didn't burn this place down while I was gone, did you?"

"We only had a couple of fires," I tell him. "But we put them out and cleaned up already."

"Then all's well that ends well." He comes in and sets down his overnight bag, then goes to the coffeepot and peers into it. He starts grinding a new batch of beans, pulling out a fresh filter. "Let me tell you, the drive from Quincy was brutal. Traffic was awful and my back has been killing me. I don't recommend driving three hours first thing in the morning without a ton of ibuprofen."

Guilt hits me again as I realize I haven't thought about the reason my dad was gone since yesterday. I'm scared of what he'll tell me when I ask, "How's Grandma?"

He sighs and rubs his face. "They're doing tests, but as of right now they think she'll be fine. Your mom is going to stay there a few more days, then I'll drive back to pick her up. You girls can manage, right?"

"Sure," I tell him, relieved. "We'll be okay."

"I knew you would." He studies the coffeemaker, which is nowhere near done brewing, finds my mug of old stuff, and takes a sip. He really does look exhausted. "But now I need to get cleaned up for the Bohmers. I knew we could count on you, Lainey. Thanks. You're the best."

⚜

The Bohmers are late. It's a good thing because it gives Dad extra time to recover. It's not so good because we like to give families time with their loved one before everybody else arrives. It lets them say a more private goodbye and arrange any photos or personal items they might have brought along for the bier.

I've been stationed in the foyer for the past forty-five minutes, ready to show them to where Mr. Bohmer is laid out in his casket. Now, with fifteen minutes to go before everything is supposed to start, I see a woman coming up the walk with a younger woman and two men.

"Good afternoon," I say as I open the door. Dad comes to greet them when they're all inside.

"Everything is ready," he says. "Mrs. Bohmer, I hope you're well."

The woman gives him a dignified nod, then I step aside as Dad leads them into the visitation room. He glances back at me, and I know my job: Wait for mourners and keep them in the foyer until the family has indicated it's okay to let them in.

Pushing back the vomitous feeling that seems determined to rise up my throat, I smooth out my skirt and wish I'd followed Dakota's advice to take aspirin before going to bed last night. The ones I swallowed an hour ago are not keeping up with the headache now throbbing behind my eyes.

My phone buzzes in my pocket. I'm not supposed to be on screens while I'm working, but I pull it out anyway.

> Last night was incredible. Even if Flossie was an elusive b&*% you were 100x better.

The corners of my mouth hurt from trying not to smile. I can't wait to get out of here and see Xander.

Cars pull up, and people start getting out. I'm preparing to open the door for the first group when a shriek pierces the quiet, followed by more shrieks and the sound of sobbing.

Dakota rushes out of the back, and we race into the visitation room together to see what's wrong. Mrs. Bohmer stands in the corner with her hand over her mouth. The younger woman and two men stand beside her, looking beyond angry.

Dad stands by the casket holding an empty beer bottle.

"Who put this in there?" he asks.

Dakota is white as a sheet of paper. All I can do is stare. It's the same bottle as the ones I hid in the trunk of my car.

Dad looks around, his eyes blazing with a fury I've never seen before.

"How did this get into the casket? Dakota?"

"Sir, I have no idea," Dakota says. He's confused, and terrified. The bottle is his, but he has no idea why it's here.

"It was down my father's pants," one of the men shouts. "You think maybe you'd remember something like that?"

"Dad struggled with sobriety," the younger woman adds. "If this is a joke, it's extremely cruel."

Normally, this is where Mom would step in to help defuse the situation, but Mom isn't here, so I'm the one who speaks, hoping I can hide how much I'm trembling.

"Obviously something's gone wrong here." I turn to the Bohmers. "Could we have a minute to talk with each other about this?"

"Are you kidding?" the other man says. "I'm not going to leave the room so you can get your stories straight. I want to know exactly what to tell our lawyer when we call her."

"I'm not leaving either," the younger woman says. "I want answers."

"I want that too," says Dad. He glares at Dakota. "Have you been drinking while working with our clients? Once this is reported, I can guarantee you'll never find a job in this profession. Consider your career over."

Dakota looks like he might be about to cry. I could let him take the blame—save myself and preserve my dad's vision of me as the good, responsible daughter. But I could never let someone lose their career over something I did.

"It's my fault," I blurt out. "I had friends over last night."

Dakota is too shocked to even look vindicated. For all the times I've treated him like a screwup, the biggest, most awful screwup has turned out to be mine.

"I'm so sorry," I say. "I never meant for anything like this to happen."

Dad's face morphs from disbelief to shocked hurt before he pulls himself to his full height and his voice turns deathly formal.

"Mrs. Bohmer," he says, "I cannot express my apologies strongly enough. You and your family will receive all our services free of charge. I know that can't begin to make up for the shock and disrespect you've experienced, but I hope it will be a start. And we will discuss any other ways that we can make this right in the coming days. But now, your guests are arriving."

"Mom?" The younger woman turns to Mrs. Bohmer, who is no longer sobbing, and I can sense my father holding his breath.

Mrs. Bohmer nods. "Let them in."

Dakota goes to open the door. Dad speaks to me through gritted teeth.

"Go to your room immediately. And send your sister down here. Tell her in no uncertain terms that she is to help without complaining or she will face severe consequences."

When I get to Astrid's room, she takes one look at my face and starts changing clothes. I don't go to my room or change my clothes. I sit at the top of the main stairs, out of sight, and listen. Every other person who comes through the door gets told what happened by one of the Bohmers, and their guests respond with exactly the kind of horror you'd expect. What hurts the most is hearing them trash my dad. I have to stay here and listen to my parents' reputation sink further by the minute, knowing it's all my fault.

I think back through last evening, trying to remember if anybody went down to the prep rooms without me. My memory of the time from when we were all down there together to when Xander and I were in the visitation room is pretty much gone.

Small things bubble back, but they don't offer any comfort. I remember sticking my tongue out at the portrait of my great-great-great-grandfather. I remember feeling abandoned by Flossic. I remember everybody dejected on the stairs. Was anybody else as drunk as I was? Is this someone's idea of a sick joke?

The service ends, and Dad and Dakota go outside to direct traffic. I venture back downstairs and busy myself putting away chairs, picking up discarded programs, anything to stay occupied while I wait.

Finally, the back door opens. Dad stalks into the foyer, followed by Dakota. They both go into the office, and I know without anyone saying a word that I am to follow.

"I have never been more horrified or disappointed in my life," Dad says once we're all inside. "If I had not seen that with my own eyes, I wouldn't have believed it. I want to know how it happened."

"Sir." Dakota steps forward. "I should have checked Mr. Bohmer more thoroughly before bringing him up. It's inexcusable that I missed the bottle. I take full responsibility."

"You should," Dad tells him. "As the last person to work with the deceased before they're presented to the family, it's your responsibility to make sure everything is as it should be. But whether you should have seen the bottle is beside the point. It shouldn't have been there in the first place. Elaine, how many people were here last night?"

"Just five."

"Who?"

"Sienna. Her boyfriend, Jaxon. Madison and Miles. And . . ." I don't want to say Xander's name.

"And the boy I warned you about? Is he the reason your judgment is so incredibly bad all of a sudden?"

Dad's cell phone rings. He ignores it.

"Sir." Dakota looks nearly frantic to escape. "Would it be okay if I go now?"

"Please do," says Dad. "I want to speak with my daughter privately."

I try to catch Dakota's eye as he leaves, to somehow let him know how terrible I feel for taking his beer, for letting this whole thing get so out of control. Dakota glances up, and it's clear: No apology in the world will make up for what I've done.

Dad loosens his tie. I'm prepared for him to continue reprimanding me. Instead, he closes his eyes and pinches the bridge of his nose.

"I don't know what to say. I'm shocked, Elaine. I warned you about Xander."

"This isn't his fault," I protest.

"Based on what I've heard about this boy, I'm having a hard time believing that."

"You don't know him like I do. All you know are rumors from a bunch of stupid small-town people."

"Do you consider the police stupid? They've found him at the old homestead more than once, messing around where he had no business to be."

"He was investigating," I say. "Ghost hunting. That's what he does."

Dad's eyes widen. "Ghost hunting? How ridiculous. And disrespectful, which seems to be a running thread with this young man. Chief Arpin thinks he's responsible for real damage out there— graffiti, fires, beer cans everywhere . . ."

I hold up my hands, waving for him to stop. He has no idea what he's talking about.

"People party there all the time. Xander can't be responsible for everything."

"If he's capable of vandalizing private property, then he's capable of vandalizing our business."

"He didn't vandalize anything."

"Well then, who did? Miles? Madison?"

"I did!"

Silence. We both stare at each other, unable to believe what came out of my mouth.

"*You* did?" Hearing him say it makes this moment feel infinitely worse.

"Yes. No." I shake my head, trying to rattle my thoughts loose. "I don't remember . . . but does it really matter? I invited people over. I let them drink. I didn't keep an eye on things like I was supposed to. It's my responsibility."

My father stares at me, his expression growing angrier with every word I speak. Finally, he manages to push out three furiously strained sentences.

"Give me your phone. And your laptop. They're mine until further notice."

Panic strikes. "Dad, I need my laptop for school. And I can't drive Astrid around if she can't get hold of me."

His phone starts ringing again. He talks over it.

"You can use the computer in the office for homework. You can have your phone when you're at school in case your sister or any of us need to reach you. But you will turn it in to me as soon as you get home. And you are not to leave this house—the only exception being the eleventh, when we drive up to Cincinnati."

"Wait a minute." An awful feeling starts to pool at the bottom of my stomach. "When?"

"The eleventh. We're visiting the mortuary school the next day with Kevin Berland. I sent it to the family calendar. Did you not check it?"

I pull out my phone, but I'm pretty sure of what I'll find before I look at the date. I peek anyway, and my stomach belly flops. It's the same weekend as DraCon.

"I can't go to Cincinnati then. I have something else planned."

"If it's the musical, Mr. Ferrara can find a substitute," Dad says. "There are other pianists around."

"It's not for school, it's a convention in Chicago. For *Dragonfly*. I promised Miles we'd go together."

Miles. Oh no. I'm supposed to be at his house soon, to watch the latest episode. He's going to be furious with me.

"A convention?" Dad says. "Why is this the first I'm hearing of it?"

"A lot has been going on, and you just told me about Cincinnati last night. I made these DraCon plans weeks ago. It's not like I *wanted* to have a conflict." I can't keep anything straight in my head because his phone is ringing again, and the sound has rubbed every one of my nerves raw. "Dad, I'm sorry, but could you please answer that? I don't think I can listen to it again."

Glaring at me, he checks the screen.

"It's your mom. How about I let you fill her in on what's happened here?"

God. Mom. She's going to be livid. But there's no way to avoid it; she's going to find out one way or another.

"Fine," I say. "Just please answer it."

He picks up and puts her on speaker.

"Tom? Elaine?" Her voice fills the room, sounding tense and puzzled. "I checked the office voicemail a little bit ago. Can anybody tell me who *Spirit Seekers* is and why they're trying to reach us?"

CHAPTER TWENTY-NINE

"*Spirit Seekers?*" says Dad. "I've never heard of them. Are they a vendor?"

"They've left four messages," says Mom.

"Oh God." I clutch my stomach as the nausea flooding my body gets worse.

"Elaine, what's wrong?" says Dad. "Are you going to throw up?"

"I know who they are," I tell him.

"I just Googled them," says Mom. "Tom, you need to see this."

I don't want to do it, but I come around to the office computer, find *Spirit Seekers,* and pull up their website for Dad and me to look at. Their logo fills the screen over a post from their blog.

AMAZING EVIDENCE FROM ILLINOIS FUNERAL HOME

The headline screams over Xander's photo of Flossie in the visitation room and a clip of the green dots moving, along with the EVP recording of her name. Underneath the photo and videos is this fine print: *We're working to learn more about this incredible spectral image and footage. We'll keep you posted on what we find out.*

"I'm not even going to ask when these things were created," Dad says. "It's very clear *where* they were created."

Mom's voice crackles over Dad's old phone. "Could someone please explain to me what's going on?"

I scramble to get closer, to be sure she can hear me.

"Mom. If I can fix this, then nothing is going on. Well, nothing as far as *this* is concerned. There are *other* things going—"

"We need to talk," Dad tells her.

"Oh goodness, I don't like the sound of that." Now she sounds like *she* wants to throw up.

I turn to my dad.

"I know I'm supposed to give you my phone, but please, you have to let me make one call. I know what this is, and I think I can handle it, but I need to do it right now."

He hesitates and then, looking more tired than I've ever seen him look in my whole life, he nods. I rush out of the office and up to my room.

Whatever it takes, whatever you have to do, you have to make this better.

"Elaine!" Xander answers video chat looking impossibly not-hungover. "Are you done with your work?"

Seeing him hurts. It actually physically hurts because I should be warm and tingly right now, looking forward to a romantic afternoon with my boyfriend. Instead, I feel sick and betrayed and unable to believe he actually did what he's done.

"Call off *Spirit Seekers*." My voice sounds like it's coming from a different person. "Right now. Tell them to delete everything they have and leave us alone."

"What?" The smile still lingers on his face. "What are you talking about?"

"*Spirit Seekers*. Your picture and videos—on their blog. Tell them to take it down."

"Hold on." I see him pull over his laptop and navigate to the website. When he sees it, he runs a hand through his hair and says, "Oh wow! This is amazing."

"It's not amazing!" How is it possible that he doesn't get it? "My parents have seen this. *Spirit Seekers* is calling us. Why would you send them these things?"

"I didn't!" he insists. "People downloaded them when they were first posted. I've been trying to get them to stop sharing this stuff, but *Spirit Seekers* has staff who search the internet for things like this. You said they contacted you?"

This is getting more confusing by the second. And I haven't even brought up the rest of it.

"They called the funeral home office," I tell him. "Oh, and somebody put a beer bottle down Mr. Bohmer's pants last night."

Xander goes pale. "What?"

"Someone put an actual beer bottle down the pants of an actual corpse in an actual casket, and it was found by the actual family before the actual freaking funeral."

I can't believe the words I just said really came out of my mouth. I've always been so careful, always dreading some kind of looming disaster, and what happened turned out to be so far beyond any disaster I could ever have imagined. What good is anxiety if it can't help prepare you for the really bad stuff?

"You're kidding," Xander says as the seriousness of it all sinks in. "Who would do that?"

"I'm wondering the same thing."

He pauses. "You don't think I did it, do you?"

I know it's not fair to accuse when I have no proof. And the bottle isn't even the biggest deal here. Right now I need to not have my family's funeral home turned into any more of a freak show than it's already become.

I take a deep breath and try to focus.

"Just . . . fix the *Spirit Seekers* thing. Get them to take down everything about us, however you have to do it."

A tall figure appears in my doorway. Dad holds out his hand.

"I have to go."

"Elaine—"

"Goodbye, Xander."

Heartbroken and so ashamed I can't even lift my head, I place my phone into my father's palm. Wordlessly, Dad scoops my laptop off my bed and tucks it under his arm, then he turns and leaves the room.

❧

I've never needed *Dragonfly* like I need it right now.

It's early evening before I can email Miles from the office computer about why I didn't come over. I don't wait for a response because he always takes forever to check email; I'm just trusting we'll be okay once he knows what's happened.

I can't hide in my room and watch on my laptop, so I curl up under a blanket in front of the family room TV and pray nobody comes in for the next fifty minutes. I lie back, searching for the comfort of the soft pillow against my head. The theme song starts, and my world begins to settle. This is familiar. This is escape. This is exactly where I need to be.

And then, all hell breaks loose. There's a battle. A rip in the space-time continuum. A choice is made. A betrayal occurs. Pax and Skye walk a razor-thin balance between safety and disaster, and just when it looks like all might be okay, the unthinkable happens.

Pax is killed.

My anxiety has ratcheted higher and higher as the episode unspools. I've been anticipating the comedown, when it's clear that the worst isn't going to happen and all this turmoil was just another trial in Pax and Skye's progression of souls.

But now everything—*everything*—is getting turned inside out.

What the actual crap?!

I stare at the screen, trying to process what I'm seeing. *Dragonfly* is just a show, but it's been so much a part of my life that I feel like it's a part of me. Pax and Skye, I *know* them. Pax's death feels like a real death.

I need to reach Miles. I need to at least let him know I've seen it, and that we can talk about it as soon as we're together. I'm heading downstairs when Dad stops me on the stairs.

"Can I please use the office computer again?" I ask. "I need to email Miles."

Dad shakes his head.

"I think you need to go to bed now," he says. "You can talk to your friends tomorrow at school."

"But Miles . . ."

"Good night, Elaine."

CHAPTER THIRTY

Driving Astrid the next day is somehow the most painful part of this whole thing, because we both know my screwups affect her too. All last night and this morning, a feeling of dread lay over the house. I heard Dad on the phone with Mom, talking about contacting our attorney in case the Bohmers bring in theirs. Then he gave us the silent treatment, heading down to the office before breakfast, leaving a black hole of doom at the center of everything.

When we pull up to school, Astrid grabs her backpack, but she doesn't hurry out of the car like usual. Instead, she stays by my side as we trudge toward the building. It's an uncomfortable truce, but I'm grateful for it.

"Can I get a ride home today?" she asks, scuffing through the leaves along the curb. "Coach is sick so there's no pom."

"Yes," I tell her. "Just meet me out here and don't be late."

"Hey! Funeral Girl!"

We both turn to see some kid I don't know—a freshman, from

the greasy, scrawny look of him—laughing with his equally scrawny, greasy friends.

"Nah, man," one of the other kids says. "She's Ghost Girl now. Hey, Ghost Girl, can I come to your séance?"

"Ignore them," I tell Astrid. "They're a bunch of losers."

But then we get inside, and heads literally turn—like in a movie when a character's done something terrible, and everybody stares at them as they walk through the halls. Astrid breaks off for the gym, and I keep my head down, heading for Miles's locker.

Sienna gets to me first. She rushes over when she spots me across the commons.

"What's going on?" she asks. "Your dad called my parents about Saturday night. Why aren't you answering your texts?"

"Because he took my phone," I tell her. "I only get it back for school, otherwise I'm cut off from everything— Ugh, seriously?" Bridget Mitchell and Alice Chen are whispering as they walk past. "*Why* is everybody looking at me like that?"

"Because those photos and videos of Xander's have gone beyond viral. They're everywhere." Sienna lowers her voice. "Did you guys plan this or something?"

She's got that swoony look in her eyes again. She thinks this is some plot the two of us have hatched. She thinks Xander and I are officially together, and who could blame her? The last time she saw us, we were.

But now?

"Xander and I did not plan it," I insist. "*Spirit Seekers* got those things somehow and put them on their website. But my dad had our lawyer send a cease and desist. They shouldn't be any-where anymore."

"Um, think again." She shows me her phone, pulling up blog after social media post after news story, some of them from major outlets, all of them going wild over the picture of Flossie, the ghostly movement in the visitation room, the sound of her name.

"It's obvious they were taken at your place," Sienna says. "Everybody knows about Xander's investigating, and who else around here owns an old funeral home? Plus, he was the one who originally posted all this, so—"

"Oh my God," I mumble. "This is a mess."

"But what *happened*? Your dad said something about somebody putting beer bottles down somebody's pants?"

She looks horrified, but also like she sort of wants to laugh. It's not funny.

Except it is.

Except it's not.

I shift my backpack to my other shoulder and ask, "Saturday night, when everybody went off on their own, did you and Jaxon go back down to the prep rooms? Did you maybe do something to Mr. Bohmer?"

"Oh my God, no!" Now she looks totally offended. "I would never do that. *Who* would ever do that? Did Miles? Did Xander? You don't think Xander did it, do you?"

"I don't know." My head is starting to hurt again. "And I honestly can't deal with Xander today. If he asks about me, tell him I need time alone. Or say whatever you want. Right now, I need to find Miles."

"I'm right here."

I turn, and he's standing next to me.

"Did you get my email?" I ask him. "My dad took my phone

and my laptop, and I couldn't reach you about *Dragonfly*, and that whole episode was absolutely awful. I wanted to text you about it, but I couldn't!"

"I got your email," he says. "But not until way after I'd already gone ahead and watched it—after I spent all day wondering if *Dragonfly* was going to get forgotten like it has ever since Xander got here."

Sienna, sensing an argument, slinks away. I study Miles's face, hoping he'll break into a smile and break the tension.

"But you know what happened," I press. "You understand, right?"

He gives a maddeningly noncommittal half shrug. "I understand, but probably not how you want."

A new and disturbing emptiness is starting to creep into the part of me that holds the things I've counted on all my life. One of those things was knowing Miles would always be there. Now . . .

"What do you mean?" I ask.

"I understand that none of this would have happened if you'd listened when I told you to be careful around Xander," he replies. "I was friends with him before anybody else, which is why I knew what I was talking about. Dude only cares about getting attention from his internet fans. I also understand that none of that seems to matter to you. When Xander calls, Xander gets top priority, no matter what."

My lower lip starts to tremble. Miles has never been cold like this.

Again, he shrugs. "I'm just being honest."

"Fine," I say. "I'll be honest too. You've always sucked at hiding how you feel, and it's obvious that you're jealous."

His face goes red, but now that I've started, I won't stop until I've hurt him as much as he's hurt me.

"You've always been the center of attention," I tell him. "*Oh, Miles is so funny! Everybody laugh at Miles!* Then Xander comes along, and he's getting attention now, and you can't handle it."

I've never seen Miles furious before—not when Madison ruined his Minecraft world in fifth grade, not when Connor Kress stole his freshman project idea and got a better score, not even when some ass from Shasta Falls tripped him during the state cross-country championship last year. But now, his eyes are ice-cold rage.

"Thanks for that analysis," he says. "You know me so well."

"Yeah, unfortunately I do."

I turn to go, racing the tardy bell but also needing to be away from him. I don't want him to see me cry—don't want him to think he's won. But the hall is so crowded. I dodge bodies, barely able to move more than a couple of steps at a time, and when I turn to look over my shoulder, Miles is the one who's no longer there.

⚜

For the rest of the day, I hide. I avoid Xander's texts. I keep my head down in choir when Madison tries to ask what's going on. And I spend every hour on the hour dodging jerks who think it's hilarious to call me Funeral Girl during passing periods. Oh, wait, thanks to *Spirit Seekers,* it's Ghost Girl now.

Last bell finally rings, and I head to my car to wait for Astrid. Slouching behind the steering wheel, I watch the parking lot empty, envying all the people who get to go home and do homework and hobbies and whatever else without worrying about ruining their family's business on top of it all.

Three-thirty comes. Still no sign of my sister. I'm starting to text her when the car door opens.

"Seriously, Astrid, I told you not to be la—" The last word turns into a scream when I realize it's not Astrid sliding into my passenger seat.

Xander waves at me. "Hey."

I clutch my hands to my chest, gasping as adrenaline races through my body.

"Xander! Honestly! There should be consent rules about getting into someone's car. You cannot just jump in and give me a heart attack like that!"

"I can get back out and knock," he offers. "But I was afraid if I did, you'd drive away."

I have to admit I might have done exactly that.

"My sister will be here any minute," I tell him. "Then we have to get home. I'll be in even bigger trouble if I'm late."

"See, that's why I'm here." His eyes are massive brown pools of sadness; even now, I feel like I might drown if I look at them too long. "Can we talk? Please? When your sister comes, you can kick me out, I promise."

Astrid probably went off with her friends. Who knows how long she could be? I rest my forehead on the steering wheel.

"Fine, we can talk. But I don't know what you want me to say."

"I swear I didn't do anything to that man," he insists. "Why would I ruin any chance I'd have of going back there? Only an idiot would sabotage the best investigation site they've ever found."

Listening to Xander, I can see Miles's face. I can hear him telling me that all Xander really cares about are his followers, and the realization that he might be right makes me sick to my stomach.

"So, to you my house is just an *investigation site*?" I ask. "It's *my* actual home."

"And amazing things are happening there." Xander's eyes are burning with that fever I've come to recognize as a sign he's falling into a ghost hunter's delirium. "Okay. I know this is going to make me sound like a jerk, but I think you should talk to *Spirit Seekers*. Or let me do it. Actually, I definitely think you should let me do it."

"Oh my God." My heart sinks as a picture forms that I should have seen a long time ago. "I thought you cared about me, but all you really wanted was to get inside my house."

I wait for him to deny it. He hesitates, and my entire body goes cold except for the searing hot lump in my throat.

"So, nothing that happened between us was real," I say. "It was all about investigating."

"Elaine . . ."

I bury my face in my hands.

"I thought you asked me to be your girlfriend because you had real feelings for me. I opened up my life to you like I haven't with anybody else, ever."

I can hear him shifting, feel him getting closer, but I don't want to look at him. I can't.

"I do have real feelings for you!" he insists. "And we're so close to doing something nobody's ever done before. We can't stop now."

"What you're really interested in is Flossie. Basically, I've been competing with a hundred-and-fifty-year-old ghost. God, I'm so stupid. I thought you *understood* me."

"I do." He pulls my hands away from my face, grasping them in both of his. "I understand that *something* needed to happen. You were the one who said you didn't want this life forever. You said you felt trapped. Don't you feel even a little bit liberated now that things are coming out in the open?"

"I do not feel liberated," I tell him. "I feel humiliated. And scared."

Xander once told me *Sometimes you have to put yourself at risk to capture something amazing.* But this risk is too big.

"My first impression was right all along," I say. "You *are* an adrenaline junkie and an attention addict. My dad said people are talking about vandalism at the homestead, and at first I defended you, but now I actually think it *was* you, because why let basic respect and decency get in the way of whatever you want, right? You probably also put that bottle down Mr. Bohmer's pants. Did you get a good photo of that? I'm sure your followers will love it, never mind that it's completely ruined *my* life."

I look away, afraid I've pushed too far. When I look up again, his face has literally fallen—as in, every one of his features has dropped two inches.

"You want to know why I investigate the paranormal?" he says. "Because I have to think there's something more than this crappy world where people can't wait to believe any stupid gossip they hear. And yeah, it matters to me what people online think. Because sometimes it feels they're the only ones who care."

His eyes are red-rimmed, but still beautiful with that little mole underneath the right one. They're also dangerous. Ever since this boy stepped in front of my horses at Harvest Home, he's turned my life inside out.

"I thought I might be in love with you," I tell him. "I thought maybe you felt the same way. But you used me to impress some stupid TV ghost hunters, and rather than realize why that's so awful, you now want me to talk with them."

"Elaine, listen—"

"No." I pull away, as far as I can without getting out of the car. "It's over. All of it."

He makes an angry, choking sound as he slams back out into the parking lot. I watch him walk away, taking in the messy hair on the back of his head, his slumped shoulders, those ratty sneakers. All the feelings I had for him, they're still here. Only now they hurt. My heart hurts. My head hurts. Even my body hurts from all the stress I've been holding on to.

Xander doesn't look back.

And there's still no sign of Astrid. I wait five more minutes, then go back inside to find her.

A couple of guys are shooting hoops in the gym. They don't know who Astrid is, so I check the locker room and then head back to the empty commons. Voices are coming from the math wing. One of them is a girl's.

"So, are you with her or me?"

The next voice is a boy's. And I'm positive I can guess who it is.

"It's not like that," he says. "Why does everything have to be so much drama with you?"

"Because you're hanging out with her when you're supposed to be with me, and it isn't right."

The boy sounds bored now. "She's my friend. I can hang out with who I want. Jeez, don't be so sensitive."

"I'm not being sensitive, I'm telling you something's wrong!" There's a silence, where I can hear my sister crying. The boy makes a sound like it's all too much.

"I can't handle this," he says. "Dang, maybe grow up a little? I'll talk to you later."

I step away as Quinn comes storming out of the hallway. He

stalks past me, and I wait until he's gone before I look back. There on the floor, hugging her knees to her chest, is my sister.

I rush over.

"Astrid, what happened?"

"Nothing," she says, and I want to shake her because that is so obviously not true.

"Come on." I help her to her feet, keeping my arm around her as I guide her out to the car. I start driving, and she sits there, silent. An odd sort of pressure has been building inside me all day, seeds of anger burrowing deep, like the anxiety I'm so used to feeling is replicating, mixing with a simmering rage that only makes the replicating go faster. Fighting with Miles, fighting with Xander, avoiding my friends, trying to keep away from conflict . . . I can't handle much more avoiding.

"I'm not stupid, Astrid. You either tell me what's happening or I'm talking to somebody—a counselor or Mom and Dad . . ."

"Don't!" she says. "I don't want them to know."

"Then talk."

She sniffles as she turns her phone around and around in her hands. "So I know you think Quinn is too old for me, but he's really cool and sweet, and it wasn't weird until Ella Schmidt decided *she* wants him too. Saturday at the warehouse, she got a bunch of her friends to basically ambush me. They told me to go home, I'm a baby, leave Quinn alone—stuff like that."

Ella Schmidt. Why doesn't it surprise me that my grade school tormentor is now tormenting my little sister?

"Is that the whole story?" I ask. "Nothing else happened?"

"Quinn isn't making me do anything I don't want to do," she insists. "Which is stupid to even have to say because we aren't *doing* anything in the first place. Promise you won't tell Mom and Dad? They already think I'm a massive screwup."

Wait a minute, what? Hearing her say that knocks the breath out of me.

"Mom and Dad don't think you're a screwup," I tell her. But I realize that they do sort of treat her like it. "If anyone's the screwup here, it's me."

She peeks at me sideways, like she's scared of how I'll take what she's about to say.

"I'm sorry all that happened with your friends, but honestly, I've been a little glad about it too. Is that really awful?"

"Maybe," I say. "Why would you be glad?"

She shrugs.

"Mom and Dad think you're amazing. You're great at piano. You're going to take over the family business. I'm just this nobody who can't do anything besides maybe dance."

"That's not true. You can do so many things, and your dancing is amazing. Besides, you've never wanted anything to do with the business."

"Maybe I would if I felt like anybody thought I'd be any good at it. You've got everything covered." She raises the pitch of her voice to imitate Mom. "'Elaine is so responsible and smart and helpful. Oh, and you look cute, Astrid. Have fun on your little pom squad.'"

If I wasn't on the highway right now, I'd reach across the seat and try to hug her.

"I didn't know you felt like that. I'm so sorry, Astrid. Mom and Dad love you. Everybody loves you."

"Everybody but Ella Schmidt," she says.

"And that's one big but . . . Pun intended."

"Shut up! Ella's gorgeous, including her butt. It's wrong to body-shame, Elaine."

"Consider me reprimanded."

We laugh—not like we used to exactly, but a laugh that connects us just the same. It's a bright spot in what has otherwise been a crap-tastic day. And it takes away a little of the ominous feeling when we pull up to home. The house looms under the gray sky, and as we walk to the back entrance, the wind whistles around from the front, making me shiver.

This place may or may not be haunted by ghosts, but my dad's anger might be even more terrifying. Astrid catches my eye as we pass the delivery bay, and I know she's thinking the same thing: It's going to be a long night.

CHAPTER THIRTY-ONE

Dad doesn't ask why we're late because he's in a meeting with a casket company rep. Upstairs in the kitchen, we look around for something to make for dinner.

"Do we have any spaghetti?" Astrid opens the pantry door. "Maybe we just heat up some sauce?"

"I think I saw meatballs in the freezer," I tell her. "Let me get something done for chemistry, then I'll boil water if you make a salad."

She gets her books out, and we work at the kitchen table until the business phone rings. We look at each other and wonder whether to cook at all—if Dad has to go on a death call, we might be eating by ourselves. But then Dakota's voice comes up the back stairs.

"Elaine, it's for you."

"Oh God, what now?" All I can think of is that *Spirit Seekers* found my name, and now they're trying to reach me directly. Who else would be calling on the business line? I pick up the phone and wince. "Hello?"

"Elaine?"

The sound of my mother's voice lifts the lid on a well of emotions I've tried to keep closed all day. I haven't heard from her since yesterday morning, and I didn't realize how much I wanted to until just this minute.

"Mom." I dash up the stairs to my room for privacy. "Why are you calling me on the business phone?"

"Because your father took your cell phone. Didn't he?"

"In theory. But he's busy, so I still have it from school today." My voice trembles, then cracks. "I screwed up."

Nothing can hold back the tears now. Big hiccupping sobs roll out of me in waves.

"Oh, sweetheart," says Mom.

"We're going to get sued," I cry. "Memories is going to take all our business, and it's my fault."

"Lainey. I know you didn't mean—"

"But I did! I must have or I would have watched people better, so the whole thing with Mr. Bohmer wouldn't have happened. And the ghost hunts here, those were my idea, so ultimately that's on me, too." There's so much I want to tell her, about Xander and how I thought I could trust him—how I thought I might actually love him and could still. All I can manage is "When are you coming home?"

"I'll be back Thursday," she says. "Grandma's recovering. It wasn't a stroke after all, and things are in hand here, so Dad's coming back to get me."

I let out a shuddering sigh. I'm so happy for at least one piece of good news.

"I'm glad she's better."

"You're the one I'm concerned about, though. I called because I wanted to make sure you're okay."

This whole conversation has me shook, because I was positive my mom would be angrier even than my dad. She's always been so focused on appearances, and this has made us look as bad as possible. Her kindness pokes at every soft spot I have.

"Nothing's okay," I say through a fresh wave of tears.

"Do I need to come back earlier? We can make an appointment with Dr. Hymans if you think it would help to talk with someone."

I realize when she brings up my therapist that it isn't anxiety that's bothering me. In fact, I don't feel anxious at all right now. I'm sad. I'm overwhelmed and sorry and freaked out about what's happened, but I'm not feeling that buzzing, finger-in-a-light-socket dread. I used to worry that some awful, nameless something would go wrong, and now something *has* gone wrong—actually many somethings. And while I'm scared and angry and a million other emotions, I am, curiously, not all that anxious.

Also, I know my mom has her own things to worry about. I don't want to stress her out even more.

"I'll be fine," I tell her. "Well, maybe not *fine*, but I'm pretty sure I'll live."

"Oh, good," she says, sounding relieved. "Just get through the next couple of days and lie low with your father, all right? Whatever happens, we'll get through this. Just know that I love you. Your father does too—no matter what. We love you, honey. Okay?"

"Okay. I love you too." I have to go or I'll cry even harder. "I need to make dinner now."

"Thank you for keeping things moving along, sweetheart. I'll see you soon."

Astrid's got the salad started when I come down from my room. I take the frozen meatballs out of their bag and put them on a cookie sheet for the oven. Dad comes up just as I'm draining pasta.

"Oh, thank you, girls," he says as he sinks into a chair at the table. "I was about to order a pizza, but this is much nicer."

We fill our plates with spaghetti, then we sit and eat. Dad asks how school was. Astrid says, "Good." And she doesn't exit the table at the first opportunity. Dad doesn't demand that I hand over my phone either. We're all making an effort.

Then, as we're finishing our last bites, he says, "So, Elaine, when we drive up to Cincinnati, you'll want to look into whatever you have to do to keep up with your classes. Make sure to get any assignments you'll miss. You can do them in the car."

My hand closes in a fist around the napkin in my lap.

"I told you I can't. I'm supposed to go to Chicago."

He swipes my empty plate away and carries everything over to the sink.

"You're not going to Chicago for some fan convention," he says. "After what happened this past weekend, why should I trust your judgment to take a trip like that?"

"What happened was wrong, and I feel worse about it than you will ever believe," I tell him. "But I can't just cancel on Miles."

"I made these plans because it's important," he says. "I'm talking about setting you up for your future."

"What if I don't want that kind of future?"

A plate clatters as it slips out of his hands.

"Why wouldn't you want it?" he says. "I thought you liked helping out here."

The pressure I've been feeling all day suddenly has nowhere to go but out of my mouth.

"Oh my God, Dad. I'm sorry but working all the time at a funeral home is exactly nobody's idea of a good time. I like being with you. I like making money. That doesn't mean I want to do this for the rest of my life."

It's almost like there's an echo, the way my words hang in the air—these words I can't take back. I can see him regrouping, trying to back off from the whole rest-of-your-life thing.

"All I'm doing is asking you to explore your options," he says.

"It sounds like you've pretty much decided which option you want me to choose."

"Well, you can hardly blame me. This business has been in our family for generations. Who else is going to take it over?"

Astrid has been using her knife to push a carrot that escaped her salad back and forth between her napkin and water glass. I can tell she wishes she'd bolted when she had the chance.

"I don't know why you think I'd be any good at it if I did take over," I say. "I couldn't even come up with decent marketing ideas."

"If you explored it more, I really think you'd be interested," he says. "Which is all the more reason why I want you to meet with Kevin and see the school."

"Can he do it another time?"

"No. He's busy."

"So am I!"

"With—what is it you call it—fandom? I'm sorry, that's not a good enough reason to be rude and cancel these plans that Kevin has already agreed to. We're going to Cincinnati."

I can feel the anger that's been taking root inside me, nudging at my skin, wanting to bloom. All my life has been *Thanks, Elaine, for dropping everything; thanks for holding down the fort; thanks for being there when we need you. You're the best.* I thought if I put all my wants and needs second, it would buy me some understanding and flexibility when it counted, but now I see how wrong I was.

I can't be "the best" anymore.

"No."

"What?" says Dad.

I push away from the table. "I said no."

He straightens to his full height, and when he speaks again, it's in that super-formal way that has always been so intimidating.

"You are in no position to say no to anything," he says. "You'll do as I say."

I'm not intimidated anymore. I force myself to stay strong.

"I can't change what I've done, and I know I deserve to be punished," I say. "But I am telling you this right now: I'm not going to visit mortuary schools. I'm not helping with the business either. You just said Mr. Ferrara could find other pianists; well, you can too. I'm not working as a greeter or a guest-book attendant anymore. And I absolutely am never driving the buggy again."

His voice follows me up the stairs to my room, calling my name. I close the door to shut out the sound. Then I stand in the middle of the room, shaking.

"Flossie?" My voice sounds small—not like someone who just stood up to her father. I clear my throat and try again. "Flossie, if you really do have a message for me, now would be a great time to let me know."

I wait, straining to catch the slightest creak or moan or whisper, trying not to miss whatever crumb of guidance the past might offer. I hear the sink in the kitchen as my dad cleans up from dinner. I hear my sister go into her room and close the door. But in this old attic filled with more than a century of memories, there is nothing but silence.

CHAPTER THIRTY-TWO

"I think I'm going to throw up."

Sienna sways outside the choir room door, one hand on her stomach, the other clutching her music, while Madison pushes a packet of papers at me and starts talking over the sounds of everyone waiting to audition for *Sweeney Todd*.

"Here, Elaine," she says. "I copied my music onto separate sheets so you can spread it out and not worry about that page turn in the middle."

"Thanks," I say. We've done her audition number so many times now that I'm sure I could play it in my sleep, but I don't tell her that because she looks even urpier than Sienna.

I want to reassure them that they're going to do great. I want them to both get lead roles. And I wish they weren't looking at me like I somehow hold the keys to their success, not when I'm barely keeping things together myself. My father isn't speaking to me. Miles has cut me off. Xander and I are broken up. Everything is a mess.

The choir room door opens, and anticipation ripples through

the crowd. Mr. Ferrara pokes his head out. He gestures at me to come inside.

I put on my encouraging, good-friend smile as I turn back to Sienna and Madison.

"Good luck," I tell them. "And please *don't* break a leg because I love you, and I don't want to see you in pain, and it will be so much easier rocking those lead roles when you're not on crutches."

They try to smile. I try to keep smiling. It's showtime.

"All right, you know the drill," Mr. F says once I'm behind the piano. "People come in and perform their song. If they don't have one prepared, then I'll give one from the show that they can sight-read. After they sing, they read from the script, and that's it. I want to keep things moving so we aren't here all night, okay?"

"Okay," I say, but it's really not. My anxiety has returned, making it hard to concentrate. I barely slept last night.

You can do this. Just relax your shoulders, your neck, your hands. Take it one song at a time.

For the past three years playing tryouts, I've had fun trying to guess who would get cast for which parts. This year I feel totally lost. Sienna was right, the lead cast of *Sweeney Todd* is small. And people are rising to the challenge like crazy. Even the people who most of the time aren't great sound better than usual today.

Sienna is my first friend to come in. She launches into her song, and you'd never know she was close to yakking just twenty minutes ago. When she reads from the script, I 100 percent believe she's a murderous meat-pie-making matron from Fleet Street, not a high school junior from Nowhere, Illinois.

Madison comes in three people after. She glances nervously at me as she takes her place, then bows her head to get ready. She looks up again, nods, and we begin. I watch her as I play, envying how confident she seems, not just in this moment but about what she wants to do with her life. I'd give anything for even a crumb of that certainty. I thought Flossie would help. Instead, I'm more confused than ever, and now I'm fighting with my dad. Did Flossie fight with her father like this, and am I doomed to repeat her mistakes?

"Elaine?"

Mr. Ferrara's voice cuts through the music. I stop playing, my brain struggling to pull out of its spiral and decipher what's wrong.

What's wrong is that I've completely blanked out and played the same page of music twice. Madison stands in the center of the room, glaring at me.

"I'm so sorry." I scramble to find where we should be and give her two measures. She finishes strong. Her script reading is good too. But when she turns to leave—the speed of her walk, the straightness of her back—I can tell she's livid.

A minute later, Madison's archrival, Jasmine Yost, is striding in, and I have to squash the urge to run after my friend. We still have fifteen more people to go.

Be calm. Act professional. Don't let anyone know.

I've gotten so good at hiding how I feel that it isn't hard to put on my here-to-help smile. I take Jasmine's music. And when she nods that she's ready, I start to play.

❧

When auditions finally end, I dash outside to find the music wing deserted. I try calling Madison; she doesn't answer. Neither does Sienna. I text as I walk to the parking lot.

> Mads I'm so sorry—I did not mean to mess up like that.

When she doesn't answer, I switch to group chat.

> Guys I'm really really sorry. Mads you still did really good in there. Better than Jasmine, trust me on that.

This finally gets Sienna to text back.

> You always do this.

Those four words hit me like a slap in the face. As soon as I'm safe in my car, I pull up video chat. Sienna's face appears. She holds her phone up and I see she's sitting on Madison's bed, her other arm wrapped around Madison's shoulder.

"What do you want?" says Madison.

I didn't really expect them to get on, now I'm operating with a barely working filter.

"I want to know what Sienna meant, *You always do this.* What do I always do?"

"You always flake out on us." Madison glares at me, tears streaming down her face. "Something important is going on, and you're wrapped up in your own drama. We're always understanding, like *Elaine is busy, it's cool,* but this time you flaked out on something that's important to *me.* You ruined my audition!"

Before I can defend myself, she gets up and dashes out of frame. I hear her door slam across the room.

"Wow." My eyes and mouth are wide circles of shock in the corner of my phone screen. "You feel like that too?" I ask Sienna.

"Mads is angry," she says. "I'm not saying it's rational, but I get it. You don't understand the pressure we're under."

If I was shocked before, now I feel like I've landed on a whole other planet.

"You think I don't understand pressure? Wow, Sienna. If you really think that, then you don't know me at all."

Her shoulders come up in a way that says she's not sure how it could be any different.

"Maybe we would know you better if you weren't always going off, canceling plans. It's sort of hard to really know somebody when they're never fully around."

"It's not like I want to cancel," I tell her. "You have no idea how much I always hate doing that."

"Then stop."

"It's not that simple. And also, how hard would it be to try and include me if I can't be there? You and Madison assume I won't be around, and then you freeze me out."

I search her face, hoping to see some hint of softening. And maybe there's a glimmer. But then she says, "Sometimes it's just easier to assume you're not going to be part of something than have you be a no-show." Her phone pings. "That's Jaxon. I should go."

"Fine," I say. "I'll see you around."

Astrid's getting out of pom practice soon, so I pull around to the front of school and find her already waiting. When she gets in the car, she doesn't even nod hello. I'm used to her silences by now, but there's something about the way she sits, so still and defeated, that feels heavier, more serious.

"Did something happen with Quinn?" I ask. "Or Ella? Or Quinn *and* Ella?"

"I really don't want to talk about it," she snaps, and fine. It's fine. Literally, no one in my world is speaking to me, so maybe I should just enjoy the silence and figure out how to not care. I put on a playlist I made the last time I was in a really crappy mood, titled *Screw Everybody*, then I hit the road.

When we get home, Dad's left a note on the kitchen table: *Elaine—Called school and told them you'll be out on the 11th. Don't forget to get all missed schoolwork for the car ride. You don't want to fall behind.*

I throw the note in the trash. It's dinnertime, but Dad hasn't emerged from the office downstairs, and Astrid's locked herself in her room. I start opening cupboards, looking for something I can make, but we don't have anything simple enough for my beginner cooking skills, plus screw it—I'm not in the mood anyway.

I grab my keys and leave a note of my own: *Going to get pizza.*

❧

I've never seen Valentino's not full of people, probably because it's the one non-fast-food restaurant around that stays open past eight and doesn't treat teenagers like the devil's spawn. For a Tuesday night, it feels like the entire school is here.

As soon as I walk in, people start whispering.

"Ghost Girl . . ."

"Spirit Seekers . . ."

"Did you see . . ."

Snippets of conversations swirl around me as I make my way to the counter.

"I heard her and her boyfriend faked it all," someone says. "Her funeral home is tanking, so they're hyping this Gillies Ghost thing for attention. It's a scam."

I keep my eyes ahead of me, my mind on what I came here for.

Don't get mad. Just get your pizzas and get out of here.

The guy behind the counter stares at me, clueless.

"We never got your order," he says.

"Yes, you did," I tell him. "I called it in ten minutes ago, and I paid for it."

I show him the confirmation on my phone. He gives a shrug. I jut out my chin and widen my eyes like *Duh!*

"Maybe you could look for it?"

Now he looks annoyed. "Wait here a minute."

He wanders into the back. While he's gone, I play on my phone in an attempt to avoid the stares.

Keep calm. Losing your temper in the middle of a pizza parlor isn't a good look.

And then I see him: Quinn. He's sitting by the old jukebox with Carson Sauer, looking like he has zero worries in the world—like it's no big deal that my sister is completely depressed thanks to him.

Counter Guy comes back.

"So, it looks like we're going to have to make your pizzas," he says.

That's it. No apology. No estimate how long it will take. And now I'm screwed. I can either wait here with everyone looking at me or I can drive someplace else.

I don't want to go someplace else. I want pizza.

Pushing myself into a corner behind the gumball machines, I screw my eyes shut, willing the pressure in my chest to subside and the guy at the counter to call my name so I can get out of here before I blow.

When I open them again, Quinn is looking right at me. He's got a weird expression on his face, like guilt mixed with an over-confident sureness that I won't call him out. And that's what finally crushes my fears, my filters, my fight to keep inside the anger I've been smothering for so long. I raise my hand and wave.

"Hey, Quinn!"

He looks away.

Now that I've given it a taste of freedom, the anger inside me stretches and grows. It propels me across the room.

"Quinn! Hey!"

I'm standing over his table, looking down on his smug, guilty face.

"Hi?" he says.

"I hear you're dating my sister. Her name is Astrid in case you need a reminder."

"Um . . . okay." He's starting to squirm in his chair.

"So you *are* dating her?" I ask. "Or are you dating Ella Schmidt, because I heard that too."

"I don't think it's any of your business," says Carson, and no. Oh *hell* no. Quinn's friends do not get to be a part of this conversation. Other people are watching now, yet I don't care. The anger is like the beanstalk in that old fairy tale, shooting up out of control with me clinging to a leaf, along for the ride.

"I'm making it my business," I tell Carson. Then I lean over, locking eyes with Quinn. "You don't deserve my sister."

"You're crazy," he tells me.

"Really? I thought I was Ghost Girl."

"Um . . . Gillies?" The guy at the counter calls out. "Your order is ready."

I keep my eyes locked on Quinn's, letting three perfect beats go by before raising my hands and popping them open in his face.

"Boo!"

"Hey, Elaine."

It's Miles, carrying both my pizzas and a warning in his eyes: *Come with me NOW.*

I give Quinn one last death glare, then follow Miles to the door. When we're out on the sidewalk, I have to fight the urge to crush him in an enormous hug. I've missed him. And I'm still so, so angry.

"To what do I owe this honor?" I ask as I snatch away the pizza boxes. "Yesterday you made it clear you're done with me, so why are you suddenly giving a crap?"

"I don't know," he says. "I was here with some cross-country guys and you came in. Just then I felt like I should go get you. I was honestly afraid you might smash Quinn's nose in."

"Yeah, well, I'm angry. Is that not okay?"

"No. I mean yes. It's okay."

"Good. Not like I needed your permission."

"So, do you feel better?"

I lower myself to the curb, letting the boxes slide to the pavement.

"Honestly, no. Ever since Saturday night, it's been nothing but one awful thing after another. I knew there was a good reason to hate Halloween."

"Halloween would have been fine if it had stayed just Halloween. We were okay when we were getting candy."

He's not saying what I know he wants to say: that everything was good before we met up with Xander.

"It was definitely fine before the beer," I admit. "I can't remember huge chunks of the night, but I do remember being sick of my life. I didn't think I wanted to take over the business. I couldn't just come out and tell my parents that, so what if I ruined things to the point where there might not be any business to take over?"

Miles sits next to me and says, "Does that really sound like something you'd do?"

"I don't know anymore!" I bury my throbbing head in my arms. "I don't know who I am, I don't know what I want, and the worst part is that I screwed up everything with the people I thought I could count on to help me figure it out. Now I'm completely alone."

Tears slide down my cheeks, plopping to the concrete at my feet.

"Hey." He pulls me to him, and it feels so good. I rest my head on his chest, and for the first time since I don't know how long, I let myself relax.

"I'm sorry," he says. "I didn't mean to leave you alone. I just . . . things have been hard for me too."

"Then why don't you talk to me?" I ask. "I know you've been stressed out with the kittens and the baby pigs and school and all that . . . I want to help. Whatever is bothering you, you can tell me about it."

"See, I don't think I can."

"Why, Miles?"

"Because it's you. You're my problem."

I lift my head and study his face, the one I've known since grade school. He's the same old Miles, but there's something more in his expression now, something guarded.

"How am I your problem?"

He closes his eyes.

"When you said I sucked at hiding how I feel, I figured it was obvious. I feel like it's *been* obvious since maybe about seventh grade, but you somehow have never seemed to see it."

Warning lights start flashing in my head like some demented Christmas display.

"Miles, don't."

This "it" he's talking about: I did see. I saw it, and I felt it, and it scared me because this *it* is not supposed to be happening between us.

"I have to say this," he says. I can see myself reflected in the clear blue of his eyes, and even though I want to look away, I can't. "I have to tell you that I love you. I've tried to keep it inside for years now. And for the past whole month I was working up my courage to tell you. I've been feeling like things need to change."

"They don't."

"That's not what you said before."

Before I was talking about Pax and Skye—a science fiction show. Right now we're talking about real life. *My* life. And I've been counting on this part of my life—Miles and me as best friends—to stay the same.

"Miles, come on—"

"I have to at least try."

He reaches under my chin and tilts my face toward his. His fingers creep up to my cheek in the gentlest of caresses. His hand moves to the back of my neck, leaving an agonizing trail of warm tingles in its wake. Slowly, almost tentatively, he pulls me in until his lips find mine.

Oh my Lord. Who knew Miles could kiss like this? I bring my hands to his shoulders, feeling the contours of the muscles—the solid comfort there. He pulls me closer, kisses me deeper, and it's like someone pushed away a sky full of clouds to reveal a friendly sun that has been waiting to shine on me. Everything inside warms up, asking *Why in the world have we not been doing this all along?*

Louder than that is a voice screaming *Stop!*

I pull away.

"Miles, I can't do this. You and me, we want different things."

"You just said you don't know what you want."

"I don't. But . . ."

His arms, which had been around me, drop. His eyes, which had been full of hope, go stony.

"You don't know what you want, but you do know it's not me," he says. "Wow."

"How are you so sure I'm what *you* want?" I ask. Miles and I have always understood each other, or at least I thought we did. But there's no secret language for this. "You could meet someone amazing any day."

"*You* are amazing!" he says. "The way you laugh when you're surprised or freaked out. When you chew on your lip because you've trained yourself not to bite your nails. The way you can be so hilariously out-there and nobody else knows it . . . I love it all. I know you so well."

"But there's a whole other version of me that I'm trying to figure out, and maybe you won't like her. Maybe you won't *let* me be her. You're happy here; I want to leave. I'm *going* to leave."

He presses his lips together, his eyes glistening under the streetlight.

"So, you think I'd hold you back?"

Yes. I do. The comfort I feel with Miles, it's dangerous. Because even if he didn't mean to do it, he'd be a pull on me here. How do I know I'd be brave enough to leave if I have a reason like him to stay?

"Please." I grab his hand, desperate to make him understand. "You're my best friend."

"I can't be that anymore," he tells me.

The heartbreak in his voice wrenches my stomach into a ball of confusion and hurt. I feel like a part of me is getting ripped away.

"I can't be what you want me to be," I tell him. "And if you can't be what I need you to be, then what is there?"

"Nothing," he says.

"Right," I say as I let him go. "Nothing."

⚜

By the time I get home, the pizzas are cold discs of congealed cheese, and no one seems to care that dinner was missed. I put the pizzas on the counter, then go up to my room.

Walking away from Miles felt so final, yet all the way home I couldn't shake the feeling that there was something unfinished between us. The *Dragonfly* poster over my bed reminds me what it is.

I take out my phone.

> What about DraCon?

He texts me back.

> I'm not going.

I know I shouldn't be surprised. And yet it really hurts.

> Okay—I'll pay you back the fees and whatever else.

259

His last response lands with a thud.

Whatever.

My room is dark except for the streetlight spilling through the window. I go over and look out, at my front yard in this small town I've known all my life. Standing here, I feel like someone else is in the room with me—another version of myself from almost two centuries ago, gazing out the same window, feeling just as lonely and lost. But I can't look for her anymore—at least not tonight.

My eyes are raw. My head hurts, and my heart feels like it's been shredded into a million pieces. All I want to do is sleep. I get into bed, curl up beneath the covers, and let the darkness take me under.

CHAPTER THIRTY-THREE

"Elaine."

I open my eyes to see Mom sitting next to me. I glance at the clock by my bed and realize it's Thursday. For the past two days I've told Dad I was too sick for school; now I've lost track of time. I can't tell if it's morning or afternoon.

"Mom." My throat feels like I swallowed sandpaper. "When did you get home?"

"About an hour ago," she says.

I sit up, letting the room come into focus. Sometime between yesterday and today, I managed to put on a pair of sweatpants, but I'm still wearing the shirt I had on when I came home from Valentino's.

"Your dad says you haven't left this room since Tuesday night," Mom tells me.

"Not true. I came out to get food." I gesture at the granola bar wrappers littering the floor around my bed. She gives me a come-on look, and I get serious. "I can't go to school. And I can't show my face around here. Everybody's mad at me."

"Hiding out in bed isn't going to solve anything."

"But it feels good."

Actually, that's not true either. My body aches from inactivity. My brain is fuzzy from drifting in and out of half dreams. And when I think about all the schoolwork I'm going to have to catch up on, my head starts hurting all over again.

Mom turns on my light, then opens my window, letting in a blast of chilly air.

"Why don't you get up and come meet me in the family room? We got apple cider on our way into town. I'll put it on the stovetop with some butter."

The promise of my favorite cold-weather drink perks me up like nothing else has been able to until now. With it comes the realization of just how gross I am. The air from outside blows a whiff of myself to my nose.

"I'm going to take a shower first."

"Good idea," she says. "More time for the spices to mull."

Twenty minutes later, I come into the kitchen with clean hair and clothes, drawn by the scent of nutmeg, cinnamon, and apples. Mom hands me a mug. I take a sip, letting the cider and melted butter warm my soul. She sits on the couch in the family room and motions me to sit next to her.

"First, I want you to know we've worked things out with the Bohmers. We paid for all of their services and made a generous donation to Mr. Bohmer's Rotary scholarship fund. They've agreed to drop everything, and we're all moving on."

"That's good," I say as I stir my drink with a cinnamon stick.

She studies my face. "I thought you'd be happier."

Putting down my mug, I reach for the afghan we keep on the ottoman and wrap it around myself.

"I'm happy we're not getting sued. Please don't get me wrong. It's, just, Mr. Bohmer is like problem two hundred seven of the million problems I have right now." I don't know how to even start explaining the past week to my mom, but I do know, all of a sudden, what could help. "I think I need to get away."

"Weren't you and your dad planning a trip for next weekend?"

So she and my father just spent three hours together in a car, and he conveniently neglected to mention the massive fight we had three nights ago. Great.

"That's problem number two hundred eight," I tell her. "Dad wants me to go to Cincinnati to visit mortuary schools. But I'd already planned to go somewhere else—somewhere that's important to me."

Mom sighs; she's starting to get the picture. "Go on."

"Miles and I were going to go to Chicago for the *Dragonfly* convention. This actor Miles loves is going to be there, but it's the same time Dad wants me to go with him." I pause to pull in a hiccupping breath. "I know I shouldn't be asking to go anywhere after everything that's happened, but it sort of feels like this is all I have left."

She sits quietly, sipping her own mug of cider. Outside the door that leads to the back deck, fat white snowflakes have started coming down.

"We've been so centered on the business that we've put too much pressure on you," she finally says. "But once your dad makes up his mind about something, it can take a near act of God to change it."

"I know."

"You say this convention is next week?"

"Saturday and Sunday. But most of the hotels are probably booked by now."

"So we'll look into Airbnbs. I'm sure we can find something."

I catch my lip between my teeth, barely daring to hope.

"You mean I can go?"

"If I go too," she says. "That's the stipulation. I won't embarrass you and Miles too much, I promise."

"Except Miles isn't going." I swipe my nose with my sleeve; the sound of his name has made me weepy again. "We sort of aren't friends or . . . anything anymore."

"Oh, Elaine. How much more drama is there with you right now?"

"Infinite amounts, Mom. My life is pretty much a bottomless pit of drama."

She sighs again. "All the more reason to get out of town."

I feel a smile stretch across my slimy, tear-stained cheeks. It sounds nice to go someplace with this new, understanding version of my mom.

"Are you sure?" I ask.

She reaches out to squeeze my hand.

"I'm not sure about anything. But being someplace that has nothing to do with business or sick family sounds like heaven right about now. What?" She frowns. "You still look worried."

The moment of happiness I'd just found is starting to crumble under the weight of what I know I'm going to have to pay for it.

"Dad is already mad at me. He's going to literally hate me now."

Mom's jaw sets and her eyes go steely with determination.

"Let me deal with him," she says. "Whatever happens in the next few days or weeks, we'll sort it out. Right now, I think you need to focus on you."

❧

"Some of these costumes are really beautiful," Mom says. "I have no idea who any of the characters are, but the creativity is amazing."

We're standing in line at the convention center, waiting to get our badges and surrounded by *Dragonfly* fans. An otherworldly Spirit of Light floats by in a costume that must have taken dozens of hours to make. A Night Queen waits at the hot dog stand wearing truly terrifying makeup, while a group of German-speaking girls goes by in gossamer dragonfly wings.

People who aren't in costume are wearing *Dragonfly* gear. Sweatshirts with logos peek from underneath winter coats. One guy wears a water-lily tank top and silver hot pants with nothing else but thigh-high boots in the freezing Chicago weather.

I almost wish I hadn't decided to leave my Skye costume at home. Wearing it reminded me of Halloween, which reminded me of everything that came after, so the wig and army jacket stayed hung up in my closet. Instead, I've got on a long-sleeved tee with a water lily across the breast, a black short skirt, and black tights. I'll save the cosplay for if I ever come back.

Right now, I never want to leave. If the first few days after *Mr. Bohmer and the Bottle* were a blur of drama, then the week leading up to now was an awkward slog that felt like it would never end. Madison and Sienna kind-of-sort-of decided not to freeze me out after they both made *Sweeney Todd* callbacks, but the final cast list goes up any day now, and if Madison doesn't get a good part, then I'm pretty sure the breakup between them and me will become official.

Speaking of breakups, Xander has only gotten more popular thanks to his Flossie photos and video. And Miles and I haven't spoken at all, except when I texted to let him know I was still going to Chicago.

He responded, **OK**. And that was all.

Now, when the guy at the counter hands me Miles's badge and Mom puts it around her neck, I push aside the guilty feeling and tell myself he could have come if he'd wanted.

It was his decision to skip out, says the reasonable voice in my head.

Yeah . . . , says the more emotional side. *But it still sucks.*

Mom's phone rings as we're stepping out of line.

"We stopped at the hotel, now we're at the convention center," I hear her telling Dad. "Oh goodness, I sent an invoice for the Mossell casket yesterday, did they not get it?"

She raises an eyebrow, asking if I want to say hi. I shake my head. My father's Disappointed Dad formality has been off the charts; the last thing I want is to try having a conversation while I'm at one of the reasons he's disappointed in the first place.

"Give him time," Mom whispers when she hangs up. "This is hard for him."

And I hate being the reason something is hard. More than once I almost changed my mind about Chicago. I almost told Dad I'd go to Cincinnati instead, but then talked myself out of it. Something deep inside told me I'd probably never get this chance again.

"Whoa . . ." I suck in a gasp. Positioned at the entrance to the expo hall is a giant poster with a bigger-than-life photo advertising tomorrow's panel with Magnus. Knowing I'm actually in the same city as the person I've been watching all these years gives me a massive thrill; I snap a photo and catch myself before sending it to Miles.

Inside the expo, we wander through a wonderland of *Dragonfly* merch and memorabilia. I see a T-shirt I know Miles would love and almost forget he isn't here to drool over the limited-edition posters, the figurines, and the handcrafted jewelry. Mom nods appreciatively at every trinket, but it's not the same. I buy a key ring for myself, plus an enamel Pax-and-Skye pin that I slip into my pocket rather than wear. It feels wrong somehow to put it on without Miles.

It's not just the stuff that captivates me, it's the people, too. Every person I see could be someone I talk to on the fan boards, or someone whose fanart or fiction I've admired. A girl bumps into me wearing a tee with a joke only hard-core fans would get, and when I tell her, "Love your shirt," the smiles that pass between us are filled with all sorts of shared things.

Then why do I feel so alone?

At first the feeling is an ache that gooses me every time I catch myself turning to show Miles a cool souvenir or point out an especially great cosplay. As time passes, it gets more hollow—a knowledge that the people I love back home will someday be a part of my past, while my future is filled with vast amounts of strangers.

But maybe it doesn't have to be that way. Madison and Sienna and I, if we want to stay friends then we should be able to. It'll take work, though; I can't just expect them to keep me in their world if I'm not going to make an effort to stay there too. Sienna was right, I have to do better.

"I'm getting hungry," Mom says. "Let's go find some deep-dish pizza."

The sun's almost down when we reemerge outside. The vast backdrop of the Chicago skyline illuminates the sidewalk, and I pick up my stride, blending in with the people who don't see the wonder in the looming skyscrapers, the chaos in the street.

A bunch of guys on electric scooters whiz past the intersection, making me hang back. I get to the corner just as the light changes. Mom wades through the stopped cars, ignoring a man who shouts at her from a taxi, while I scramble to keep up, feeling every bit the small-town girl that I am.

"You still with me?" she calls.

"Just trying not to get run over," I say, flinching when a delivery truck blares its horn at me.

Mom follows her phone to a pizza parlor, and we duck inside. No one looks up when we enter; everyone has their own story to focus on. I could create a new life in a city like this—someplace with no expectations or assumptions about who I am or what I'll do. The distance between me and here is just a few steps and a hundred miles. I can see it. I can feel it. For the first time, I'm not just dreaming of something in some vague someday. For the first time, I know.

I really could go anywhere.

CHAPTER THIRTY-FOUR

Anticipation wakes me up early the next morning. Today's the day—the panel with Magnus!

I pull out my phone, expecting a string of crazy-excited messages from Miles. In these first few minutes of consciousness, the reality of our new non-relationship hasn't clicked into place.

From the fan boards to Twitter to TikTok, people are chattering about the panel. I've even got a text from Saidah in Kansas City, who we connected with at a virtual watch party for last year's season finale. But there's nothing from Miles.

There is, however, something from Xander.

I know I shouldn't open it. I don't know why I do. Maybe because, in this hotel room in the middle of a massive city, I'm conversing with people from literally all over the world. *So what's one little message from Dodson?*

I tap the green bubble and a photo fills the screen: me at Halloween peering out through Skye with pink hair cascading over one of my black-rimmed eyes. Underneath the photo is a text.

You said I only wanted you so I could investigate at your house. That's not true. This is the reason I wanted you. You're smart and beautiful and you're going to go places. I sort of wish you'd go places with me. I know I've screwed up in massive ways, but this thing between us was real. It is real. If you gave me a second chance it would mean more than you'll ever know. I hope Chicago is great. I miss you.

I toss my phone to the foot of the bed and cover my eyes. I told the little winged hearts to go flutter around someone else's head. I took that floaty feeling I always get around Xander and slammed it into a trunk that I've kept shut tight for the past two weeks. Now he's trying to nudge open the lid. The fact that it's budged, even the tiniest bit, is proof I didn't close it tight enough. I remind myself to think about his actions, not his words: the way he put Flossie out into the world and what happened as a result; the idea that it might have been him who planted the beer bottle on Mr. Bohmer. Xander is bad news; I know it.

But then there are those photos—the ones that make me look confident and fearless. And those eyes. And that brown-sugar mole . . .

Quit it. Just stop right now. I can't let Xander tempt me anymore. I have to be strong.

"Are you awake?" Mom comes in carrying a to-go tray of coffee and a bag of something warm and sweet-smelling. "There's a bakery down the street, so I walked over and got breakfast."

My stomach growls as I take a doughnut from the bag and a cup of hot coffee from Mom. She sits next to me on the bed, looking pretty in jeans and a sweater. Usually she wears skirts or suits be-cause she's always out in the community representing the business. It's nice to see her relaxed.

"I forget how much I love this city," she says. "When I was fin-ishing college, I had a chance to come here for an internship, but it didn't work out."

"You could have gone anywhere," I tell her. "What made you want to go to the middle of nowhere and live in a funeral home?"

She smiles as she adds sugar to her drink. "I guess the short an-swer is that life takes you all sorts of unexpected places."

"Not for me if I take over the business. The only place life will be taking me is straight back to Dodson."

I swirl my coffee in its paper cup, remembering when I drank from the nursing home's finest china and talked with Xander about escape. We agreed being trapped was one of the worst things that could happen to a person. He told me to break free. Somehow, I en-visioned freedom coming with a side of clarity. I imagined it being a lot less messy.

Mom pulls apart a croissant. She puts a piece in her mouth and chews thoughtfully. "One thing's for sure, this whole thing would be a lot easier if you and your father weren't so much alike."

This makes me do an actual double take.

"Alike how? Dad never doubts anything. He loves being a funeral director."

"You don't know him as well as you think you do," she says. "There are so many things he wants to say that he doesn't. Times when he puts on a smile because it's what someone wants or needs to see. I'm almost nervous to think about how the transition would go if you did take over—two pressure-cooker personalities trying to work together could blow up in everyone's faces."

"But if I don't do it, will we have to close?"

"Oh, honey, I don't know." She puts down her croissant, looking at me with care and concern. "And I don't want to put that on your shoulders. The business was changing even before your dad started his career, but he felt called to do it."

"See, I have no idea what that feels like," I tell her. "I don't know what I want to do next month let alone in the next ten years."

"You don't have to know."

"Yes, I do if I'm going to mortuary school. If I do that, then I'm saying I've chosen."

One thing I love and hate about my mom is that she never denies when something is hard. I'm right and she knows it. Pretty soon, I'll have to make a decision.

She points to the doughnut I've been neglecting, reminding me I need to get moving. I gobble down half, then pull myself out of bed. Right now, the only thing I have to decide is what to wear for the panel.

"Thanks for breakfast, Mom. I'm going to go get in the shower; I want to be there when they open the doors so nobody steals my seat."

※

"I heard Magnus is chronically late because he counts the Jolly Ranchers in his dressing room, and if there aren't exactly twenty-three watermelon and twenty-four blueberry, he throws a fit."

I'm sitting in my assigned panel seat, listening to none other than Nelson showing off for his followers in the row directly ahead of me. He looks just as dorky in person as he is online, and he sounds ten times more pompous. People are either hanging on his every word or giving him major side-eye.

I might not believe Nelson's explanation for why Magnus is late, but Magnus has definitely kept us waiting. Fifteen minutes have passed since the doors opened and people rushed to their seats. Next to me sits one of the German girls we saw yesterday. Mom spotted the group of them again this morning and offered her ticket—the one that should have belonged to Miles.

"I won't appreciate it nearly as much as you will," she said. The girls drew straws, and now I'm accompanied by Franziska, who doesn't need to speak English to tell me how excited she is. I know because I'm right there with her.

Butterflies keep fluttering into my chest, making me unsure whether to burst out giggling or run for the nearest trash can to puke. Miles would have taken my mind off the jitters. He'd be doing goofy impressions, telling dumb stories—anything to make the time go faster. He also would definitely be telling Nelson what an ass he is. But since Miles isn't here, I'm left staring at the stage with its two empty chairs, listening to *Dragonfly*'s most annoying fanboy run his mouth. The event is being livestreamed, so I have no idea how many eyes are actually on this ballroom. Miles could be among them, though. He wouldn't miss it.

We've just hit the twenty-minute waiting mark when a guy in high-water jeans bounds onto the stage. He tells us he's James from *Fandom Today*, he's excited to be here, *blah blah blah* . . . I blink while James blabbers, and suddenly there he is: Magnus Tiedemann. In the same room as me. This is really happening.

Magnus-as-Pax is tall with blue-tipped brown hair, and he speaks like someone who grew up in New Jersey. Real-life Magnus is shorter than I'd expected, with a shaggy blond mullet and the slightest Dutch accent. *Fandom Today* James shakes his hand, then turns back to the crowd.

"We're here to celebrate the influence *Dragonfly* has around the world," he says. "An influence so powerful that the recent episode featuring the death of Pax was the most tweeted about event in the show's history."

I dip my head, stifling a laugh because I can hear Miles snorting in the back of my mind. James is talking like this is the Nobel Peace Prize, not a fan panel for an over-the-top sci-fi show. At least Magnus seems to appreciate how campy *Dragonfly* is. When James finally allows him to speak, he gives an almost sheepish smile.

"Let's just say I'm floored that all of you care so much about me," he says. "Maybe I need to get out more."

The crowd screams approval. Magnus smiles again. He doesn't seem at all like the kind of guy who'd throw a fit over Jolly Ranchers.

"*Dragonfly* has been my life for the past six years," he says. "And believe me, I know how much I owe the fans. I don't do many events, but I felt like this one was important, especially given recent story developments."

James and Magnus sit and start their discussion. James asks whether Pax is really dead; Magnus diplomatically refuses to answer. They talk about Magnus's background, about what it's like to work on the show, about the other actors. And then the organizers fan out, selecting people to ask questions. Some actually have questions to ask. Others just want to talk. Overwhelmingly, what they want to talk about is the meaning behind Pax's death. There are so many theories and angles, but all of them are missing one element. I wait for someone to bring it up. Finally, I lift my hand.

Don't chicken out. They might not even call on you, so stay calm and see what happens.

Someone puts a microphone in my face.

"Um . . ." I test out my voice, hoping it's not too loud. "Hi, Magnus. I'm Elaine. My friend Miles and I have been watching *Dragonfly* since it started, and I'm not hearing anybody talk about what all this means for Skye. They're two parts of a whole—or at least they were supposed to be. I don't think we can talk about what happens to Pax without talking about her too."

"That's an excellent point," Magnus says. He sits forward. "What do you think this means for Skye?"

It's hard trying to condense everything I've been thinking into a couple of simple sentences, but I go for it anyway.

"I think she's going to have to figure out who she is alone. But maybe that's necessary? I don't know where the show is taking this whole thing, but maybe she needs to be on her own. And maybe, even though it's painful, it's something that has to happen for things to keep progressing."

"I can't give away any spoilers, obviously," Magnus says. "But I'm pretty sure you're onto something."

The microphone is still in my face, so I keep talking.

"I thought it was pretty obvious all season that they were planting hints something like this was coming. And I told Miles I thought things were going to have to change. He didn't want to believe it, but then he can always see the good in a situation. He sort of balances me out when I get too pessimistic, and usually I'm not pessimistic with him because we both get how hilariously weird this show is. But in this case, I knew I was right. We had this whole fight about it, and now I'm not sure what to do because, even though I want Skye to be able to progress on her own, I don't want her to lose what she had with Pax. The whole thing is in uncharted territory now, and that's scary, you know?"

I realize I've been blabbing. I also realize that it sounds like I'm talking about more than just a TV show. Suddenly I'm back in Miles's truck, in my pink wig and army jacket, sitting next to him in that trench coat with his eyes smudged black and his hair spiked up in that alarmingly hot way that made me feel flustered like I'd never experienced with him before. And I'm sitting on the curb outside Valentino's, feeling the comfort of his arms around me, the surprise when he kissed me. I didn't want to admit how right it felt, like the runes on Skye's hands matching the seal on Pax's heart. I'd insisted Skye didn't love Pax, but is it possible Elaine does love Miles?

"I don't see anyone with you," *Fandom Today* James says from the stage. "Did Miles not come?"

"He wanted to. We just . . ." I can't stop stammering. "I mean *he* just . . . he couldn't make it."

"I see," Magnus says with a smile.

"But he's your biggest fan. Seriously. He should be here."

"It does look that way, doesn't it?" Magnus's smile deepens. "Well, if he's not watching from home right now, then tell Miles I said hi."

The microphone moves away; James and Magnus move on, and soon the panel is ending. Magnus's bodyguards whisk him out of the room as people swarm the stage. Many of the ones who don't are staring at me, whispering. Nelson even looks like he might be about to come over. I start pushing through the crowd, frantic to get out, when I feel a tap on my shoulder. I turn, ready to tell Nelson where to shove whatever stupid comment he's about to lay on me, but it's not Nelson, it's one of the panel organizers.

"Magnus asked me to give you this," she says. "For Miles."

She hands me a bag, and when I look inside, I know I really need to get out of here before anyone around me sees.

Inside the bag are Pax's spectacles. And from the worn look of them, these aren't one of the replicas you can buy out in the expo hall. I am holding one of the signature props from the show.

Clutching the bag to my chest, I hurry out to the main concourse, looking for Mom. I find her with her phone in her hands, looking stricken.

"Elaine," she says. "I have terrible news. There was a car accident last night. Miles and your friend Xander are in the hospital."

CHAPTER THIRTY-FIVE

"Why, why, *why* can't I get hold of anybody?"

Screaming through my teeth, I check my texts for the hundredth time in case I missed a message, but there's nothing. Nothing from Sienna. Nothing from Madison. Nothing from Miles or Xander. I've called them. I've texted. I've DMed on every possible app, and it's like they've vanished from the face of the earth.

"Maybe the signal's bad out here." Mom takes her eyes off the road to give me a reassuring knee squeeze. "I'm sure someone will get in touch as soon as they can."

"But what if they can't? What if it's really serious? It would have to be really serious for them to go completely silent, right?" I wince as my teeth graze a raw spot on my chewed-up lip. "How much farther?"

"About fifty miles," she says. "I'm driving as fast as I can."

I continue texting everybody I know. I check their social media and the social media of everybody *they* know. I refresh and refresh the *Daily*'s website looking for any tiny detail about what happened.

All I can find is that the crash occurred around midnight at the market stand on Devil's Backbone. The other driver ran the stop sign and hit the back of Miles's truck. That person was taken to the ER, then released. And two of the people in the truck were admitted to the hospital with injuries that aren't considered life-threatening, which doesn't ease my mind since "not life-threatening" could mean anything from bumps and bruises to irreversibly paralyzed. Speed was a factor, but they don't suspect alcohol or drugs.

My best source of information turns out to be Astrid. Some of her porn friends were at a bonfire last night at the quarry, and they're saying Miles was headed there. Astrid texts that Sienna was in the truck too. And while she doesn't think Sienna was hurt, she doesn't know why she wouldn't be answering her phone.

> Maybe she's at the hospital? When Sophia got her tonsils out she said the wifi is crap in there.

I put my phone down, giving my eyes a break while my brain cells continue their lightning storm inside my head. I've chewed my lip bloody and started in on my nails. Screw it. If anything excuses going back to an old habit, it's not being able to reach your friends who could have been maimed in a horrific car crash.

Now that I know the outline of what happened, I have more questions. First, why was Miles with Xander? Somehow I can't see them being Saturday-night-party buddies anymore.

Second, if Miles was driving to the quarry, why would he be on Devil's Backbone? The quarry is nowhere near there.

And if Miles was in the hospital this morning, did he see the panel with Magnus?

For a minute I hope he didn't. I don't remember exactly what I said, but I know it was pretty personal. Would he be mad I said it in front of all those people? Would it make things even more confusing between us?

Right now I don't care. I just want to know he's okay.

I send him another text.

> WTF is going on? Are you OK?! What happened, and where is everyone? I'm going crazy not being able to reach you please answer your phone!!!!!

Wow, that escalated quickly. I take a deep breath and try again.

> Miles. I'm worried and I miss you and I'm on my way home. Please be OK.

I send this one, not expecting an answer. Then, my phone buzzes with that repetitive pattern that means someone is actually calling. The name lighting up the screen isn't Miles; it's Xander.

"Xander?" I turn in my seat so it won't be as easy for my mom to hear. "What happened? Where are you?"

"At home," he says. "They let me out of the hospital about an hour ago."

I let my head fall back against the car seat, letting a little stress go, because if he's home, then maybe things aren't so bad. He sounds tired, but nowhere near death.

"What's going on?" I press. "Are you okay?"

"I broke my arm and my face is banged up, but when I think about how it could have been, I will take this and freaking gladly."

"What about Miles?"

"I think he's okay too. I couldn't find out much. I think they want to keep him there another night."

"Oh God." If he's staying longer, things must not be totally all right.

"Really, Elaine, it's so much better than it could have been," Xander reassures me. "We got hit hard, but it was in the back of the truck. We spun around, and it was seriously a miracle we didn't flip. For a minute I thought we were going to be three more crosses out on that road."

"But what were you *doing*?" All of my questions need answers *now.* "Why were you even there to start with?"

"I'll explain when I see you," he says. "*When* can I see you?"

"I'm going to the hospital. Then I need to get home."

"What about tomorrow at school?"

His intensity scares me—almost as much as the way my pulse jumps at the thought of those bottomless brown eyes. He's pushing hard at the lid of that trunk I'd slammed shut. Once I let it open, all the things I jammed inside will be impossible to put back.

Remember what you promised yourself: None of the bad stuff would have happened if it wasn't for Xander. Someone who could mess with your family's business like that isn't someone you can trust.

"I'll be at school," I tell him. "And you can see me there if you want, but I don't think it's a good idea for us to talk."

"I just want to . . ."

"I need space and it's too soon." I bring a hand to my mouth, searching for a remnant of fingernail to bite before clenching my fist and shoving it into my lap. "I'm really sorry about the accident, Xander, but I can't let you in anymore. I meant what I said. It's over."

Besides the day I was born, I've never been inside the hospital. I know I'm lucky—no broken bones, no appendix needing to be removed, I've never even needed stitches. And so, because I am a hospital virgin, it's only natural that a hospital would freak me out.

At least that's what I tell myself when I step inside the lobby and immediately want to cry.

The sterile in-between of the place, the smell of best efforts and things that must be endured for people to get better, makes me well up. I think about Miles in one of these rooms, and about the people who only leave when someone like Dakota or my dad comes to fetch them. I don't know what I'd do if Miles was one of those people.

"Elaine!"

Sienna is rushing over, a slight limp slowing her down. Jaxon stands nearby, looking ready to defend his girlfriend against anything, man or machine, that could try and hurt her again. I meet her halfway and pull her into my arms.

"Sienna, I'm so, so sorry. I haven't been there for you and Mads, and I wasn't here for you this time either, and I'm going to do better from now on, I swear."

I have no idea where that apology came from; it just started pouring out, and now Sienna's crying too, and I'm sure we look like a soggy, tragic mess together, but I don't care. I'm so happy to see her.

"I've been trying to call you! Why didn't you answer?"

"I don't know where my phone is," she says, sniffling. "It flew out of my hands when we crashed, now it's somewhere in Miles's truck. The police wouldn't let me go back and look for it."

"But you're okay?" I hold her at arm's length for an inspection.

"I have a bruise on my shoulder from the seat belt," she says. "And my knee feels like somebody hit it with a sledgehammer, but I walked away. Xander and Miles got it worse."

Terror. For the hundredth time in the past five hours, I'm gripped by this fear of what I'm going to find out.

"Is Miles still here?" I ask.

"He has a concussion. I think the doctors want to observe him some more before they let him go home."

Tears come faster now, mixing relief with lingering worry. Miles isn't paralyzed or in a coma, which means my worst fears aren't coming true. Still, I won't truly feel better until I see him myself. While Mom goes to the front desk to find out where we need to be, Sienna brings me over to where she and Jaxon have been sitting. She offers a drink of her Coke; I'm so thirsty my voice rasps.

"Tell me everything. Astrid said there was a bonfire at the quarry. But if you were going there, then why were you at the Backbone?"

"We went to the homestead first," Sienna says. "Miles was taking me because Jaxon had an away game and Madison didn't want to go. Xander started texting around for a ride, and I told Miles we should give him one. Then when we picked him up, he was all obsessed with getting to the homestead. He wanted to get a better shot of that misty thing he got a picture of in the barn on Halloween."

I'm squinting, trying to make sense of what she's telling me.

"And Miles took him?" It's unimaginable to me that this could be true.

"Only because I said I wanted to go to the homestead too. But now I wish I hadn't." Sienna's eyes widen. "Elaine, he was beyond obsessed. You know how he can be intense sometimes."

I shiver, remembering the sound of his voice, the dark of his eyes. "Yeah, I do."

"Well, this was way worse. When we got there, a bunch of older guys were smoking weed and shooting beer cans off the gravestones. Xander totally chewed them out, saying they were being disrespectful and ruining things for everybody else. I was seriously afraid *we* might get shot. But that's not what really freaked me out. The whole time he was investigating, he kept saying what he had wasn't good enough. He was getting super upset about it, and Miles and I finally had to drag him away."

"Dude has a problem," says Jaxon.

"I know you don't want to talk to him, but maybe you should. Hey," Sienna forces me to look her in the eye. "Are *you* okay?"

My face is probably a soup of different emotions as each new feeling contradicts the previous one. I miss Xander, but I just told him I didn't want to see him. I want to know why he'd get so mad at stoners shooting beer cans, but I don't want to admit I might have been wrong accusing him of vandalism. And I really don't want to do any more ghost hunting, but I can't stop thinking about Flossie—especially after what my mom said about Dad and me being alike. Is there any chance Xander could help me reach her still?

And what about Miles? This morning seems so long ago, sitting in the panel at DraCon, realizing how much he means to me. Before I do or think about anything or anyone else, I need to see him.

❧

A nurse leads Mom and me to a place where the staff look more serious and the people in the waiting room look more tense. Miles's parents are sitting in the corner with the remnants of a take-out lunch in front of them. They rush over when they see us.

"Lainey!" Mrs. Drummond pulls me to her as if I were one of her own kids. I can feel her heartbeat through her blouse, and over her shoulder I see leftover panic lighting up Mr. Drummond's eyes.

"The kids said you were out of town," he tells me. "I hope you didn't leave something important to come back here."

"There's no way I wouldn't get back as soon as I could. Can I see Miles?"

"He's sleeping," his mom says. "And they're trying to limit traffic in and out of the rooms, so they're only letting family back there."

"Oh . . ." My shoulders slump; I feel like crying all over again.

"But he'll be home tonight or tomorrow," Mr. Drummond adds. He gives me a reassuring dad pat. "It'll be all right, Lainey. He'll be happy knowing you were here."

Looking around, I realize someone is missing.

"Where's Madison?"

"Getting some air." Mrs. Drummond points down the hall to a bank of windows looking out on a garden. "You should say hi. She'll be glad to see you."

"Go on," Mom tells me. "I'm going to stay and chat for a few more minutes. I'll come get you when it's time to go."

Outside, I find Madison on a bench alone. She looks so still and small. All this time we've been friends, I never realized how much of a presence her twin brother was—until now, when I see her without him.

"Hey." I sit beside her. "You okay?"

She shrugs.

"I'm sorry I wasn't here when this happened. You guys were right that I bug out too much. I already told Sienna I'll do better, and I will."

She nods.

"It sounds like Miles is going to be fine, so that's good, right? Maybe he'll go home tomorrow, then we can all give him crap about his driving skills. I know that's one of your favorite topics."

She smiles the tiniest smile, but she still doesn't speak. I take the spectacles Magnus gave me out of my bag and place them in her lap.

"Can you give him this?" I ask. "There's a lot of *Dragonfly* stuff tied up in it and I know how much you hate that, but I think having it would cheer him up."

She nods again, her shoulders starting to shake.

"Oh no!" I wrap my arms around her. "I know it's scary what happened, but everything's going to be okay!"

"I'm just really sorry too," she sobs. "I've been awful."

"If this is about the musical, forget it. You were right, I was obsessed with my own problems, and I didn't pay attention and that wasn't fair to you."

"No, I mean the beer bottle. I'm the one who put it in the casket."

I drop my arms, not sure I heard her correctly.

"*You* did it? Why?"

"I don't know." She covers her face with her hands. "I was just so mad. I was sick of tagging along with Jaxon and Sienna, and then you and Miles . . . And the more I drank, the madder I got that I'm always the one who follows the rules. You all think it's funny, but maybe I'm tired of being the mom in the group, you know? I sort of wished I'd get caught and get in trouble; then maybe you guys would look at me some other way. Or maybe Miles would get blamed, and people wouldn't think he was so funny anymore. But it turned into such a mess. You can tell your dad it was me."

With her delicate features hiding behind those small, pretty hands, it's impossible to picture Madison creeping through my basement, slipping into a forbidden room. But I get it, if not exactly what she did, then the desire to be a completely different person. I also see how easy it's been to look at Miles and Madison as a unit. *Sometimes siblings have secrets,* he told me once. We all assumed we knew her, and we were wrong.

Then there was me, assuming Xander could have planted the beer bottle on Mr. Bohmer. I was wrong about that too.

What else was I wrong about?

"My dad doesn't need to know who did it," I say.

Madison peeks through her fingers. "Are you sure?"

If she only knew half of what's been going on at my house, she'd feel better about the bottle. I want her to feel better; I know how terrible that guilt can be.

"Mr. Bohmer was only part of the story," I tell her. "Dad was going to be mad at me eventually. That just sort of provided the warm-up."

She nods, tracing the shape of Pax's spectacles with her finger.

"I'm always jealous of how you and Miles are together. It's like you're this genius mind meld with all your *Dragonfly* stuff. You call him instead of me about the important things. And Sienna is this amazing singer who's definitely getting a lead in *Sweeney Todd,* and she'll get into whatever school she wants, too, no problem. I feel so nothing next to all of you."

"You are *not* nothing," I say, hugging harder than ever. "And this musical is just a blip on the screen. If you don't get a lead this year, you'll be a lock for the lead in whatever they do next year. After that, you can get out of this place and be your amazing self somewhere that really appreciates your amazingness."

This earns me a genuine laugh.

"That'll be nice." She rests her head on my shoulder. "I'll miss you guys, though."

And that's what starts me crying all over again, hearing someone else say what I've known was coming all this time.

"I know," I tell her. "I'll miss you too."

CHAPTER THIRTY-SIX

The business line is ringing when we get home.

"Oh goodness, what now?" Mom says in her wine-o-clock voice. "It's supposed to be dinnertime."

She picks up and immediately looks confused. Dad comes into the room as she's saying, "Una momento. No hablo española."

Dad turns to me and says, "Run get Dakota."

I find him in the foyer, switching out the flowers we keep under Great-Great-Great-Grandfather Leathan's portrait.

"Hey . . . um . . ." I don't know how to speak to Dakota after everything that's happened. I owe him such massive apologies that it's impossible to figure out where to start. I take the old flowers from his hands. "Mom and Dad need you on the business line. Please. I'll throw these away."

Except I don't. I eavesdrop as he picks up the phone in the office. He listens for a second, then says, "Hola, buenas tardes. Me llamo Dakota y hablo español. Estoy aquí para ayudarles."

He continues conversing in fluent Spanish. I recognize a few words from my Spanish class at school, but it's embarrassing how little I understand. Dakota laughs, he reassures, he sounds confident and in control—like a real funeral director, even if I only get a fraction of what comes out of his mouth.

He emerges from the office and looks surprised to still see me there.

"Tell your dad it's taken care of," he says. "The Larretas are coming tomorrow at eleven to make arrangements for their mother. I'm putting it on the schedule so I can be there to translate."

I realize I still have a handful of wilted flowers. I shove them behind my back and say, "I didn't know you spoke Spanish."

"I speak Mandarin, too. Nowhere near fluent, but I can carry on a fairly decent conversation if needed."

"That's really great. It was a huge help to Mom and Dad."

He holds out his hand, waggling his fingers. Blushing, I give him the still-dripping stems.

"Your parents are going to need more help soon," he says. "This community is getting an influx of Latinx families. You haven't noticed?"

Our community hasn't ever been that diverse, but now I realize I have seen more people at school who look different from me. I hadn't thought about it much. Apparently, I should have.

"These small towns are changing faster than you think," Dakota continues. "If you really want to serve the community, you're going to have to broaden your cultural literacy."

I know he's right; it's one more way my parents have assumed things would stay the way they've been for so long. They don't mean to exclude anyone, but that's not an excuse.

Dakota moves past me to the back room to toss the flowers. The conversation could end here, except ending it now will only move the things I need to say to another time. It might be easier for a moment, but anxiety will turn every unsaid thing into a spiral until I get it off my conscience.

"I know things haven't been that good for you," I begin. "Mostly because of me, and I don't even know how to say I'm sorry enough times to make anything better." He doesn't disagree. He just stands quietly, letting me go on. "You probably wish you could be someplace else. I know I would if I was you."

Dakota crosses his arms as he leans against the door frame.

"Can I be honest with you?" he says.

"Yes." I'm about to get shredded. He's going to tell me just how terrible I am, which I totally deserve. I put on my best I'm-listening smile. At the very least, I owe him that.

"Memories did invite me for an interview," he says. "And I thought why not hear what they had to say? I'll have to find a job soon anyway. We agreed I'm not a good fit for them. However, I did meet someone who might be a good fit for me."

"You're dating someone from over there?"

"He's their office manager. It's only been a few weeks, but so far it's really good."

Him. Oh.

"That's great, Dakota," I say. "But why are you acting like you need to hide it?"

The corner of his mouth quirks in a way that says he thinks my idealism is cute.

"This is still a small town," he says. "And I don't know if things are changing *that* much. Also, who knows where I'll be next year or after that? If I don't stay here at Gillies, there aren't a lot of other options in this area. Memories is looking for freelance embalmers. At those corporate homes, it's not uncommon that the funeral director doesn't prepare the bodies, and that personal touch is something I really believe in. I don't want to freelance, I want to run my own business."

"Maybe you can take over this one," I suggest.

"I don't know if I'm the right fit here, either."

"Same."

He undoes the top buttons of his dress shirt, revealing the MORE SCI LESS FI T-shirt underneath, and gives me the realest real-talk look I've ever seen.

"I get that there's a lot of family tradition involved here, but you of all people should know this profession isn't something you should do unless you really want to."

"Was it something you always wanted to do?" I ask.

"No. But I'm fascinated with anything spiritual, and I really like helping people. The more I do this, the more confident I am that I'm making the right choice. I got a degree in chemistry before I started to think this could be the career for me."

I laugh, picturing Dakota in a lab surrounded by beakers. "Oh man, I wish I'd known about your chem skills before AP started kicking my butt this year."

"I could tutor you," he offers. "If you trusted me enough."

"I might take you up on that, but only if I get really desperate. It's not because I don't trust you, it's just I'm pretty sure I'd drive you up a wall." I look around at the formal foyer and into the office, where the shelves are stacked with casket catalogs, the top hat for the buggy costume spilling its black veil to the floor, and the calendar on the wall contains every community event recorded by Mom. "I just don't want to disappoint my parents."

"They'll figure it out," Dakota says. "And you don't have to commit right away. Lots of schools have pre–mortuary science programs—you could start there and change majors if you decide it's not right for you. Also, Astrid might surprise everyone. She's been hanging around with me, asking questions when she thinks you guys aren't looking."

"Ha. Really? Everybody thinks she has no interest in the business whatsoever."

"I have a feeling it'll be a couple of years before she's ready to admit that this could be a cool job. And you shouldn't be afraid of taking a couple to think it over too. Okay?"

It's the first time anyone's suggested I could come back to this— that maybe it's possible to try something else first. I want to hug him. Instead, I say, "Okay, Dakota. Thanks."

He closes the backroom door, then shoos me out of the foyer and back up the main stairs.

"But seriously," he says. "Whoever takes over this place should at least know a little Spanish."

♣

Madison texts just before midnight, while I'm brushing my teeth.

> He's coming home—he's feeling pretty good.

Before I can text back, she's on video chat. And the look on her face is not happy.

"What's wrong?" I ask. "You just said Miles is coming home, so is he *not* okay?"

"No he's fine. You just might not be." She winces. "He doesn't want to see you."

I hear her words, but this is Madison. A lot of the time what she says sounds a lot worse than what she actually means.

"He's tired, right? I mean obviously he's not going to want to see me *now*, but—"

"No, Elaine," she says. "He means ever. Well, maybe not *forever* since you're obviously going to see each other at school. But you coming to visit, stuff like that, he says no. Did you guys have some kind of fight?"

"Not exactly."

I almost wish that night outside Valentino's had been a fight—fights are things you can move on from, be forgiven for, put behind you. What happened between Miles and me was more like an earthquake that brought down everything I thought we'd built over all those years of being so close. It's starting to look like rebuilding could be impossible.

"Did you give him the spectacles?" I press, still not willing to believe that this is where we end. "Did he watch the panel?"

"Yes, and I don't know. When I told him you wanted to see him, he said . . . Ugh, Elaine, you don't want to know what he said."

She's trying to save my feelings, but I *do* want to hear it. I need to.

"You can tell me, Mads."

"Fine." She winces again. "He said *I'm not rescuing her anymore.* Are you going to freak out? I shouldn't have told you."

"I'm not freaking out."

What I'm doing is worse, because most of the time, freaking out means overreacting. What I'm doing now is realizing that Miles is right. I took him for granted. I expected him to always be there, no matter what he was feeling, no matter how much it hurt him. All I could think about were my own feelings; now it's his turn to think about his. When something like that is true, you can't freak out about it. All you can do is let it sit, painful and heavy, on your heart.

"I'm exhausted from the hospital," Madison tells me. "I'm going to bed. Just so you know, I don't think either of us will be at school tomorrow."

"That'll make this whole thing easier—at least for a day," I say. "Sleep tight, and tell Miles . . . wait, no. Don't tell him anything. Night, Mads."

She signs off, and I pace the bathroom, replaying our conversation over and over until the loop tangles with my own thoughts in a spiral to end all anxiety spirals.

Of all my coping strategies, the best for nighttime is a cup of herbal tea. I go down to the kitchen, being careful not to make any unnecessary noise. Dad was still his super-formal-disappointed self tonight, even after all the drama with the wreck. I'd rather not try to make conversation if he gets out of bed to see what I'm up to.

Lucky for my nerves, nobody wakes up. I climb the stairs back up to my room, holding the mug in both hands. I use my shoulder to push my door open, and freeze.

There she is.

She's facing the window with her back to me, and she is as real as the woman I saw before that little boy's funeral years ago. Her hair is in a braid down the middle of her back, and she wears a white long-sleeved shirt and dark skirt, her waist curving in a way that could only be possible with a corset.

I screw my eyes shut, then open them again. She's still there.

My throat feels thick, like in a dream where I want to scream but can't get out any sound. This is my chance to speak with her—to ask all the things I've been dying to know.

Her head moves; I hold my breath. I see her profile as she glances over her shoulder, as if she can sense but not see me. I listen too, and become aware of a sound repeating at odd intervals. It sounds like something hitting the window glass. *Ping!*

Ping! . . .

Ping! . . .

My phone goes off, sending me scrambling to silence it. When I look up again, she's gone.

I run to the window and turn in a circle, spilling tea all over the floor. There's nothing where she was, not even a cold spot.

"Flossie?" My voice works again. I listen, furious with myself for letting the moment pass.

Ping!

Someone is outside, throwing pennies at my window. I check my phone and see Xander's just texted me.

> I'm here—come down—please.

I look out again to see the silhouette of a boy on the sidewalk.

Is this a ghost-story version of *Romeo and Juliet*? Is Flossie somehow having me relive some key moment from her life? Maybe it happened like this: pebbles on glass; a silhouette below; a girl creeping down the stairs and out the back door to meet with adventure or even escape. I was wrong about so many things with Xander; maybe Flossie is letting me know it's okay, this butterfly feeling in my stomach. That whatever is about to happen could be the answer I've been looking for.

You're smart and beautiful, and you're going to go places, Xander said. *I sort of wish you'd go places with me.*

I circle around the house to find him under the streetlight. He turns when he hears me, and I gasp at the sight of him. A cast encircles his left arm, and the right side of his face is bruised. The darkest, angriest spot covers where his mole should be. He looks so broken.

"Xander?" I whisper. "How did you get here?"

"I took my dad's car," he says. "I needed to see you. I couldn't wait."

I look up at my room. From this spot, where Xander has been pitching pennies, the window is a vertical black rectangle—the perfect frame for a body.

"Did you see her up there?" I ask him.

"Who?"

"Flossie! She was standing in my window just a minute ago. Looking out."

"No," he says. "I just saw you."

"That wasn't me, that was her."

Or was it? In a wisp of *Dragonfly*-esque surreality, I get the flipped-mirror feeling that maybe it's me people have been seeing all this time. Maybe *I'm* the Gillies Ghost.

"She was there, I swear. I went downstairs to get some tea, and when I came back, she was at the window, right before you texted. When my phone went off, she disappeared."

Xander's entire body stiffens.

"You're saying you saw a full apparition? Really? Just now?"

"Maybe she wanted me to see you out here," I tell him.

"That makes total sense." He reaches for my hand, and when his fingers meet mine, the heat I've always felt at his touch races up my arm. He leads me to the porch steps, where the lighting is dim and romantic. We're heading for a kiss—one that I know will decide things once and for all. Miles has made it clear where he stands, and now Xander is standing here. All I have to do is follow the signs.

Before I kiss him, there's something I have to say.

"I know you didn't put the beer bottle with Mr. Bohmer. And I shouldn't have accused you of vandalizing the homestead. I said some really terrible things, and that was wrong."

"Let's face it, I didn't exactly do a great job of inspiring trust," he replies.

"Still, let me make it up to you?"

I step closer, circle my arms around his waist, and crush his lips with mine. I can feel his cast against my back, his breathing quicken as I kiss him even deeper, and the butterflies come rushing back. My mind swirls, my skin burns, everything inside me starts humming with that addictive adrenaline rush.

He pulls away.

"I have something to tell you," he says. "Please don't get mad until you hear the whole thing. Promise?"

At this moment, I would promise him anything.

"Yes," I say. "I promise."

"I didn't contact *Spirit Seekers* that first time. I swear I didn't. But when you told me they contacted you, I did send them an email. I wanted them to know I was the one who took the video and picture of Flossie. It's only fair I should get credit."

"Everyone knows who captured those images," I agree. "If they're already out there, people should know it's your work."

"That's what I thought too. Anyway, the producers were impressed. We've been emailing back and forth, and they actually might want to come to Dodson to investigate. That's why we were at the homestead. I needed to get better evidence to convince them it's worth it."

I remember Sienna telling me how intense Xander was last night, how he seemed obsessed. Now I know why.

"You can always go back there," I tell him. "Some investigations are harder than others, right? I mean, look at what happened here— some nights it was totally dead."

He shakes his head, and I'm starting to become aware of the

energy coming off him. It's scattered and intense—definitely not romantic.

"No, but see, they aren't interested in the homestead no matter what I do." He scrubs his hand through his hair. "I was hoping I wouldn't have to ask this but . . . they want to come here. To the funeral home."

Every one of my instincts is suddenly screaming to get free of the dizzying effect he has on me. I step out of his arms.

"We've been over this," I tell him. "Thoroughly."

And by *this*, I mean my thinking there was more to the two of us than ghosts. I thought Xander was drawn here by a desire he couldn't resist. I thought maybe the car crash gave him some kind of revelation about our relationship. I thought he drove here in the dead of night because he couldn't wait to share it with me. Or maybe you just love someone, and you want to be together no matter what. I thought that was why Xander was here.

"I know everything got messed up before," he says. "But we were just getting started. We could do it better now. We could be a team."

I pull in a deep breath, still attempting to make sense of what's going on.

"My dad would never let that happen."

"You could convince him," Xander presses. "I know you've been doing marketing for your parents. And you said Memories is really big competition. Having a show like *Spirit Seekers* film at your place would be incredible publicity. It would blow them out of the water."

Xander's eyes may burn with that dangerous fire, but he's also right. Memories doesn't have the history we have. They don't have the story, the family connection. Unless they're hiding something up their sleeve, they could never top being featured on *Spirit Seekers*.

And where could *Spirit Seekers* take me? If I worked with them, could it open other doors too? Maybe Xander and I really could go places together.

He reaches for my hand. I let him take it.

"Maybe you're right that Flossie has a message," he says. "The guys at *Spirit Seekers* are professionals. They could find out what she wants and what it means. They could give her a voice."

I can't deny I want more information about this girl who looks like me and who's become a family legend for daring to choose another path. If someone could help me understand why she's here, it could answer so many questions about my own life and what I want to do with it.

But what Xander's asking is too big; I can't decide something like this so quickly.

"I need to think," I tell him. "I'm not saying no. I just *don't* know."

"When *will* you know?" he presses.

"When it's not two a.m.? You have to give me time."

"We don't have very long. That's why I couldn't wait until tomorrow. They want to come soon. Maybe even this weekend—at least to scout and see if they really want to do this."

"I have to talk with my parents," I tell him. "This isn't some secret ghost hunt; this has all sorts of risks for my entire family."

"Sometimes you have to put yourself at risk to capture something amazing."

The intrepid thing to do would be to tell him yes and figure things out later. But something holds me back—the voice I've associated only with anxiety now sounds like a friend I should trust, and right now it's saying *wait*.

"Give me until Wednesday morning," I say. "I know this is important to you. Okay? I get it. And I swear I won't keep you waiting. I just need to figure this out."

"Wednesday?" In the dark, the streetlights reflecting in Xander's eyes look like flames. "You promise?"

"I promise."

He pulls me to him, kissing me hard and heated. I close my eyes and try to lose myself again, searching for that exhilaration I love more than anything else. He pulls away and rests his forehead against mine.

"Thank you," he says. "So much. You're the best."

CHAPTER THIRTY-SEVEN

How do you get through a Monday when you've had no sleep, you're on a secret deadline to make a decision that could change your life, *plus* your best friend—the one you miss more than you ever thought possible—is recovering from a car crash and doesn't want to see you?

You zombie-walk it.

I feel like some undead thing shuffling from class to class, grunting whenever anyone speaks to me, mindlessly driven by the hunger to make it to 3:00 p.m. so I can go home and spiral out in the privacy of my own room. So, when drama erupts outside of fifth bell, I don't pay attention—until I hear my sister's name.

"Dude, Astrid Gillies is going *apeshit* on Quinn Hofstetter!"

I hear the guy next to me say this just as my phone starts blowing up with the school rumor mill spreading news about a fight. I usually steer clear of that stuff, except it's my sister. Fighting.

What the eff?

I sprint to the commons, where a mob has gathered around the snack bar. Pushing my way through, I see Quinn against the soda machine. Astrid has her chest to his, and she's not alone. Ella Schmidt stands beside her, glaring at Quinn.

"You didn't think I'd actually talk to Ella, did you?" Astrid is saying. "Well, guess what? We compared texts."

"You thought you could play us off each other?" Ella says. "Eff that misogynistic BS, Quinn. Astrid's actually a decent person, unlike you."

Quinn's eyes are darting from the crowd to Astrid to Ella, cluelessly astonished at having to face some consequences for his actions.

"Hey, Astrid, come on," he says as he tries to rest a hand on her arm. She swats it away.

"Leave us both alone," she tells him. "And don't ever touch me again."

People start whistling, chanting for a fight. Just when it looks like Ella might actually throw a punch, one of the vice principals appears and motions for all three of them to come with her.

I follow them to the office.

"I'm her sister," I tell the secretary, pointing to Astrid's back as she goes into Ms. Chambers's room. "I'm the one who'd drive her if you send her home, so I should probably hang out here."

The woman nods, and I go sit on one of the chairs against the wall. Ten minutes later, Astrid comes out. Inside the office, I can still see Quinn's knees; apparently, they aren't finished with him yet.

"What's happening?" I whisper.

"They said I could go home and enjoy a Quinn-free rest of the afternoon," she tells me. Ella comes out next and shoots a satisfied look our way. She raises a hand. Astrid raises hers. They fist-bump the air between them, then the girl who used to torment me in grade school walks by without a second look.

"You actually talked to Ella?" I ask as we head through the parking lot. "You're braver than me."

"I sneaked a look at Quinn's phone," Astrid explains. "Let's just say I realized Ella's not the bad guy here."

"Hey, Ghost Girl!"

We're passing the music wing door; the seniors who vape there start laughing when we look over.

"When's your haunted-house party?" one of them calls. "I want to come!"

I unlock my car, and Astrid tosses in her backpack.

"Ghost Girl. Funeral Girl," I say. "I don't get why they think that's such an insult."

Astrid shrugs.

"It's normal for people to be interested in what we do," she says. "They just have a dumb way of showing it."

"Dumb isn't even the word. It's just exhausting, this fascination people have. I sort of wish they could see how not-interesting it is. It's just a job."

"Yeah, but it's more than that too."

After months of sullen silences and defensive snapping, having Astrid speak to me still feels weird. As I pull out, I consider whether to take a chance and ask another question. I'm dying to know if what I've heard is true.

"Dakota says you've been hanging out with him, learning about the business when no one else is looking?"

She shrugs again. "Dakota doesn't make me feel stupid."

"I'm sorry if I made you feel that way. I didn't mean to."

"It's not just you," she says. "And honestly, I'm starting to not care. This stuff is actually pretty cool."

She's fishing in her bag, pulling out a lip gloss, no sign of turning on me if I push further. So I go ahead and push.

"Are you ever going to tell Dad you think that?"

"I don't know." She swishes the gloss on her lips, then checks herself in my pull-down mirror. "I like flying under the radar. That way nobody can decide for me until I'm ready. And for the record, I don't think anybody should decide for you, either."

When did my sister get so grown-up? I've been watching it happen, feeling sad about the changes but not seeing the whole picture. I saw her pulling away. I saw her struggling. I didn't see her getting stronger too.

"I'm sorry people assumed you wouldn't be interested in the business," I tell her. "And I'm sorry I let Mom and Dad assume only I could do it. I guess I still think about you as little, but you're not anymore and it's been kind of hard accepting that."

I glance over to see a smile creeping across her face.

"I don't make it very easy sometimes," she says.

"You really don't."

My phone pings. I glance at it, thinking it'll be Sienna asking why I'm not in choir.

> I saw the panel.

It's Miles.

I suddenly feel completely, freezingly naked. The panel seems so long ago. I can't believe it was just yesterday morning.

"What's wrong?" Astrid asks. I push my phone into her hands.

"I am totally trusting you right now," I say. "I need to answer that text, but I don't want to crash the car. Just write *You did?* and then tell me what he says."

"Okay. He's responding." She reads from the screen. *"Yes."*

I squint, trying to keep my eyes on the road, resisting the urge to snatch back my phone.

"Yes what? That's all he said was *yes*?"

"It's your turn," she tells me. "What do you want to say back?"

"I don't know. He told Madison he doesn't want to see me."

"Do you want to see him?"

If Astrid wasn't in the dark about everything that's happened between Miles and me, I'd tell her that was the stupidest question I've ever heard. Instead I say, "Hell yes. So much."

She starts texting.

"What are you saying?" I shriek. "Read that to me before you send it!"

"I wrote, *I'd really like to see you but I understand if you don't want to see me.* Oops! I just hit Send—you were fine with that, right?" Before I can answer, she says, "Oh! He's responding again! Little dots . . . little dots . . . *okay.*"

"What? What's okay?"

"That's what he said. *Okay.*"

Ugh. Miles is not going to make this easy. Does that single word mean he's okay with me coming over? Or is he just saying okay to acknowledge what I've said? Why does he have to pick now to be all cryptic?

Pulling up to home, we stop in the drive for Dakota, who's heading to the garage where we keep the van. He motions for me to roll down the window.

"You guys are early," he says.

"Yeah . . ." I think I'll keep what happened at school between Astrid and me. "The power went out, so they sent everybody home."

"Cool," he says. "Hey. We just got a death call from some new place I've never heard of. Barton. Where is that? It's not even on Google Maps."

Astrid leans across the seat and says, "Barton is tiiiny. It's over by Lester. I can come along and show you."

She gets out of the car, motioning for me to stay where I am.

"You need to be someplace else," she tells me. "Go! I'll tell Mom and Dad where you are."

"Are you sure?" I can't believe this is happening: Someone else is going to help Dakota.

"Yes," she calls as she follows him into the garage. "Tell Miles I said hi."

I can see him from a block away, sitting in his front porch swing, wrapped in a blanket. He has his eyes closed, head tipped back, gently pushing himself back and forth with his foot.

He opens his eyes when he hears my car door slam and watches me climb the porch steps with an expression I can't read. I've always thought I could tell what was on Miles's mind. All this time there were things I never saw. Or maybe I missed them on purpose.

I wait for him to get up, go inside, and leave me out here alone. I wait for him to tell me to leave—to tell me *anything*. There's only a wary look that doesn't say *stay* but also doesn't say *go*.

I sit next to him, pulling my coat around myself for warmth.

"When you told us you wanted to wear a prom dress to your funeral, I didn't think you meant this season."

He laughs softly, and the sound brings back the hollow ache in my chest.

"I sort of feel lucky I'm still in one piece to get into a prom dress," he says. "For a minute while my truck was spinning, I thought I was going to end up in two or three pieces. Of all the not-fun parts of this experience, that was the most not-fun of all."

"Yet you somehow still manage to look better than Xander."

His laugh this time sounds bitter.

"Most of my hurts are in places you can't see," he says.

"Well, I'm really glad to be seeing you like this and not, you know, at my house in one of the prep rooms." I've been trying to be light and semi-funny and not bombard him with all of my emotions at once, but it's impossible. I'm now crying for what feels like the millionth time. "I'm sorry. I just, I missed you in Chicago, and I realized how much I take you for granted, and then I thought maybe I wasn't going to get to see you again, and . . . can I hug you? Please?"

"A hug would be nice," he says. "Just don't be offended if I flinch. I'm still finding bruises I didn't know I had."

He leans in and I wrap my arms around him, burying my head in his neck, breathing in the smell of his freshly showered skin. His arms come up and he hugs me back. Then he lets go, almost like he's putting a fragile thing back on a shelf.

"You said I look better than Xander. I guess that means you've seen him?"

"He came over last night," I say. The whole visit has a dreamy quality; it's hard to believe that it actually happened.

"So, are you guys, like, officially back together and all that?"

When I open my mouth to answer, I realize Xander never asked about getting back together. He came all the way to my house, and what he really wanted to talk about was *Spirit Seekers*.

"We didn't actually discuss our relationship," I say. When I tell Miles what we did talk about, the suspicion that's been lurking in the back of my mind comes into clearer focus: For Xander, ghost hunting and me always go together. I'm an opportunity tied to what I can give him.

To be sure I'm right, I ask Miles about Saturday night. "When you were at the homestead, investigating, did Xander tell you what he wanted the evidence for? Did he mention me at all?"

Miles sighs, and I can hear the weariness in his voice as he speaks. "When we got back in the truck to leave, he asked when you'd be home. I told him I didn't know—you have your own life, and that bothered him. A lot. He wasn't happy you were out of town."

As I think about this, I'm beginning to suspect that the reason for Xander's unhappiness wasn't that he missed me. Miles lets the silence stretch, and for once I'm grateful. I need to let everything sink in. Maybe last night feels so unreal because so much of it *wasn't* real, especially the part where I thought Xander and I were finally surrendering to some fated romance.

Years ago, on one of the rare nights my dad felt like he could slip away from the business, he took us all camping. I wanted to help build the fire, so I doused a pile of sticks and papers with lighter fluid and lit a match. The flames roared up, big and satisfying, only to fizzle out within minutes.

"That's because you didn't give it any real fuel to burn," Dad explained.

Thinking about Xander now, I see that dying campfire. It's amazing how quickly things cool when I realize there's nothing besides his obsession with the supernatural to keep the flame going.

Miles shifts; I can tell he wants to be done talking about Xander.

"Those spectacles are pretty amazing," he says. "You must have made a real impression on Magnus."

"Actually you did," I tell him. "You would have loved DraCon. You should have kept the tickets and gone instead."

"No," he says. "I wanted you to go. Without me. We don't always have to do everything together, and I never wanted to stop you from going wherever you want. Also there's the internet, so I didn't miss the important stuff. I finally watched the panel this morning. It almost sounded like you didn't hate me."

"I could never hate you."

He makes a "hm" sound, which nearly breaks me because I don't know how to cut through this chilly carefulness between us. What I do know is that the difference between Miles and Xander has never been more clear.

Xander showed me things about myself I'd never seen. But it was always through his lens. I've always looked at myself through other people's eyes—hiding from their curiosity, shrinking from their stupid nicknames, muting the things that make me special because I was anxious, because I didn't want to disappoint anyone, because I didn't know myself well enough yet. And even though Xander looks like escape, if I went with him, I'd be trapped in another way: With Xander I'll always be Ghost Girl.

Miles has only ever expected me to be Elaine. All the different versions—he's accepted them, even the one who let herself get consumed by a false fire. I thought love had to be hot and new and adventurous. I was scared to admit it could be cool and calm and steady too. I know now that I can travel as far as I want. I can be as many different Elaines as I need. But I've always felt the most like myself when I'm with Miles.

"I don't hate you," I tell him, "because it's impossible to hate someone you love."

I turn my body to his, looking for permission to kiss him, but he won't meet my eyes. Even though he's sitting right next to me, there might as well be a mile between us.

"I've been wrong," I say. "About a million things, but most of all how I feel about you. I love you. I do. I was scared and too stupid to admit it, and I don't know how you still deal with me after all the crap I put you through. The fact that you *are* still dealing with me just proves even more how wrong I was."

I pause, hoping with everything I have that the chill between us will melt. He keeps his eyes on his hands in his lap. He doesn't move, doesn't speak, doesn't betray so much as a hint of what he's thinking. My heart feels weighed down by the realization that it's too late.

"Maybe I should get out of here."

Finally, he speaks. He says, "You can go."

I nod. I get up. I force my feet to move, one in front of the other, to the edge of his porch, prepping for the reality that this is the last time I'll be here as his potential girlfriend, as his friend . . . as anything. Once I go down these steps, it will all be over.

"Or you can stay and try me one more time."

I turn back, not sure I heard him correctly.

"Try what?" I ask.

He holds open his blanket, a hint of the jokester I've always loved flickering in his eyes.

"I know you pretty well after all these years," he says. "And that first time I kissed you, I could tell you liked it. Not saying I knew you'd be here now, like this, and if I said I didn't lose hope more than a few times since that night I'd be lying. But if you're serious about what you just said, maybe try me again and see how this time goes?"

I retrace my steps and sit beside him again. He wraps me in the blanket, enveloping us both in its warmth, then he waits. It's my move, and I know what to do. I close my eyes and I kiss him. He kisses me back, then pulls away, his crisp blue eyes searching my face.

"Do you mean it?" he says.

I find his hand and squeeze it in mine.

"I *so* mean it. We may not be endgame—or maybe we are. Maybe we don't actually want different things, or maybe we do. But we should find out, right? Maybe we owe it to ourselves to—"

"Hey," he interrupts.

I stop talking. "What?"

"Take out the parsley."

Like always, Miles is right; I don't need to tell him, I need to show him. So I take his chin in my hands and bring my lips to his again, and the difference is so clear that I can't believe it took me this long to understand. Xander was fast and dizzying, but it was a thrill that goes nowhere except an inevitable crash. Miles is slow and deep and heavenly, like a mug of buttered cider, like the happy sigh when your skin gets used to a hot bath, like a place you never want to leave.

Sometimes the bravest, most intrepid thing you can do is just let yourself be happy.

"Miles." I don't want to stop kissing him, especially not to revisit a sore subject. But I did promise Xander an answer.

"Hm . . . ?" He's kissing my neck now. And it's so amazing I almost forget what I wanted to say.

"I know you've rescued me from my problems way too much, and this isn't that, I promise. I don't need rescuing right now, I think I just need advice."

I tell him about how I'm operating under a Wednesday deadline to let *Spirit Seekers* scout at my house and how I'm starting to think it might be okay.

"Maybe I should tell Xander yes and talk my dad into it," I say. "What do you think?"

Miles strokes my hair and stares at the clouds across the street. It's so soothing that I almost want him to put off answering so we can sit here, just like this, for as long as possible.

"I think it's up to you if you want to let someone else tell your story," he says.

Your story. Those words spark an idea that starts to flicker around the edges of my imagination.

"It *is* my story," I say. "Maybe I could tell it."

"About Flossie?"

"I'm not sure if I'll ever find out her whole story. But what about the story *behind* her? Xander says he looks for ghosts because he wants to believe there's more to the world. That's what people who come to the funeral home want too. It's sort of the whole reason we have funerals."

"I think I get it," says Miles. "Wait, no, I don't get it at all."

"Hold on a minute."

I run to my car, get my notebook, and bring it back to the porch.

"I'm just starting to figure it all out," I tell him. "But if you're up for it, I'd really love your help with this."

CHAPTER THIRTY-EIGHT

stay at Miles's house until his mom kicks me out. Not just kissing, although a *lot* of that happens. Most of the time is spent in the kind of back-and-forth that makes watching *Dragonfly* with him so good. I come home with a full notebook and an even fuller heart to find Xander in our family room with my dad.

They both turn to me with perfectly neutral expressions—as if the past two weeks were a glitch in the matrix and they're nothing more than two people with no history, just chatting on a normal Monday night.

"Xander. What are you doing here?"

"I came to see you," he tells me. "But you were out, so I started talking with your dad."

My father, for his part, doesn't look furious. It's way too weird. I set my things on the kitchen island and say, "Can Xander and I talk privately?"

"Of course," Dad says. He starts to get up, but I motion for

Xander to follow me instead. We go down the back stairs to the patio outside.

"Xander? What's going on?"

"Don't be mad," he says. "I had to see you again."

I brace for him to try to kiss me, working up the courage for what I know I have to do, which is break up with him—officially and finally.

Instead he says, "We have unfinished business with *Spirit Seekers*. I couldn't wait."

I don't know why this surprises me, considering everything I've learned and realized over the past twenty-four hours, but it does. And even though I know it shouldn't sting, I still flinch. He's not here for me, he's here for Flossie.

"I told you I'd decide by Wednesday morning. You couldn't wait?"

"This is too important," he says. "We have to plan it out. We can't just make it all work at the last minute."

The truth about what's really going on hits me with sickening clarity.

"So you went over my head and talked to my dad."

"He was surprisingly open to it once I explained," Xander says. "He wanted to know more about the photos and the videos. I told him about Flossie because I knew you wouldn't."

"You *knew* I wouldn't?"

He takes me by the shoulders, the cast on his arm pressing into my sleeve, and looks into my eyes.

"I know you need someone to get you to do the hard things," he says. "I can be that person."

"Xander," I warn. "You need to stop talking right now." Because

I do hard things every day. I work with the dead. I help comfort their grieving loved ones. I balance all that with my friends and my other interests, and nothing about that is easy, but if there's one thing I'm sure of it's that I don't need Xander's help.

"You never would have found Flossie without me," he says. "She's showing herself for a reason."

"Flossie isn't yours to talk about."

"Yes, she is," he insists. "She happened to me too."

"It's not the same. This isn't your house. It's not your story."

"It's my investigation, though." He's still holding my shoulders, still looking into my eyes. In his, I see a hole I used to think I could fill. But it's obvious now how impossible that is. If Xander gets what he thinks he needs, he'll only want more.

"Elaine, come on," he says. "This is all I have."

"You could have had me."

I can see it all plainly now. Xander is a boy who stands in the middle of parades, who lets himself almost get run over, and lets the same thing happen to other people in order to get what he wants. Maybe he's trying to get his parents' attention. Maybe he's on a mission for the world to take him seriously. Maybe he has problems so deep I couldn't help no matter how I tried.

I bring my hands to his, pull them away, and step backward.

"Even if *Spirit Seekers* does come. Even if you get all the evidence you're looking for and all the followers and fame, you'll always be chasing something, Xander. I'll never be enough."

He doesn't try to convince me I'm wrong. He just looks at me with those beautiful bruised eyes and says, "Don't you want to know why Flossie's here? What she wants?"

The answer comes in a voice I now recognize as fully my own.

"I know what she wants. She wants me to run away. But not

from here, from you. You can take *Spirit Seekers* to the homestead if you want. The funeral home is already being used this weekend."

"By a funeral?" he asks.

"No," I say. "By me."

Dad stands at the deck door with a glass of whisky in his hand when I come back upstairs. He looks surprised to see me alone.

"Is Xander gone?" he says.

I don't know what my face looks like. I cried when we said goodbye, even though I didn't want to. And now my eyes are probably raw and red. I do my best to pull myself together.

"He's gone," I say. "He shouldn't have been here in the first place."

Dad motions for me to sit on the couch next to him. He takes a long sip before he speaks.

"When Xander first showed up here tonight, I wasn't happy to see him. But it turns out he does have some talent with this investigating thing. I've wondered why you seemed so interested in the stories about Flossie. Is this why?"

"Yes. I've actually seen her."

"You have?" He looks at me with wonder.

"Yes. Have you?"

He shakes his head.

"The honor of communing with ghosts appears to have been reserved exclusively for you. I don't know if I'm glad about that or envious. But Xander seems to think there's something here worth exploring."

I don't disagree. Being with Xander taught me a lot of things, including some pretty fundamental truths.

"People are curious," I say. "About this place and what we do here. To be honest, after the past few weeks, I'm more curious too."

He finishes his drink and gets up to pour one more.

"This job puts food on the table," he tells me. "It keeps a roof over our heads and clothes on our backs, but it also touches one of the great mysteries of existence. It's a privilege and a huge responsibility. Even without ghosts, you've seen things no one else has seen. You know things most people your age will never know—or at least not for many more years if they're lucky."

"I know," I say.

"So, you can see why I might think you'd be the perfect person to carry on the business."

I do see. Now. But we've never talked openly about it. Until this very moment, I don't think I would have been able to say what I say next, which is "I just want to have a choice."

He nods. He sighs.

"When I was growing up, I didn't have that. Family helped family. It was duty."

"But Mom said you felt called to do it."

"Sometimes I'm not sure where calling and duty separate," he says. "But it was never a decision I regretted. And I would never want you to have regrets in your life, Lainey."

"I'm not saying I absolutely will never take it over," I tell him. "I'm saying I don't know right now, and I don't know how to make that okay. I'm scared to be the reason everything ends."

He gazes into his glass, then outside again, where Mom's pots of tomatoes and roses are empty now that winter is almost here.

"Endings are a part of life," he says. "I of all people should know that. And sometimes life has to be uncertain, which is something I've never been good at." He swirls his drink in the glass, and he's quiet for so long that I start to wonder if this is going to end with another silent treatment, not because he's mad at me but because neither of us knows what to say anymore. He lets out another sigh.

"Maybe we should let that *Spirit Seekers* show film here. It'd be publicity for sure, and these days any publicity seems to be good. Maybe this is the kind of thing people want to see."

"Maybe," I say.

I know he and Xander are right: The Gillies Ghost would get us attention. But people aren't going to choose our funeral home because we have a ghost; they're going to come to Gillies because we take good care of their loved ones, because we comfort them and we help them understand, as much as that's possible.

"What if I had a better idea?" I say. "I can't promise it'll be as cool as a ghost-hunting show, but I think it could be even better in the long run."

I take my notebook out of my bag and show him what Miles and I worked on this afternoon. I explain what I want to do—how I could talk about the things I know, and how for some people it could be helpful in a rough time and for others it could just be interesting, and how I might not know what I'm going to do for the future but this is something I can do now.

Dad listens. He asks questions. Finally, he says, "We'll have to talk with your mom of course. She's the final word on these things."

"I think she'd love it," I tell him.

"And you'd film it all here?"

"Yes. Everywhere. That's the point. We take people all the places they don't normally get to see. Show them the things they wonder about and take away some of the mystery. You'd have to trust me on this."

He flips back through the notebook pages, scanning here, taking time to read there.

"I like this," he says. "People have so many questions. You can answer them in a way they'll understand."

"It'll be accurate and respectful. But also fun. It can even be funny, too."

"It's joy in the face of sadness," he says. "The juxtaposition of the universe."

"Right," I say. "That's exactly what it is."

CHAPTER THIRTY-NINE

"Where do you want this set up?"

Miles stands with a ring light in his hands next to a tripod with a waiting camera. I scan the foyer, looking for the best background for our first episode, and for the hundredth time in the past three days I wonder what made me think I could create a web series, much less star in it.

"I don't know," I say. "Xander's the photography expert, not me."

"Xander's still at the homestead playing TV star with his *Spirit Seekers* friends."

"They're not filming anything, though. It's just a scouting team."

"Well, I can't say I'm heartbroken he's there and not here." Miles puts the light down and comes over to where I'm standing under the portrait of Great-Great-Great-Grandfather Leathan. "Let's do this instead."

He pushes me against the table, and I don't care whether the OG disapproves. Miles and I are not going to get anything done if we keep this up, but it's so hard to stop.

"Hey! I just did her makeup." Astrid's voice pulls us apart. "You're going to mess it up!"

"And Elaine wonders why we're behind schedule." Madison has just come through the front door with Sienna trailing on her heels.

"We're not behind," Miles tells her. "Things are flexible. It's a flexible schedule, right, Elaine?"

"Well . . . we *have* been putting stuff all over social media about a premiere on Tuesday," I say.

"That's three days away."

"That's no time when you think about editing and everything else we need to do."

"Fine." He gives me space, which allows me a better view of Sienna and Madison. They're giggling and nudging each other, acting shady.

"So, Elaine. We were jerks," Madison says.

"We were *complete* jerks about the musical," says Sienna. "Before you say *it's okay*, it's not okay."

"We feel bad about it," says Madison. "So, we made something for you."

Sienna hands me her earbuds and her phone, then they come around, one at each shoulder, to look at the screen with me.

"Imagine an old TV-show intro," says Sienna. "Like a montage of pictures and a logo and all that stuff."

"I can put it together," adds Madison. "But for now just use your imagination."

Sienna touches Play and a bouncy, retro-sounding song starts. The black screen shows the lyrics while a recorded Madison and Sienna sing in harmony.

Funeral Girl—She lives in a funeral home.
Funeral Girl—You've got questions, and that's okay!
Death's not as scary when you know some facts.
She's got answers so go on and ask
Funeral Girl—She's your friend at the funeral home.

I take out the earbuds when it's over. "Oh. My. God."

"It's your theme song!" crows Sienna.

"Do you hate it?" says Madison. "I think she hates it."

"You don't have to use it if you don't want to," Sienna adds.

"No." I start cracking up as the lyrics, with all their unrhyming kookiness, replay in my mind. "It's so good. I love it. You wrote this?"

"Madison did. I wrote the music bed and the harmonies."

"I actually do think I hate you," I tell them. "Because now I'm not going to be able to get that out of my head."

"It's catchy, right?" Madison is clearly proud of herself.

"An ear worm in the best possible way."

"And . . . I've got it!" Miles has set the camera up in front of the casket in the front visitation room. Dakota and Dad hauled it out for a prop, just in case; now Miles walks me over and positions me in front of it. Astrid starts fussing over my makeup, and when I turn my head so she can touch up my highlights, I see something I've never noticed before.

It's a photograph, framed, on the wall between the visitation rooms. As I get closer, I can see a girl posing on what looks like a busy dock, a massive ship behind her. She is dressed for travel— trunks at her feet and a hat perched smartly on her head. Her eyes hold a hint of excitement, her chin tilting up in a most intrepid way.

I take the picture down and look at the back. *Florence Irene, 1897* is written there in white script.

I've lived in this house all my life and I've never examined all the pictures on the walls. They were just part of the old-fashioned décor; I used to think they were boring.

Then I realize: This is the place where Flossie was standing when Xander took her photo. This is where we heard the three taps. Is this what she wanted me to find?

I haven't seen Flossie since the other night in my room. I want to, but I haven't exactly had time to look. This photo tells me a lot, but it creates more questions too. If Flossie did travel, did she go by herself or was there a boy involved like in the old family legend? If she really ran away and broke her father's heart, why would he hang her photograph in his parlor? Maybe there was a whole other dimension to their relationship that no one knew about. There'd have to be, right? Nothing is ever as simple as one moment or one chapter.

Whether I ever learn the whole thing or not, I do know this: Flossie and I may look alike, but her story isn't mine.

"Hello? Are we ready to go?" Madison's behind the camera now, impatiently tapping her foot.

"Yes, sorry!" I hurry back to the casket and grab Astrid's mirror for one last check. "Is my hair okay?"

"It's great," says Sienna. "You look pretty but relatable. Knowledgeable but approachable."

"She looks amazing!" says Miles with an extra-wide grin. He stands behind Madison and positions a stack of cue cards at eye level. "Remember, only use these to stay on track. Don't read, just be yourself."

"Got it, be myself." I roll my neck, crack my knuckles, and bounce three times for luck. "Okay, let's do this."

Miles gives me that smile that says he'll be here no matter what. Astrid checks my lipstick one last time. Madison hits Record. Sienna gives me the signal to go. I stand up straight, look into the camera lens, and smile.

"Hey, I'm Funeral Girl."

CHAPTER FORTY

There are no dead bodies in my house—at least not at the moment—which is a good thing, because if someone was to come to make plans for a funeral right now, they might not appreciate the sight of me making out with Miles while dressed in a Victorian undertaker's costume.

We're outside by the buggy, in plain view of anyone who might drive or walk by. Normally it wouldn't be the best advertisement for Gillies Family Funeral Home, but since *Funeral Girl Explains Everything* has become such a hit, I've been amazed what I can get away with.

"Did I ever tell you how hot you are in a corset?" Miles asks as he takes a bit of my ear between his teeth.

I close my eyes, savoring the warm rush that runs down my spine whenever he touches me. "You don't have to tell me because I'm wearing the thing. Thank God it's April and not August or I'd be a smelly, disgusting mess."

"I love it when you talk sweaty to me," he murmurs. "But seriously, the first time I saw you in this thing, back at that stupid parade, I could barely keep my tongue in my mouth. And of course you were oblivious."

"*So* oblivious. *So* stupid." Tipping his head backward, I leave kisses along the ridge of his neck. "Aren't you glad I've seen the light?"

The sound of a clearing throat forces us apart. Xander stands on the sidewalk with his camera.

"Excuse me," he says. "But we should get going on this while the light is still good."

"Sorry," I say, and adjust my collar back where it belongs. I'm still getting used to having Xander around, but we need him. When *Spirit Seekers* decided not to film Dodson, he joined our team as videographer, photographer, and person-in-charge-of-anything-else-visually-related, which has taken our production values up immensely. It's awkward sometimes, but everybody knows their job, and they all do it amazingly.

Miles helps brainstorm and write each episode. Dad fills in when we need an expert. Sienna does set dressing and the occasional appearance when I need a character to help explain things. So far, she's been a pall bearer, a coroner, and several corpses in various stages of embalming and presentation. The episode on near-death experiences, where Jaxon played a paramedic and Sienna woke up and snuck a kiss, was our most viewed episode ever.

Madison, meanwhile, handles the business side, and it turns out she's ridiculously good at it. In the five months we've been doing the biweekly web show, we've got thousands of subscribers and engagement through the roof. Companies have even started asking about sponsorships. And it's not just people our age who are watching. People in the community tell Mom they can't wait for a new episode. Guests at visitations ask for Funeral Girl by name. Like it or not, I'm the new face of Gillies. Just this morning, Madison gave us the latest breakdown over coffee and scones.

"None of us should be quitting school to become YouTubers or anything," she said. "But these numbers are really respectable."

So respectable that *Teen Life* magazine asked us to take over their Instagram for a week. I did an interview yesterday with their reporter. We talked about competition from other local funeral homes—*Eh, not worried about it.* About my thoughts on life and death—*Can't have one without the other, so live and die fearlessly.* About those mysterious photos and video that are still floating around the internet—*No comment.* And about whether I'm destined for a career as a funeral director—*No idea. Sorry not sorry.*

Dad and Mom made an appearance too. They said all the right things, about being proud of me and letting me choose my own path. Xander's going to photograph them later, on the back deck with the trees blooming. Astrid said no thanks to being part of it, but only because she's got pom practice. It's competition season, which trumps funeral-home stuff any day.

But the main goal at the moment is creating five days' worth of content. We'll do some behind-the-scenes posts. A tour of the living quarters. Also some AMAs. But the centerpiece is this photo shoot of me with the buggy.

For it, I put my own spin on the Victorian undertaker's costume. I spray-painted the corset silver and put it on the outside, over the high-collared shirt. I got my hair cut in a bob that Astrid dried straight with pin curls at my temples, and the top hat has a new veil of dark purple tulle that flows around me like an otherworldly vapor.

"You look like a steampunk goddess of death knowledge," Miles tells me as he helps me up to the driver's seat of the buggy.

"It's a definite improvement over the Harvest Home look," I say. "This is much more me."

"I don't think that's going to work," says Xander, examining the angle from down below. "She looks too small with the rest of the hearse in the shot, and if I shoot up close, you can't see the hearse at all. Plus the whole thing looks weird without the horses."

"What if you got in the back and sort of sat on the casket?" Madison suggests.

"Good idea," says Sienna. "The pink will look good with her outfit."

Miles helps me back down and around to the rear of the buggy. I've never been in the back before; I don't think anyone has.

"I don't know if I can get in," I tell them. "It's probably locked."

But when I turn the handle, it clicks loose easily. The door creaks as I open it. There's a musty smell inside, and the mauve casket is incredibly dusty. I try to sit on it but can't straighten my back because of the low ceiling.

"There isn't enough headroom," I tell everyone.

"Could we take the casket out?" asks Xander. "Or push it farther back so you're sitting in front of it?"

The boys try to push, but the casket won't budge. I climb back inside and look around.

"Let me see if there's something in the back holding it up."

Crouching, I creep to the opposite end of the chamber. I search along the floor for anything that might be keeping the casket from moving another foot or two. As I survey the back space, something in the far corner catches my eye.

Florence G

It's a shaky, old-fashioned-looking script that looks like it was done with a pocketknife. Next to it is a carving of a heart pierced by an old-fashioned key.

I explore every other inch of the interior to see if there are other carvings, but it's just her name. And the little heart, like any teenager might put after their signature. It's been here all this time, patiently waiting for me to discover it—a fist bump across more than a century.

Miles pops his head through the back door of the hearse.

"You're taking long enough," he says. "What's up?"

I turn and clap my hands together to get some of the dust off.

"Nothing," I say. "There's a board here keeping the casket in place. I'm going to move it, then you guys get ready to push."

I pry up the board, Miles and Xander move the casket to create a perfect sitting spot, and I don't tell them what I've found. I won't tell anyone. This small discovery feels private. This is just for me.

❧

We shoot until the golden hour has almost passed—until Xander has just enough time to capture Mom and Dad, and Madison and Sienna have to get to musical practice. *Sweeney Todd* opens in two weeks with Sienna as Mrs. Lovett and Madison as the Beggar Woman, which isn't the role she originally wanted but is still important and she's happy with it. When they're not working on *Funeral Girl Explains Everything,* they're singing and acting their hearts out onstage.

I change into jeans and meet Miles on the front porch with bottles of Dr Pepper and a bag of Doritos. He's scrolling through fan comments on the latest *Dragonfly* episode. So far Pax is still dead, but now there are hints he could possibly be resurrected, and people are dividing into camps: those who can't wait, and those who've decided they like the show better without him.

"Magnus is keeping his mouth shut," Miles tells me. "Which is pissing people off as much as you'd expect. You should see Nelson's latest take."

"Can we get the season finale already?" I ask. "Supposedly all will be revealed, then Nelson can disappear back into his mom's basement for another year."

"I assume we'll have the watch party at my house," Miles says as he takes a handful of chips.

"Absolutely. I'll bring popcorn."

"Then they're saying next season will be the last."

I twist the cap off my soda, catching the fizz with my mouth before it can overflow.

"I know things have to end," I say. "But knowing doesn't make it any easier."

"And then what happens?" His question is about more than *Dragonfly*, and we both know it. I gaze out at the street, listening to the birds and the neighbors chatting and the sound of lawnmowers— the soundtrack to life in my hometown.

"I guess we leave it open?" I say.

"Maybe you'll keep on with *Funeral Girl*," he suggests.

"It depends where I am. If everybody's at different places for college, I don't think it'll be possible."

"Anything is possible. You can be Funeral Girl wherever. Or don't. Whatever. You make the call."

"And that's why I love you," I say. Our fingers meet inside the chip bag. I grab his handful for myself. He grabs me in retaliation, and we share a Dorito-y kiss before going back to stuffing our faces.

Miles rests his head on my shoulder. I rest my head on his head. Cars go by the way they do every day, the way they will long after both of us are no longer here.

Who will I be then? I like that I have no idea. I can be anyone. It's all up to me.

ACKNOWLEDGMENTS

Thanks so much to my publishing team for once again helping me transform a good idea into a real story. Holly Root, along with everyone at Root Literary, thank you for being my cheerleaders always. Wendy Loggia, Hannah Hill, and Alison Romig, thank you for your patience and your most excellent notes, always challenging me to go a little deeper and do a little better.

On the home front, I have to thank Jules Hucke for early manuscript reads. Also Becky Roell for confirming many details of what it's like growing up in the funeral business. Thanks also to young Sara Bennett, beat reporter, who started hanging out at a family-owned funeral home in one of the communities she covered, asking too many questions, thinking, There's probably a good story here. Who knew older Sara Bennett Wealer would someday agree?

Finally, eternal thanks to my husband, Adam, for loving and understanding and supporting me. Thanks also to my daughters, M and B, just for being you. I cherish you all more than you'll ever know.

What if a mysterious website could tell you everything you *didn't* want to know about your future?

On sale now!

ABOUT THE AUTHOR

Sara grew up in Manhattan, Kansas (the Little Apple), where she sang in all the choirs and wrote for the high school newspaper. She majored in voice performance at the University of Kansas before transferring to journalism school. She now works in marketing. Sara lives in Cincinnati with her husband, two daughters, and a growing menagerie of pets. She is the author of *Now & When*. When she's not writing, you can find her at the ballet, or obsessively watching ballet on YouTube and Instagram.

sarabennettwealer.com

Underlined

A Community of Book Nerds & Aspiring Writers!

READ

Get book recommendations, reading lists, YA news

DISCOVER

Take quizzes, watch videos, shop merch, win prizes

CREATE

Write your own stories, enter contests, get inspired

SHARE

Connect with fellow Book Nerds and authors!

GetUnderlined.com • @GetUnderlined

Want a chance to be featured? Use #GetUnderlined on social!